DON PENDLETON'S

STONY

AMERICA'S ULTRA-COVERT INTELLIGENCE AGENCY

MAN®

DOMINATION BID

A GOLD EAGLE BOOK FROM

W⬤RLDWIDE®

TORONTO • NEW YORK • LONDON
AMSTERDAM • PARIS • SYDNEY • HAMBURG
STOCKHOLM • ATHENS • TOKYO • MILAN
MADRID • WARSAW • BUDAPEST • AUCKLAND

Recycling programs
for this product may
not exist in your area.

First edition October 2014

ISBN-13: 978-0-373-80447-4

DOMINATION BID

Special thanks and acknowledgment to
Matt Kozar for his contribution to this work.

Printed in U.S.A.

DOMINATION BID

CHAPTER ONE

Minsk, Belarus

Night settled on the city as a blanket of fog rolled across the Svislach River and obscured the lights of Upper Town. Atlantic currents made the air feel dense as heavy humidity was normal to the city this time of year. However the rare lack of wind made the air stifling and Oleg Dratshev, used to the clear and crisp bite of northern Russia, found it a chore even to breathe.

Within a stone's throw, Dratshev noted the smooth and precise movements of his shadowy escorts: four FSB agents assigned to monitor his every move. The Soviet secret service agents were constant companions with orders to protect him. Failing that, they were to ensure no one else could ever exploit his unique skills.

Dratshev had initially resisted the idea of coming to Minsk when he'd received orders direct from his Moscow masters—not for fear of his personal safety but simply because he preferred a more rural setting. Minsk epitomized the fast pace of Euro nightlife, a life simply not for him, but Dratshev knew such orders weren't a suggestion. He watched the fog for a little longer before fishing a pewter and silver cigarette case from the pocket of his custom-tailored slacks. He lit his last cigarette and then leaned against the metal bench and considered his future.

Electromagnetic pulse weapons were his specialty and the reason for his transfer to Minsk. Representatives from the FSB's special operations section were to take charge of Dratshev's brainchild for practical testing in the unforgiving mountainous terrain of northern Belarus. To this point, the tests had been solely based on computer models. Now the time had come to demonstrate the capabilities of the EMP small-arms applications, code-named ZEMKOV, and prove once and for all the theories that had constituted the past fifteen years of Dratshev's life.

As would any scientist in his position, Dratshev wondered of the far-reaching implications for the world. The science behind his invention was hardly new, but the practical applications scared him beyond his wildest imaginings.

He wanted to see it work, to see those things that had only existed in the neurons of his brain come to life. He did not relish the actual physical results.

Dratshev wondered if he was experiencing similar emotions to those of his predecessors—perhaps the creators of the atom and hydrogen bombs or space-based missile-defense systems. Only time and the writers of history would tell. It was difficult to imagine that, at barely thirty-five, he might well be judged by revisionists as a monster—a purveyor of death by simple virtue of his ability to conjure a weapon with enormous destructive capabilities.

The whisper-quiet pop, like that of a balloon, intruded on his deeper thoughts. He turned to his right in time to see one of the shadowy forms drop to the damp grass like a stone.

Dratshev felt the panic rise in the form of increased heart rate and a cold lump in his throat. The sound repeated, this time more like twig snapping, and Dratshev saw a second FSB agent fall.

Dratshev ripped the cigarette from his mouth and jumped to his feet. He looked for the other two agents who had been walking a perimeter to his left a minute earlier, but they were no longer visible. Dratshev whirled and ran up the hill at the back side of the bench along the river. He had difficulty finding purchase on the grass, damp from a hard and recent thundershower. His lungs burned with the exertion. He'd never been a physical man and the several bouts of pneumonia he'd battled as a child in the climates of Siberia and other similarly brutal environments made such activity more difficult.

Dratshev heard something behind him and turned long enough to catch a man he recognized as one of his escorts closing the distance. Dratshev slowed some, the sight of Kurig flooding him with hope. Kurig waved at him, shouting for Dratshev to keep running and as he got closer Dratshev spotted the pistol in Kurig's other hand. A new burden of dread gripped Dratshev's chest—it felt as if it might squeeze the life from him.

Finally, mercifully, Dratshev reached high and level ground. Directly ahead he spotted the road and the sparse traffic darting along the paved trail that wound through a commercial section of Minsk. Some of the businesses lining the far side of the street were closed, but a few were clubs and bistros open late. Dratshev knew the protocol for this instance, a protocol in which he'd drilled hundreds of times. If separated from his FSB bodyguards and under extreme emergencies, he was to find the most public venue he could and place a call to the special number he'd committed to memory. Someone would always answer that number, his handler and contact had assured him. Always.

Dratshev turned once more to see if Kurig had made progress, most assured he'd find the bodyguard now on his heels. Instead he caught just a glimpse of Kurig as the FSB agent fell. Dratshev saw the muzzle-flashes from Kurig's pistol a moment later, heard the reports from the weapon as it echoed in the thick air.

Then the shooting stopped and Dratshev heard no more, saw no more movement from Kurig. It could've been the distance obscured by the mist but Dratshev knew better. Kurig was dead.

And Oleg Dratshev was now utterly and undeniably on his own.

MUSIC OF ORIGINS somewhere between punk and electronic dance blared from the speakers inside the club. The bass thumped irregularly in unsynchronized contrast to the regular thudding of Dratshev's heart. A crowd of partying youths squeezed against him at every turn, making it impossible to discern friend from foe from neutral party. Dratshev willed his mind to remain focused. Logical, coherent thought had been a mainstay of his success for years and there was no reason to think it wouldn't serve him now.

That's why his government had protocols for this kind of thing. Not to mention that whoever had taken out the FSB detachment assigned to protect him wouldn't attempt to kill him where so many witnesses could identify them. Even if his enemies weren't afraid of the local police, they had very good reason to stay out of the sights of the FSB. That particular organization had a reputation of not only protecting its own but of becoming quite nasty when attacked without provocation.

Dratshev continued to take in his surroundings as he pushed his way through the throng of young men and women dancing, shouting and drinking.

One Emo chick—long dark hair framing a bony face doused heavily with makeup and black eye shadow and lipstick—offered Dratshev a smile as he passed. He returned the smile but pushed through. No time for socializing.

Dratshev liked his women, to be sure, but anyone could pose as much of a threat or hindrance as a good cover. Dratshev couldn't afford the distractions right now, anyway. Best to keep his mind on business.

When Dratshev finally reached the back of the club, he searched for lighted signs against the wall pointing to the washroom. In places such as this, such hallways leading to them would also have pay telephones and that's what he needed most right now.

He considered the cell phone in his pocket but wouldn't risk turning it on until after he made his call. They would need the GPS signal from the phone to locate him, a signal that could be used by his enemies as much as his allies. Sure enough, when Dratshev found the hallway leading to the restrooms he found a bank of payphones.

Dratshev reached into his trouser pocket and withdrew a handful of coins. He dropped enough in to buy him initial credit to get an international operator to dial the special number.

Fortunately a door separated the hallway from the main club, so at least he could make out the female voice on the other end of the line.

"Yes, go ahead with your traffic."

Dratshev gave his code name and ten-digit ID number. He answered the challenge question with the correct pass phrase and then waited while the woman routed him to his handler.

After a number of agonizing minutes elapsed the familiar voice of his handler came on the line. "What is it?"

"I've been compromised."

"Where's your security team?"

"They were neutralized."

The handler swore. "This isn't good."

"I believe under the present circumstances that would probably be an understatement. Can you send me help?"

"Nearest team is at least an hour away. Where are you? Is your phone on?"

"No, I didn't dare turn it on until I could verify contact with you."

The handler hesitated in his reply. Dratshev found this odd. The handler finally said, "Of course…per protocol."

"Yes, per protocol."

"Okay, turn it on now. I will verify your position and then activate the closest unit. You are to stay exactly where you are until they contact you. Pass phrase will have changed by then, however. Please remember this so they do not kill you on sight."

Dratshev frowned at this revelation on first hearing it, but then remembered the time difference. Per SOP, the FSB preferred to utilize UTC for all date-time references. By referencing Coordinated Universal Time, challenges and passwords remained consistent irrespective of geographical location anywhere in the world. Providing an incorrect pass phrase or challenge would most likely result in either termination of communications or, in the case of FSB assets, simply termination since it would be assumed an asset was either operating under duress or compromised beyond recovery.

As Dratshev reached inside his jacket to activate his mobile phone he replied, "Understood. I will hold hear and await extraction."

Dratshev hung up, turned and proceeded into the restroom. He considered his options while he relieved himself. He could simply occupy one of the stalls and wait but that would leave him without any means of escape if the enemy found him first. Conversely, waiting out in the main part of the club would make him more conspicuous to any party that entered and might search for him in the crowd.

Either choice presented risks but the latter one made more sense. At least he could move around and use the crowd for cover if he spotted trouble before it spotted him.

Dratshev washed his hands and returned to the club proper. He shuffled along the edge of the crowd until he could find a free space at the bar. It took the service staff nearly two minutes to notice him. The bartender took his order for vodka, neat—Dratshev decided to limit it to one so as not to dull his senses. While he waited for his drink, Dratshev kept searching for threats. So far, it didn't appear anyone posed a threat. When the bartender returned with his drink, he paid up including tip but sipped from the tumbler rather than hitting it all at once.

"Hello!" a voice called in his ear, the speaker's lips so close her breath tickled his earlobe.

Dratshev turned with surprise to see the Emo chick from earlier. He tried for his best smile. "Hello."

"I watched you walk past me," she said, again leaning close so he could hear.

He reciprocated in like fashion and they continued that way throughout the conversation. "And?"

She shrugged. "You looked like maybe you wanted to say something."

"Perhaps."

"Just perhaps?" She grinned and winked. "You mean you're not sure you wanted to say something to me?"

"Oh, I wanted to say something but I wasn't sure how you'd take it. At least not coming from an old man like me."

She laughed. "You're not old!"

"Sometimes I feel old."

"Well, maybe I could make you feel younger."

"I bet you could at that."

"So now who's being inappropriate?" She tapped just above her very ample cleavage.

"Some would just say you're honest."

She nodded vigorously and then extended her hand. "I'm Mishka."

He nodded and shook her hand lightly. "Oleg."

"You're not from Minsk?"

"You got me. I'm on vacation."

"Where are you from originally?"

Dratshev thought about lying at first but remembered his training. The closer to the truth the easier to remember details if a discrepancy rose. Half-truths with leanings toward reality were the best.

Dratshev replied, "Moscow. Well, just north of there actually."

"That's crazy! I was actually born in Krakow."

"Is that right?"

Mishka nodded; a freshly wild look in her eyes. "It is so nice to meet another Russian."

"You don't meet a lot of Russians here in Minsk?"

"Not really. I mean…at least none that stay around very long."

"But actually, I'm on vacation. So I won't be staying that long, either."

"You'll probably stay longer than you think."

Dratshev couldn't be sure what she meant at first but then he noticed just the slightest shift in Mishka's gaze. He knew the telltale signs and he turned his attention toward the dance area in time to see several men approach from various directions.

He'd been betrayed! There could be no other explanation. Oleg turned from the men and tried to leave but he found Mishka blocking his path. He went to shove her aside but something stung his side. It felt as if a needle had been shoved into the space between his third and fourth ribs.

Dratshev's mind began to swim and then he felt woozy and it became suddenly difficult to breathe. He heard Mishka scream and begin to shout in a dialect he didn't recognize, but then it didn't much matter because the periphery of his vision turned spotty. Stars danced in front of his eyes and his lungs burned not with the scar tissue of his past but more like that sort of respiratory attack brought on by suppressive chemicals.

With his head becoming foggy, his vision spotted and his capacity to oxygenate inhibited, Oleg Dratshev knew that to continue fighting and resisting would become futile. At long last he succumbed to the sweet rapture of what he assumed would be death and blacked out just a heartbeat after he felt his knees become wobbly. Then he hit the thinly carpeted floor of the club.

CHAPTER TWO

Oleg Dratshev woke to a dull ache in his head and a thick, dry tongue. When he ran his tongue inside his mouth he came away with a pasty feeling similar to what he might have experienced after a night of drinking. At first he thought maybe he'd been blindfolded but that quickly gave way to the sensation of dark, ominous shapes surrounding him.

Around him he perceived the steady, rolling drone of what could only be the vibrations caused by plane engines. Slowly his surroundings took shape and he realized he'd been secured to a reclining chair. His arms felt heavy and he reached to rub his eyes but the motions were stopped short. He felt his wrists and realized they were encircled by thick leather restraints. The subsequent jingling were those of chains attached to the restraints.

Low-watt, recessed lights above him came on and bathed his prison in a warm, red-orange glow. A door in the far wall of the compartment opened and two men entered. The first man was tall with a thick neck and muscular build. The man who followed stood much shorter. He was dressed with impeccable taste in tan slacks and a tailored silk shirt. Under the light, Dratshev found it difficult to determine the color but it looked perhaps aqua or azure in hue. He had black hair, dark skin and a neatly trimmed black beard with mustache.

The man sat in a chair directly across from Dratshev's. The expensive leather creaked under his weight. The bigger man stood behind him with his arms folded.

"Good morning, Dr. Dratshev," the seated man said in near flawless Russian. "I trust you enjoyed your nap."

"Who are you?" Dratshev asked, his voice sounding muffled in his own ears.

"We'll get to that in a moment," the man replied with a pleasant smile. "Would you like something to drink? Water perhaps?"

Dratshev thought about a moment and then nodded. The man gestured to his companion, who immediately turned and left the compartment.

The man said, "The drug we used will leave you severely dehydrated. I'd suggest when my assistant returns that you sip the water rather than gulp it, as you might be tempted. I would not want to see you vomit, as this would only dehydrate you more."

"You haven't answered my question," Dratshev said with a new sense of defiance.

"Fair enough. My name is Ishaq Madari. This will probably not mean anything to you."

It didn't and Dratshev saw no reason to pretend otherwise.

Madari continued. "I regret that I had to take such extreme measures to make your acquaintance but I can say with assurance that I have so long wished to meet you."

"You may not feel the same way when my people discover that you have kidnapped me."

"Perhaps," Madari replied, inclining his head. He looked around the compartment a moment, appearing to gather his thoughts. "Once we've landed safely I will certainly make every effort to provide more comfortable accommodations. For the moment, however, I'm afraid this is the best I can do."

The big man returned with bottled water. He opened the cap and handed it to Dratshev, who took it and tipped it high to his lips.

"Easy, Dr. Dratshev, please. As I said, too much too soon will make you ill."

Dratshev remembered and resisted the urge to take more than a couple of swallows. When he'd finished drinking he asked, "Why you have done this? Do you realize who I am?"

"I do!" Madari clapped his hands like an excited child and then steepled his fingers and touched them to his chin. His dark brown eyes gazed on Dratshev with intense curiosity. "I would surmise there's very little I don't know about you, in fact. Your work in the field of electromagnetic pulse weapons is practically legendary in some circles. Oh, please, Dr. Dratshev, there's no reason to look so surprised. The FSB lacks proper security precautions. Information can be had for the right amount of money, and money is a resource of which I have no short supply."

"I don't know what you're talking about."

Madari smiled and shook his head as if Dratshev had told a crude joke. "I'd hoped you'd have enough sense not to play such games with me. I'm aware of your fierce loyalty toward your government. I understand loyalty more than you could ever know. I used to have the same toward my own government."

"And what government is that?"

Dratshev could see his ploy to glean as much information from his captor as possible wasn't lost on Madari. It was a standard tactic his FSB instructors had taught him early in his career. As a military scientist, kidnapping was an all too real and constant threat. This wasn't lost on those within the Russian government and they insisted on putting Dratshev through regular training so he would know how to handle most scenarios.

"I was born and raised in Libya, and a prominent member of its government. But that time has long passed. Like you, I was loyal to them and they betrayed that loyalty because of certain political views I had. Had I been a wiser man, I would've kept those views to myself but I believed in them so much that they ultimately became my undoing. So now I am an exile."

"A very touching story," Dratshev said as he took another sip. "However, it doesn't change the fact that you have illegally seized a Russian citizen. My government will not sit still for this."

"Please, Dr. Dratshev, let's not squabble. You are my honored guest. And when I've obtained from you what I need you will be released back to your government unharmed."

"Ha! You've killed my security team, drugged and kidnapped me. Those are hardly the actions of a gentleman."

"They were extreme measures, agreed, but wholly necessary."

"Just what is it you want from me?"

"Ah, now that's the part I think will intrigue you most. I know you were transferred to Belarus to begin practical testing of your EMP theories and designs. I fully intend to give you that opportunity. Imagine that you will be able to expand your work beyond your wildest imagination."

"That would be very difficult to imagine."

"But true, nonetheless." Madari sighed. "It may come as a surprise to you, but your government has been less than honest with you in the advancements they've made on your prototype designs."

"Dishonest in what way?"

"In just how far they've gotten in the manufacture. They've been purposefully slow implementing your designs, fearful what would happen if they moved up the timetable, I would guess."

"And how could you know this? Even if it's true, it wouldn't make any sense. Stalling progress of my research is hardly in their best interests."

"Not when it comes to certain parties that may not be known to you—parties that have the direct confidences of your president. You see, there are conservative elements within your government that have been attempting to persuade investors buildup of conventional armament is the key to restoring Russian military superiority. They see technical advancements as merely fodder to be stolen by others and used against them. This is why they've done everything in their power to slow the manufacture of your prototypes."

Dratshev shook his head. "Then why go to such great lengths to protect me? Why not simply kill me?"

"I do not have the answer to that question, although I have frequently considered it." Madari gestured at him. "However, I think you are sufficiently intelligent enough that you have pondered this point yourself, and most likely formulated your own answer."

Dratshev had, in fact, and it was something he'd dared never utter for fear it might become a reality. Those inside the government who preferred conventional military might would never have risked assassination for fear of alienating those holding the power of the purse. What impressed Dratshev, however, was Madari's refusal to conjure some story in answer to Dratshev's question. Madari's simple acknowledgment of ignorance demonstrated a rare and unusual sense of honesty. Dratshev had to admit he actually found that refreshing.

"This is all interesting," Dratshev said, "but it still doesn't drill down to the reason you've gone to these lengths."

Madari smiled and then stood. "I believe it would be wiser to wait until you are more lucid to engage in such a conversation. All in good time, Dr. Dratshev."

Madari whirled on his heel and as he headed for the door he added, "In the meantime, please consider yourself a guest and, should you need anything, perhaps food or a blanket, my assistant will be happy to get it for you. You should take every opportunity afforded you on this point. We're still six hours from our destination."

When Madari was gone, Dratshev took time to inspect his bonds. As he'd suspected, the restraints circling his wrists were thick leather fastened by chains. Escaping such bonds would be impossible. He looked at his legs and noted they were also secured in like fashion.

Finally, Dratshev laid his head back and closed his eyes. Best to get as much sleep as possible and wait for a more opportune time to make his escape.

Sooner or later, he knew such a solution would present itself. It always did when one exercised patience.

ELEVEN MEN WAITED as their leader studied the facility through a night-vision scope. To local residents, it appeared to be nothing more than what it was advertised: a research center run by the department of agriculture.

Colonel Jack Cyrus knew it to be otherwise, which was why he and his team were in rural Iowa.

Cyrus lowered the scope and passed it to his second-in-command, Riley Braden. "Interesting. The security appears to be minimal."

Braden took the scope and performed his own inspection. "I agree, sir."

Cyrus tried not to wince at the "sir" despite the fact he understood it. It was protocol but difficult to hear coming from a man that had not only been his peer throughout their respective military careers, but also his friend since high school. In private, they addressed each other by name but out here in the field they had to set an example and chain of command in front of the others.

Braden continued. "Ten-foot fence with cyclone wire. No visible sentries, so probably armed security inside."

"Rent-a-cops, at best," Cyrus replied.

"And probably not that many."

"Intelligence says they walk rounds with e-point checks at regular intervals. That means they can't cover the whole area at one time."

"I'd concur with that assessment," Braden agreed. "What's your plan?"

"We have to assume a facility of that size will have full video- and audio-camera surveillance." Cyrus turned to Braden. "I see a training opportunity here, Major. What do you think is the best course of action?"

Braden didn't hesitate in his reply. "Two teams. Breach the northeast corner of the perimeter fence. First team will locate the power sources and neutralize them, including generators. Second team makes entry to the building and then sends two to retrieve the data while the rest deal with any human elements. Outer team will provide perimeter and egress security, as well as mission failsafe."

Cyrus nodded, impressed with his friend and colleague. "Excellent tactical plan, Major Braden. Exactly what I would've done. I'd say the decision's been made."

"Thank you, Colonel."

"You'll lead the inside team."

Braden looked surprised. "I don't know the job."

"You know it as well as I do."

"Yes, sir, but I was trained to do it only in the event you could not."

"Nonsense. There's no difference."

"Sir, with all due respect, I strongly suggest you reconsider."

Cyrus didn't look at Braden as he responded in short fashion, "I already have, Major. It's not a request. You will lead the primary team and you will accomplish the mission objectives as they've been given to us. Understood?"

"Yes, sir."

"Then let's move out."

Braden nodded and turned to the team members he would now be leading on the mission. As he briefed them on the change in plans, Cyrus sighed. He'd considered sticking to the original mission parameters but he wanted his friend to take credit for what he knew would be another success. Their employer, who'd expressed reservations about bringing Riley Braden into the fold from the beginning, had to know that Braden had as much command ability and skill as Cyrus. This would be Braden's chance to prove it without even being aware Cyrus was putting him to the test. Cyrus had learned long ago one mark of a good leader was to set up those in his command to succeed whenever possible. Not only did it boost morale but it also instilled confidence in self—not to mention what it did for unit cohesion.

The teams automatically performed a last check of equipment and then broke into approach formation. Every man knew what to do, where to stage in relationship to every other man, and what their individual responsibilities. They'd trained for this dozens of times until they'd had it down like clockwork.

The exterior team arrived first and two men went to work on the fence, cutting links with the marked precision of professionals. Cyrus knew they'd practiced, but his chest swelled with pride as he watched them in action. Within thirty seconds they'd made the ingress.

With a nod from Cyrus, Braden gestured to his team and they moved through the hold. The two squad weapons men took point and then Braden. The remaining trio proceeded after him. They moved across the field at a breakneck clip and located the power boxes stationed on the exterior of the main building.

Braden knelt and flicked his thumb twice at two of his team members. The demo guys went to work on the boxes, priming them with the charges. Braden risked a glance over his shoulder and saw Cyrus making his way through the fence in the same way Braden's team had just a minute earlier.

Once the charges were set, Braden and his men broke from their positions and headed toward the rear door where they'd planned to make their entry. They were nearly there when the charges blew the power boxes apart. Every interior light in the building went out, as well as power to a small external building. One of the men blew the lock off the door with a small roll of self-detonating plastic explosive and within seconds Braden's team had gained access.

"You have five minutes." Cyrus's voice resounded

in Braden's headset. "Mark T-minus five, starting now. Radio silence from this point."

"Copy," Braden replied.

The six men pushed up the darkened corridor, moving smoothly as one unit. They followed a standard fire-and-maneuver pattern, leap-frogging in pairs as they approached their objective.

They reached the data room unmolested and Braden gestured for four of his men to fan out while the other would provide cover while he made his entry. The door proved no match for the pencil detonator that shot the bolt lock inward as if it had been fired from a potato gun. Braden eased the door open and snatched the red-lens flashlight from his equipment harness.

He managed to get about three feet inside before bullets crashed into the chest of his comrade and drove the man into the door frame. Braden wondered how he managed to avoid a similar fate even as he threw himself the floor and a fresh volley burned the air where he'd stood a millisecond earlier.

Braden brought his Steyr Aug Para into play and triggered a burst in the direction of the muzzle-flashes. The rounds bounced off a solid object marked by the sparks from their impact. It took Braden a moment to realize that he'd been firing into bulletproof glass.

Braden rolled onto his back and yanked an HE grenade from his harness. He primed the hand bomb and tossed it overhead before jumping to his feet and rushing toward the door. He threw himself around the corner and landed on his belly just as the grenade blew. Red, yellow and orange flame whooshed through the open door.

"We're blown!" he shouted at his men. "Retreat!"

None of them had to be told twice, two taking point

and two more providing rear cover with Braden between them. The men dashed up the hallway at full sprint and exited the building in time to see a firefight had already ensued between Cyrus and his team.

Braden and his men spread out and engaged whatever targets presented. The air came alive with reports from dozens of automatic weapons on both sides. To the observer it would've seemed as if a small war had erupted in the USDA's "research facility" and it would've been a bizarre sight, at best.

Braden managed to rendezvous with Cyrus, miraculously avoiding death in the process.

"What happened?" Cyrus demanded during a lull in the shooting.

"Ambush," Braden replied as he sighted on an enemy gunner and squeezed the trigger. "They were waiting for us."

"Blown immediately? From the start?"

"It would seem so," Braden said through clenched teeth as he fired at another target, missing by a narrow margin.

"You've ordered a retreat?"

Braden nodded.

"We can't stay here," Cyrus said.

"You mean you want to leave them?"

"They have their orders."

"Sir, we have to—"

"Do it, Major. Just do it!"

Braden didn't hesitate, knowing orders were orders. He and Cyrus scrambled to their feet and fired a few extra short bursts to help cover their escape through the perimeter fence. They had a vehicle waiting in the woods, a late-model custom van. It was obvious they'd been expected, so the success of their getaway was by no means guaranteed. But one thing Cyrus and Braden agreed on as they made their way to the van, there would be a day of reckoning.

There would be payback and it would be a revenge of the sweetest kind.

CHAPTER THREE

Stony Man Farm, Virginia

The five battle-hardened warriors of Phoenix Force sat attentively as Harold Brognola, head of the most covert special operations agency in America, opened the briefing.

"We're long on intelligence and short on time, so let's get right to it," Brognola said. He looked at Barbara Price and nodded.

Price, Stony Man's mission controller, tapped the key on the table-top keyboard in front of her and the operations center conference room lights dimmed. A moment later the face of a young man with dirty-blond hair appeared on the 72-inch LED screen at one end of the room.

"Gentlemen, meet Dr. Oleg Dratshev. This picture was taken about ten years ago when he was age twenty-five. For more than a decade Dratshev has been Russia's foremost military R and D scientist in the areas of electromagnetic pulse weapons. He holds several advanced degrees and his work has been financed directly by the Kremlin. Two days ago he disappeared."

Price paused for effect and met the gaze of every Phoenix Force warrior before she continued. "Dr. Dratshev is highly respected by most members of the military scientific community. His security was handled by the FSB. He was taken by a party or parties unknown, and thus far no ransom demand has been made. The Russian government has attempted to keep his disappearance a secret, but it was hardly possible given that he disappeared shortly after arriving in Minsk and the grabbers left the bodies of four FSB agents behind."

Phoenix Force's team leader, David McCarter, cleared his throat and asked, "Do we know why he was in Minsk?"

Price shook her head. "We don't have any positive proof but we believe he may have been there to oversee the test demonstration of some prototype weaponry he designed."

Calvin James let out a low whistle. "Funny they'd think testing weapons of that size in a foreign territory would be something they could keep a lid on."

"Well, the buzz running through the highest channels at both the CIA and NSA would indicate they weren't testing high-energy weapons," Price replied.

"Wait a minute," Gary Manning interjected. "Are you saying Dratshev has come up with a design for EMP application using small arms?"

"It would seem so," Price replied.

Each of the Phoenix Force members muttered curses under their breath and an icy tension settled on all present.

"That's unthinkable," Rafael Encizo said. A Cuban native and one of the original Phoenix Force veterans, Encizo was the team's resident specialist in maritime operations and an expert knife fighter.

"As far as we know," Price said, "the capabilities of EMP in small arms are still little more than an untested theory. But we do think that given how long Dratshev's been working on the project, coupled with the Russian government's continued financing of his research, those capabilities are a very real possibility."

"Excuse me," Thomas Jackson Hawkins said, raising a hand in automatic reflex.

"T.J.?" Price acknowledged with a nod.

"I was under the impression EMP was still somewhat poorly understood. At least from the perspective of safe weaponization."

"I think Bear could give us a more expert opinion on that concept," Brognola said. "Aaron?"

The other man in the room differed more than the rest in just the fact that he was confined to a wheelchair. By any standards Aaron Kurtzman had an IQ nearly off the charts and the uncanny ability to collect, sort and manipulate copious amounts of electronic data into logical chunks of intelligence. Those talents, coupled with his leadership of all of Stony Man's computer-based operations, had saved the lives of every field team member on occasions almost too numerous to quantify.

Kurtzman grinned, happy as always to be in his element. "From the standpoint of physics, electromagnetics is a relatively simple principle to grasp. Think about the Earth. Surrounding our atmosphere is an electromagnetic field, which is generated by the Earth's core of molten metal spinning at thousands of miles per hour. At least that's the generally accepted scientific axiom.

"That field helps contain our air and moisture, but more importantly it protects us from the cosmic radiation generated by the sun. Now suppose that you could harness such a field on a microcosmic level and confine it into a narrow beam, a particle beam of sorts. By creating the initial energy and then liberating said energy, a pulse is formed that has all the magnetic force behind it with one distinct difference—it can be focused at a single point."

"Sounds more like you're talking about a laser," McCarter remarked. The fox-faced Briton furrowed his brow. "Is there a difference?"

"Big difference," Kurtzman replied. "A laser beam has to be intensely focused and remain constant to weaponize it. This requires an intense amount of sustained energy. That's where we draw the line between science and science fiction. But with an EMP, the energy is already contained within the pulse. It then becomes merely a matter of focusing it."

"But wouldn't the same principle apply?" James asked. "I mean...wouldn't it take as much energy to build up an electromagnetic charge as a laser beam?"

Kurtzman shook his head. "Not according to what Dr. Dratshev's many years of research has revealed. Somehow, Dratshev has discovered a way to generate that energy at the atomic or even subatomic level."

"Or at least that's what our intelligence agencies have surmised," Price said.

"Unfortunately we don't have the time to give you a full physics lesson right now," Brognola cut in. "The important thing to know is that Dratshev has found some way of doing it, and now he's fallen into the hands of someone willing to go to great lengths to possess that knowledge. Someone we deem to be extremely dangerous."

"But how can we know they're dangerous with any certainty?" Hawkins asked.

It was Gary Manning, former member of the RCMP and a self-taught expert on nearly every terrorist organization in the world, who answered. "Because anyone bold enough to go up against the Russian government and, in particular the FSB, is just plain crazy."

"Or fanatical, at least," McCarter added.

"In any case," Price said, "we have to assume the worst. Dratshev's abduction must be deemed a direct threat against the United States and her allies until otherwise verified. That's why we've activated Phoenix Force."

"And Able Team," Brognola added.

"We're going to work together on this one?" James inquired.

"Not exactly," Price said. "Not too long after we received the news of Dratshev's disappearance, an incident occurred at a U.S. Department of Agriculture research facility in a rural area north of Des Moines, Iowa."

"Uh-oh," McCarter said. "If memory serves, Barb, isn't that—?"

"Yes, it's a data backup warehouse for a special sector of international satellite operations overseen by the NSA."

James looked at McCarter in amazement. "How the hell did you know that?"

McCarter shrugged. "I read the classified CERN bulletins."

Hawkins chuckled. "The European Organization for Nuclear Research bulletins? What a nerd."

"Don't forget mission controller's pet," Encizo added.

"Moving right along to the incident?" Brognola prompted

"Go ahead, Barb," Manning said. "I'm listening."

Price smiled. "An armed force of about a dozen men breached the USDA facility and was engaged by security personnel. A number of men were killed on both sides, and about half of this mysterious team managed to escape. Unfortunately there were no survivors to question."

"Any idea who they were working for?" James asked.

"No," Price said, shaking her head. "All of the deceased were American citizens with military experience, however. So we're thinking some sort of mercenary group."

Brognola said, "The NSA apparently got wind something like this might take place and so they beefed up security just in case there was something to it. Turns out they were right."

"Then they must have some idea what this team was after," McCarter said. "Breaking into a bloody NSA data facility is a risky op. The stakes had to be high."

"We won't know for sure until Able Team can get there and start an investigation of its own," Price replied. "What's interesting about this attack, though, is that the particular data sets stored there by the NSA include covert operations in Belarus and a number of surrounding countries."

"Which is where Dratshev disappeared," Hawkins concluded.

"Right," Brognola said.

Price added, "That's why we think the two incidents are connected, and thus far the intelligence we've gathered would seem to support that theory."

"What we don't understand yet is what domestic interest would launch an operation on U.S. soil and why," Brognola pointed out.

"Well, it sure wasn't whoever snatched Dratshev," Encizo replied. "That wouldn't make any sense."

"Unless they were trying to divert our attention."

McCarter shook his head. "I'd have a lot of trouble

buying that, Hal. First, it would imply that our own people snatched Dratshev. Second, it wouldn't make sense to put good resources as such risk for the purpose of creating a smoke screen."

"That would be an expensive diversion," Price conceded with a nod.

"And we're not dealing with idiots or amateurs in any case," Manning remarked. "That much is obvious."

Price said, "Well, we figure Able Team will be able to tell us something soon enough. Meanwhile, we're sending you to Belarus. You'll pick up whatever clues you can."

"Are we sure that's the best place to start?" McCarter asked.

Price nodded. "We have a CIA contact there who's been shadowing the FSB team sent to retrieve Dratshev when he contacted his handler and reported he'd been compromised. An insider told our contact there was a significant delay notifying the backup team."

"So this was an inside job," Hawkins observed in his typical Texas drawl.

"It would seem so."

McCarter scratched his jaw in consideration. "Any possibility the Russians staged this whole thing?"

"It's always possible," Price said with a shrug. "But to what end?"

"Maybe they wanted to throw everyone off Dratshev's trail? Think about it. They fake his abduction and then everybody starts looking for him in all but the obvious place. His own backyard."

"We posed that as a potential scenario to our CIA contact and he didn't think it was likely," Brognola said. "He's convinced the kidnapping is real and the threat is viable, mostly due to the amount of scrambling the FSB's doing. They've apparently crawled under every rock and into every crevice of the city."

"Okay, then I guess it's off to Minsk we go," Mc-Carter said.

"If there's any more intelligence that comes our way while you're en route," Price said, "we can always divert you."

The five warriors nodded in concert.

"Good luck, men," Harold Brognola added.

CARL LYONS WAS enjoying an icy swim through a Mississippi tributary in northern Minnesota when the waterproof GPS device around his wrist sent a very mild tingle along his skin.

Lyons pushed his body against the strong current, his muscular arms and shoulders propelling him through choppy waters that would have bested a lesser man. This was just one of the many feats that had earned Lyons his Ironman nickname.

Lyons reached shore and climbed from the water onto the trunk of a fallen tree. He swung his legs over it and planted his feet on terra firma. Beads of water dribbled from every part of skin that had taken on a golden-bronze tone under three days of the early summer sun.

Lyons checked the device as it signaled him again and then set off into a half-mile trot until he reached the spot where he'd left his two companions. He found them both fast asleep, a rock pit smoldering with red-orange wood coals the only remainder of the campfire they'd started the night before.

Lyons put his hands on his hips and shook his head. "Pathetic." He then walked over and kicked the soles of their feet.

The first man, husky and muscular with gray-white hair, awoke with a start. "What's the big idea, Ironman?" Rosario "Politician" Blancanales demanded. "That's no way to wake up a friend."

The other man had barely stirred, although that hardly fooled Lyons. He knew that both of them were trained well enough they'd probably detected his approach while he was still out of sight. Those same instincts, forged from years of combat and training, were the ones that had registered Lyons as an entity that didn't pose any threat.

Hermann "Gadgets" Schwarz yawned. "Yeah. Really, Ironman, you have no class."

"Shape up, boys," Lyons said. "I got buzzed."

Schwarz looked at Blancanales and rubbed one eye. "He's not a very nice person."

"Old age has made him cantankerous," Blancanales replied.

"Stuff it," Lyons muttered as he reached into his backpack and retrieved his cell phone.

Lyons issued a voice-coded command and the phone automatically dialed the secure satellite uplink to the communications center at Stony Man Farm.

When Price answered on the second ring, Lyons said, "You rang, Mizz Daisy?"

"I did," she replied. "I'm sorry to cut your vacation short but we have big trouble. We just finished briefing Phoenix Force and they're getting ready to depart for Belarus. We need you guys to head to the location I'm sending to your phone via secured traffic."

"Can I have a clue?"

"North of Des Moines, Iowa. A research facility belonging to the USDA."

"Understood. We'll head for the car now." He looked

at Blancanales and Schwarz and grinned as he added, "Tweedledee and Tweedledum were only sleeping."

"Probably trying to catch up."

"We'll get all the sleep we need when we're dead."

"Not funny, Carl."

"Yes, Mother."

"Get moving and call me back when you're on the road. I can talk to all of you via the car phone."

"Roger that. Out."

Blancanales watched expectantly as Lyons disconnected while Schwarz had simply rolled over and started to drift. "Where we headed?"

"Some USDA facility in Iowa," Lyons replied.

"AMERICAN MERCS OPERATING on American soil?" Lyons said into the roof-mounted speaker once they'd returned to their car. "That's bizarre."

"I think you've understated it," Blancanales said from behind the wheel.

From the backseat Schwarz asked, "So I assume you think they were after something in the data vaults, Barb?"

"That's our thought," Price said. She explained their theory as it related to the disappearance of Dratshev.

"The timing does seem noteworthy," Blancanales agreed.

"So what's our approach?" Lyons asked. "I assume the FBI and NSA are already knee-deep in this. Are we going to run into territorial dick flexing?"

"Probably," Price replied. "But you'd hardly be able to avoid it, no matter what. We did manage to put in a good word with the FBI's SAIC, who's been appointed as the lead in the investigation."

"And who is this FBI Special Agent In Charge?"

"You'll want to make contact with a guy named Robert Higgs. He's a veteran investigator and one of the FBI's most decorated agents."

"What's our cover?"

"Use your BATFE credentials," Price replied. "If you come in expressing only interest in the weapons that were used, that should buy you at least some partial good will. Learn what you can and then funnel the information back to us."

"Understood," Lyons said. "We'll get the info out of them."

"Just find out everything you can and report back to us as soon as possible. It's important we determine how this fits in to Phoenix Force's mission before they reach Minsk," Price explained.

"We'll do our best," Blancanales said.

"As always," Schwarz added.

After they disconnected, Lyons tendered a grunt.

"What is it?" Blancanales asked.

"Just something really odd about it all."

"You think the Farm's right about a connection between Dratshev's disappearance and this assault on the NSA data vault?" Schwarz asked.

"I wouldn't dismiss it out of hand," Lyons replied. "They're usually right about those kinds of things. I wish we could take a more direct approach, though. Seems more and more that we're being forced to fight bureaucratic red tape in our missions."

Blancanales chuckled as he met Schwarz's gaze in the rearview mirror. "Sounds like Ironman's got a bit of nostalgia for the good old days."

"Can you blame him?" Schwarz replied. "He makes a good point, actually. Used to be we could go in, kick ass and take names. Now we have to walk on eggshells just to keep our cover."

"Exactly," Lyons agreed.

"Look at it this way, Ironman," Blancanales said. "Those are opportunities to build your skills in normal social interaction."

"I have skills," Lyons rumbled. "Aim and squeeze the trigger. Playing nice-nice wasn't anywhere in my job description."

"Well, guess we have to adopt the maxim that the only easy day was yesterday."

"Yeah," the Able Team leader replied. "But that doesn't mean we have to like it."

CHAPTER FOUR

Rural Iowa

A foul mood came over Special Agent in Charge Robert Higgs as he stared at the half-dozen bodies strewed across the grassy field of the USDA research facility. Higgs had been on a lot of crime scenes but this one had to be the most unusual.

A paramilitary team breaks into a supposed USDA site, engages in a gun battle with a security force armed more like commandos than federal rent-a-cops, and a bunch of people get killed. Higgs derived some comfort at the thought there were no innocent bystanders or civilians numbered among the casualties—that was the only thing about this that didn't set his gut on fire.

Higgs was a teetotaler by any standards, but right at that moment he could've used a stiff belt of something stronger than the lukewarm coffee in the paper cup. He downed the remainder and then turned to look at one of his men who stood nearby holding an electronic clipboard.

"So what's the verdict?"

Nick Winger sighed before replying. "Total of nine casualties—seven of them fatal and two with serious injuries. We got six bodies out here and one more inside the main building."

"And the two injured were from the grenade?"

Winger nodded.

Higgs shook his head. "What a mess. And we don't have a clue yet why this even happened."

"You'll get to the bottom of it, Bob."

"You got more faith in my abilities than I do, Nick."

"Yes, sir, maybe I do."

"It's interesting the team from the NSA didn't have much to say."

"What can they say? They're a bunch of computer geeks. Special detachment specialized in recovering data from systems damaged by disasters."

"Yeah, we both know that's bullshit," Higgs replied. "I've worked with those guys before. They're actually specialized in recovering data for natural disasters— things such as floods and tornados and fires—not bombs and grenades and bullets."

"Well, I suppose the applications are similar in nature."

"We'll see." Higgs sucked air through his teeth. "Ask me, I think they're a scrub team. I think this place did a little more than just agricultural research."

"If it did, they're not going to tell us," Winger pointed out.

"Excuse me, sir," another agent said. He approached with three men who were dressed in suits, ties and sunglasses.

More government types, Higgs thought, but he said, "What is it, Mackenzie?"

"These guys just arrived from BATFE. They asked to speak to you." Mackenzie paused and then more quietly added, "They asked for you by name."

Higgs scanned the grim faces of the three men and then nodded at Mackenzie. "I'll take it from here."

The fit blond one of the group said, "You're Higgs? Name's Carl Irons."

Higgs shook the hand offered him. Irons had a strong, firm grip and there was something special about the way he carried himself. In fact, all three of them moved and acted with confident authority, and Higgs surmised almost immediately they weren't who they claimed they were, despite what they claimed.

"What's your interest here?"

"Some place we can talk private?"

Higgs looked at Winger and nodded. The man glanced at the three newcomers and then turned and departed without saying a word.

"Okay, what's up?"

WHEN LYONS FINISHED giving Higgs the cover story about their interest in the guns that were used, the FBI agent spent a long time staring at him.

Finally he said, "You don't actually expect me to believe that story."

"Frankly, I don't care if you believe it or not," Lyons said with a scowl.

"Uh…look, Higgs," Blancanales said easily, stepping forward to avert a pissing contest. "We're not interested in jumping on your case or even taking credit. You have to admit—" Blancanales waved in the direction of the carnage "—that this is an awful lot to handle. If you'd just let us inspect the weapons that were used, we'd be able to trace them a lot faster than your labs probably could."

"The FBI might even have turned to our people anyway for that support," Schwarz added with a shrug. "So there's really no reason for you not to cooperate with us."

Higgs shook his head, keeping one eye on Lyons. "I'm more than happy to show a little interagency cooperation. But the fact is I expect honesty out of anyone I deal with. In other words, no bullshit and no cockamamie stories like the NSA data-recovery geeks who showed up on a whim—very similar to the way you boys did—with some fish tale about specializing in disaster scenarios."

"Just what is it you're trying to get at?" Blancanales asked.

Higgs couldn't seem to help but tender a snort of derision. "Okay, let me be more direct since I'm asking the same courtesy from you guys. First, BATFE agents don't typically operate in threes. They'd send a single field agent and maybe a backup man. That's SOP for them, just as it is for us. Second, I've worked with plenty of BATFE agents before. You guys don't move like them, talk like them or act like them. You're professionals, although professional *whats* I'm not yet sure. My guess is troubleshooters, maybe CIA or NSA, but that's less likely than maybe DHS. Maybe you're on a page that's not even in the official playbook."

Blancanales couldn't refrain from flashing the guy a broad grin. "Okay, so you're obviously much smarter than our people gave you credit for. Fair enough." Blancanales looked at Lyons. "I can't be more specific without your approval."

Lyons exchanged looks with Higgs and then nodded.

Blancanales said, "You're right, we're not on any page in the official playbook. I can't get into it right now but what I can tell you is we got backing. Big backing."

"How big?"

It was Schwarz who answered, "Okay, well, you know that big white building in Washington? You know—the one with the big pillars in front?"

Higgs stared at Schwarz a moment and then mumbled, "I see."

"Actually, you *don't* see," Lyons said. "If you get my meaning?"

"I get you," Higgs replied.

Lyons said, "As to the reason for our visit, let's just say we're after the same thing the NSA boys are after. Only fact is we already know what information was contained in that data vault. We're way more interested in finding out who wanted that information and why."

"And if I cooperate and help you find them, I'll close my case, as well."

"That's the general idea, yeah."

"Okay, then I guess there's no harm in telling you what we know so far. Especially since it isn't a hell of a lot."

Blancanales folded his arms. "We're all ears."

Washington, D.C.

DAVID ERNEST STEINHAM stared out the vast array of windows from the fifteenth story of his office building. He smiled at the breathtaking view of the Potomac, and with good reason—he'd paid a small fortune for it.

But Steinham also knew he'd earned every penny of the millions of dollars his company had made. Steinham had started Dynamic Core Defense Industries in the late eighties, not too long after the Reagan presidency started granting massive contracts for companies willing to perform the latest in military R and D. Steinham, an eager young college graduate, had jumped at the opportunity and built his empire from the ground up.

Year after year, DCDI would innovate new defense solutions and, year after year, the government would renew with the company under an even more lucrative contract. Over the nearly past thirty years, Steinham's company had made billions and managed to remain privately owned. They also had the dubious reputation of being one of the largest government-contracted employers in North America.

Steinham turned at the sound of his office door opening. The two men who entered looked stressed and weary, despite the fact they both wore pressed suits and were clean-shaved.

"Gentlemen," Steinham said, waving them to leather chairs and love seats arranged in a hexagonal shape around a low, lead-crystal coffee table. "Please sit down. I'm sure you're tired."

"That would be an understatement, sir," Jack Cyrus replied.

Steinham waited to take his seat until after Cyrus and Riley Braden were comfortable. "Can I get you anything?"

The men shook their heads.

Steinham crossed his legs, tugged at the crease line of one pant leg and said, "I've reviewed your report very carefully, Colonel Cyrus. I'm terribly sorry for the loss of some of your men."

Cyrus cleared his throat before replying, "Thank you, sir."

"Have you managed to contact the others who survived?"

"We have, sir. They're all fine, no injuries."

"And you're certain every one of those you were forced to leave behind was dead?"

Steinham could see the flush of embarrassment mixed with anger on Cyrus's face. He'd probably not appreciated the way Steinham had phrased that particular question, but then, Steinham didn't give a good damn. Cyrus understood quite well who paid the bills, and Steinham had been quite clear in his expectations before ever agreeing to hire the mercenary leader.

"All those of my men who were left behind are confirmed KIAs, sir. You have no reason to be concerned about security."

"And I assume no reason to believe they will manage to trace any of those men back here."

It was Braden who spoke up. "Begging your pardon, Colonel?"

Cyrus nodded and Braden looked at Steinham. "Sir, I was the one who personally vetted every one of the men on our team. I can assure you that nothing in their identities or covers could be traced back to you, DCDI or any of your affiliated holdings."

"Thank you, Major Braden. I'll take you at your word. With that matter dispensed, the only thing left to discuss is your failure to retrieve the information on the most probable entities responsible for Oleg Dratshev's disappearance." Steinham looked Cyrus in the eye. "You understand, Colonel, the very seriousness this failure on your part to accomplish the mission objectives?"

"I do understand," Cyrus said, obviously trying to remain calm. "But you must realize that the reason we failed is the same reason I lost a half dozen of my men. We were set up."

"And you have proof of this?"

"He has me, sir," Braden said. "And again, begging your pardon, Colonel? I was *there,* Mr. Steinham. Our failure to accomplish mission objectives had nothing to do with incompetence. We executed the plan exactly as we told you we would. Security forces there had been beefed up and they were actually waiting inside the data vault."

"Yes, that's exactly what Colonel Cyrus's report indicates," Steinham said. "But that's not enough to prove you were set up."

"I would tend to agree with you, sir," Cyrus replied. "But it does indicate they knew we were coming. And they specifically waited until we were well inside the perimeter to engage us. Had this been a legitimate federal op, they would've hit before we ever got the chance to get inside."

Steinham shook his head. "What's your point exactly, Colonel?"

"My point, sir, is that they seemed fully intent on destroying our entire team. I think they wanted to make sure none of us got out alive. Had we not been split into two teams, they might well have gotten away with it."

Steinham considered this and finally nodded. He had to admit there was significant merit to what Cyrus and Braden had told him. "I'll agree someone or something definitely wanted to keep the incident on the QT. But it's still disturbing because in any case, it would indicate we have a security leak inside DCDI. We can't have that. Ever. So, gentlemen, I will leave it up to you to find the leak and plug it."

"And how do you suggest we plug it?" Cyrus asked. The hard, level gaze Steinham made Cyrus reply, "I see."

"Now since we weren't able to obtain the information I'd hoped from the data vault, I was forced to pursue a secondary line of inquiry. I got a very interesting response."

Steinham rose and poured himself a drink from the fully-stocked wet bar. He didn't offer either of his guests anything. They were technically on duty and would've refused, so Steinham figured why bother.

Ice clinked in the tumbler as Steinham continued. "I would doubt either of you is familiar with electromagnetics beyond the most rudimentary facts, so you'll indulge me while I elaborate.

"DCDI got involved in the physics of EMP weapons about ten years ago. In fact, I funded an entire department devoted solely to such research. But after three years and employing some of the best minds, we weren't making enough headway so I shut the project down."

Steinham poured his brandy and then returned to his seat before continuing. "Then we got wind through our connections inside the intelligence community of backchannel talk regarding Dr. Oleg Dratshev. They were mostly rumors, but they were enough to get my attention and, based on what I knew from our time of research here, those rumblings sounded very promising.

"I tried every way I knew to persuade Dratshev to come work for me but he is a staunch socialist and a man of—how can I say this?—eclectic tastes."

"It would seem somebody beat you to the punch," Cyrus said.

Steinham gave the remark serious consideration. "Perhaps. Although I would not have dismissed hiring your team to perform a similar action, Colonel, much of what we do here is still scrutinized by government overseers. I have to take my hat off to whoever managed to pull off Dratshev's abduction. Of course, we may now never know who that is given your failure to retrieve information on his disappearance from the NSA's data storage network."

Cyrus seemed to squirm in his seat on that remark, something that gave Steinham a small measure of satisfaction. He couldn't really blame Cyrus. He'd given the mercenary tougher jobs and the colonel had come through with an unusually high record of success. Based on that fact alone, Steinham had to admit there was some merit to the military man's theory they'd been set up. But by who? And what were the chances this incident would eventually be traced back to him despite Cyrus's assurances the operation couldn't be linked to DCDI?

Steinham took a swallow of brandy, letting its smooth burn linger in his mouth and throat before he spoke. "But given we don't have that intelligence, we must now draft an alternate plan to obtaining Dratshev's whereabouts."

"You have a suggestion, sir?" Braden asked.

Steinham couldn't resist tendering a knowing smile. "As a matter of fact, I do. Some connections I have within the military community indicate that the FSB has launched a full investigation into Dratshev's disappearance. There's every indication that if they are able to locate him, they will most likely kill him. I believe your particular talents are well suited to preventing that from happening, Colonel Cyrus."

"You want to send us overseas, then?" Cyrus asked.

"It wouldn't be my first choice but…yes. I think sending you to Minsk to make contact with my man there would be the most prudent course of action. However, I don't want you to go personally. I need you here for another operation."

"I'm afraid I don't understand."

"I'd like to send Major Braden." Steinham pinned Cyrus's adjutant with a serious gaze. "This operation will require a bit of stealth and an uncanny ability at improvisation. Outside of you, Major Braden is the only person I'd trust to do that."

"You'll forgive me for saying so, sir," Cyrus replied, "but we had an agreement that my men answer to me and only me. You're not permitted to give my men orders."

"Be careful, Colonel Cyrus," Steinham warned. "I don't need to be reminded of our agreement. And I'm not attempting to give Major Braden orders. I'm merely suggesting that if he is not put in charge of the mission, I won't move forward with it. Unfortunately that would force me to turn to other resources perhaps more…flexible."

Cyrus didn't say anything, so Steinham decided to let him stew on it awhile. He knew the guy would give in. His contract with Cyrus wasn't exclusive, after all, and all present knew that fact all too well. If Steinham decided to go another way, that would signal his termination of their contractual relationship.

Steinham and DCDI had developed into an extremely lucrative contract for Cyrus's group. To lose that contract would likely mean financial ruin.

Steinham let the thought play a bit longer as he downed the last of his brandy. Then he said, "But let's not rush to any decisions just yet, eh, Colonel? Your team has been invaluable to me and I would not like to sever the ties between us just for the sake of expediency."

"Nor would I," Cyrus replied quickly, his face reddening ever so perceptibly.

Good, Steinham thought.

"So do you have a specific plan in mind, sir?" Cyrus asked, probably more in hope of changing the subject than in any real interest in the operation.

"I think sending a very small team to Minsk would be prudent," Steinham said. "No more than three, at most. You may hand-pick them, of course, provided one of them will be Major Braden. I can then give you details on how to make contact with the CIA agent there. Beyond that, I don't care about the details of the operation—you may plan them to the last letter. I only ask that you keep me apprised and if you have the opportunity to retrieve Dr. Dratshev you will do so at whatever costs necessary. We cannot afford another failure."

Cyrus looked at Braden. "Major?"

"Yes, sir, I believe that can be arranged quite easily," Braden replied.

Cyrus nodded and returned his gaze to Steinham. "It looks like we have a deal, sir. We can be ready to leave within three hours."

"Excellent," Steinham said. "You've made the right decision, Colonel. You won't regret it."

"I hope not," Cyrus muttered.

Steinham believed the mercenary thought the remark had gone unheard. But Steinham had heard it—and he would certainly remember it.

CHAPTER FIVE

Beginning his third day of captivity, Oleg Dratshev rose, bathed and dressed in the expensive slacks and shirt provided by his captors. If nothing else, Madari had proved to have excellent taste in clothing, much like Dratshev, so to this point the Russian scientist had found his conditions tolerable.

In fact, he had to admit his "captivity" to this point had been surprisingly comfortable. He'd been free to roam Madari's estate and surrounding grounds at will, not to mention fed and quartered in the lap of luxury.

As a purist and amateur homeopath—the only social vice being tobacco and the infrequent consumption of quality vodka—Dratshev had found it difficult to shake the effects of the drug they'd used to incapacitate him. His muscles still ached and he still experienced occasional nausea. Most of that had now subsided and Dratshev found it increasingly difficult to pass the time.

Madari obviously understood this well. In fact, Dratshev's host hadn't spoken to him since his arrival, apparently content to leave him be until Dratshev reached a more lucid and compliant state of mind. The quiet knock at the door, answered by one of the four large guards assigned to watch the prisoner, signaled Dratshev's seclusion had finally come to an end.

Dratshev looked at the door from where he'd been

seated and just finished the last plate of a massive break-fast served to him an hour earlier.

"Good morning, Dr. Dratshev," Madari said as he took a seat at the opposite end of the table. "I take it you're feeling better."

"I am."

Madari nodded with an expression of satisfaction. "I would assume the fact I've left you to your own devices the past couple days wasn't lost on you."

"It was not." Dratshev downed the last of his luke-warm tea with milk.

"You've finished your breakfast, now, and you appear well rested. Good. We may then continue our conversa-tion from the other day."

Dratshev held up a hand. "While I'm grateful for your hospitality, and I choose that word only to show my defer-ence to your kind treatment of me, I must again politely decline to assist you."

Madari's face remained passive. "I'm sorry you've chosen to take that position."

"I'm sure. You undoubtedly have scruples and were careful not to mistreat me."

"Mistreating you wouldn't serve a purpose."

"It wouldn't," Dratshev said. "Any more than employ-ing vicious means would prompt me to cooperate with you."

"One thing you should understand about me up front, Dr. Dratshev, is that I'm not an animal. My refraining from brutish treatment is a conscious choice—the only thing I feel separates us from the animals of today's so-ciety. I've seen enough bloodshed and misery to last a couple of lifetimes. There is nothing as detestable to me as senseless violence."

"Yet you chose to take me by force," Dratshev said.

"Would you have come with me voluntarily?" Madari smiled and splayed his hands. "But the point you make is conceded. I did what I did only out of necessity, as I've already explained."

Dratshev sighed. "I don't suppose you have any cigarettes."

Madari turned immediately to one of his men, who disappeared through the door, and then returned his intent gaze to Dratshev. "Might I be bold to suggest that the fact I've not harmed you would at least buy me an audience?"

"Only foolish men refuse to listen," Dratshev said.

"My purpose for bringing you here is, quite simply, that I believe in the merits of your research. You see, Doctor, I was once a very high-ranking member of the Libyan government. My position in that government was not too dissimilar from your own—military research and development, although in an unrelated field."

"So you're a scientist, too."

Madari laughed. "Hardly."

The guard returned with a pack of cigarettes and matches. Madari waited until Dratshev had lit one before continuing, "It was my job to see to the security of scientists, much as those within your own FSB were assigned to do. This is why it was I took you from them with little effort."

Dratshev exhaled a cloud of blue-gray smoke. "I can assure you that they will find out."

"In due time," Madari admitted. "But only when I'm ready to tell them. This will be very soon provided I can pique your curiosity."

"I've already told you that I'm completely loyal to my country. I won't cooperate with you."

"Fair enough, but please at least afford me the opportunity to enlighten you to a few facts. The first being that you were betrayed by your own handler."

"Phah! I don't believe you."

"You might if I told you that the team sent to extract you was only a few minutes away."

Dratshev wasn't sure he'd heard Madari correctly at first, but then he recalled the handler telling him the retrieval team had been an hour out. "That proves nothing."

"It does when you consider our agent was able to positively identify you just minutes after you placed the call to your people."

Dratshev remained silent.

"Oh, yes," Madari said. "The very seductive young lady who engaged you in the club... She works for me. In fact, you will see her again very soon."

"What does that prove, sir?"

"It proves we had eyes on you the moment you entered Minsk. We knew your travel plans, your location and your purpose for being there. All of it. That information all came courtesy of your handler. You see, despite any faith you might have in the volition of the FSB, there's no question everyone has a price. Your handler came rather cheaply.

"But let's forget that. The other more telling fact is that none of your prototypes was in Belarus. There was no secret development factory north of the city. The government of Belarus would have never permitted such activity by the Russians within your country, to say nothing of the half dozen foreign intelligence agencies with a presence there."

"You've still not provided proof. I won't take your word alone for it."

"You don't have to, Dr. Dratshev. I haven't brought you here to tell stories. I've brought you here because I *do* have prototypes of your designs."

"To what end?"

"As I explained, I was once a prominent member of the Libyan government. I was also a leader within what most of the world has dubbed the Arab Spring. But my reasons for that involvement were based solely on my desire to see the Libyan government leave behind the chains of despotism and tyranny that have so long plagued it, and enter into a new and true form of democratic government. A government elected by the people, not by sedition and fear."

"A noble goal, if true," Dratshev said, inclining his head to show respect for the idea. "But somewhat naive, don't you think?"

Madari seemed unmoved. "Is it? You seem to forget my background. I've spent most of my adult life around scientists and I understand how they think."

"Is that right?"

"It is. Stop and consider for a moment why you do what you do, Doctor. The mind of a genius is not motivated by something so abstract and banal as patriotism or thirst for power. Most are also not given to fame or fortune, despite their gigantic egos. No, Dr. Dratshev, I imagine you're motivated by what most of your kind are—scientific curiosity and the thrill of discovery."

"And that's what you're counting on with me?"

Madari produced a gentle laugh. "That's exactly what I'm counting on. Come on, admit it. You *are* curious about the prototypes."

"Perhaps," Dratshev said with a shrug, although he knew Madari was too clever to be fooled. "But I won't help you perfect them."

"Well, I'm determined not to take no for an answer," Madari said as he stood. "Would you be kind enough to accompany me to the range?"

Dratshev stubbed out his cigarette, pocketed the remaining pack and matches, and rose with a shrug. "I suppose there's no harm. And it's not as though I have a choice, eh?"

"Take heart, Doctor," Madari replied. "I think you're about to be impressed."

As they walked down the long corridor that terminated in an exit, Dratshev said, "I must admit you have a very nice home."

"Thank you."

"I don't suppose you'd care to tell me where we are."

"Of course," Madari said. "We're in the Greek Isles. Although you'll understand if I'm not more specific than that. Not that you could escape. Not unless you are an excellent swimmer and impervious to sharks."

"I'll take your word for it. I am curious about another matter."

"You're going to ask where I learned to speak Russian."

"Very clever."

"Not really," Madari said. "As I noted earlier, I have a comprehensive understanding of scientific curiosity. Although, I'm hardly an enigma to be solved. While most would consider a native of the Middle East who lives in the Mediterranean and speaks fluent Russian—and I admit that on the surface it's odd—you'll remember I was trained in security at a military R and D facility in the northern region of Libya. I spent many years there. Some of our scientists were from other countries, including a few from the former Soviet Union. I spent four years training in a number of languages. I also speak English and Spanish. And Arabic, of course."

"Of course."

The pair walked the rest of the way in silence and it wasn't until they reached the range that Dratshev understood why he'd not seen it during his earlier romps through the massive grounds. The range was accessed off a secured, gated entrance obscured by foliage woven directly into the chain links of the gate.

They passed through a narrow path created by a natural break between two hedgerows that stood well above their heads. They emerged on the other side and Dratshev immediately recognized the familiar sunken bunkers and supply buildings that probably housed an array of weaponry.

"My security team utilizes this as their training grounds, as well."

"Impressive."

"Not yet," Madari said with a chuckle.

Madari led him to one of the short, squat buildings and rapped twice on a heavy metal door. The door opened and two men emerged, each carrying the oddest-looking weapons Dratshev had ever seen. They literally looked like something out of a science-fiction movie. The barrels, or what Dratshev assumed to be barrels, were thick and extraordinarily long—he estimated nearly nine feet. Directly behind the barrel was a boxy, transparent chamber containing some type of coiled tubing. The stock had a brushed steel finish but there were flutes in the superior line of the stock that looked like bubble levels.

Dratshev's mouth dropped open as he realized they were filled with liquid helium.

Madari looked wholly satisfied. "I can see from your expression that our designs aren't that far off from your own."

Dratshev clamped his mouth closed before responding. "Hardly. They're not even close, actually."

"Nice try, Dr. Dratshev, but I'd advise you to stick to the truth. You're really not much of a liar." Madari took one of the weapons and hefted it. "These are our phase-two prototypes, actually, the closest we've been able to come to your original design specifications. But I can assure you your government hasn't come anywhere close to building anything like it. The barrel, you'll note, is still too long to make the weapon practical in small-arms applications, but we've had difficulty producing sufficient energy pulses through anything shorter. This is one of things I hope you can help us with."

"I've already told you—"

"Yes, yes, I know." Madari extended the weapon. "Here, you may hold it."

"I don't wish to hold it."

"Please."

Dratshev folded his arms, determined not to be swayed by Madari's charms. And yet…something about seeing a prototype EMP of his design, even if they hadn't gotten it nearly correct, seemed irresistible.

"Please," Madari reiterated.

"Very well," Dratshev said, taking the weapon gingerly from his captor-host.

It proved much lighter than he'd expected and he nearly dropped it from over-compensation. The barrel made it top-heavy and he had to angle it slightly to prevent the thing from landing in the gravel-and-dust floor of the range. Dratshev took a minute or two to examine the finer details and on closer inspection confirmed his suspicions about the liquid helium.

Finally he looked at Madari. "How did you—?"

"You're going to ask how I knew about the specifications. As I already explained, everyone has a price. Your handler has been extremely cooperative."

"My handler knew nothing about the designs."

"On the contrary, your handler knew *everything* about your designs. He intercepted the plans you sent to the manufacturing facility. He also arranged your transfer, without authorization from your government, I might add."

Dratshev didn't want to believe it, but his gut told him Madari spoke the truth. So he'd been set up from the beginning. And Dratshev's handler had probably come up with some story to their masters at the Kremlin about how Dratshev had arranged his own abduction as a means for defection. The leaders in Moscow were certain to have assumed by now that Dratshev was a traitor. Any FSB detachment sent wouldn't be on a search-and-rescue mission—Moscow would send an assassination team. And Dratshev knew they wouldn't rest until he was dead.

"Ah, I see the light has come on," Madari said with a knowing grin. "You finally understand the truth. You see, Dr. Dratshev, I didn't really kidnap you. I saved your life."

"And now you think I owe you something for that."

"Not at all." Madari shrugged. "It makes no difference to me if you continue to maintain your loyalty to Mother Russia. But understand that if you don't cooperate with me, I will be left with no other alternative."

"And that is?"

"To liberate you."

"I like that," Dratshev replied with a scornful laugh. "It sounds much better than kill me."

"No, I literally meant I would free you. You'll find me a very literal man, sir. As I've told you, I'm not an animal or a murderer. If you refuse to cooperate, I will set you free."

"And then what?"

Madari shrugged, clasped his hands behind his back and replied, "Then I'm certain the FSB will have no trouble finding you and terminating your life—this I can most assuredly guarantee you. This is really to say that releasing you poses absolutely no liability to me. And even if you managed to escape, chances are good you'll be on the run for the rest of your life. The odds aren't in your favor, to put it bluntly."

"It seems to have escaped your notice that if I'm dead, you will be unable to complete building of the prototypes."

"It doesn't matter." Madari favored him with a wan smile. "If you refuse to cooperate, my situation hasn't changed. And with you dead, I alone possess the knowledge and research, which I will put up for auction to the highest bidder."

"You seem to forget my government has the information, as well."

Madari shook his head. "Not all of it. Dr. Dratshev. My arrangement with your handler goes back considerably. Five years or better now, I think. He's only given your people part of the information and none of the prototype specifications. Those have come straight to me and I have lined your handler's coffers handsomely for that information."

Dratshev had heard enough and could no longer contain his temper. "None of this makes any sense, Mr. Madari."

"Please, call me—"

"Don't interrupt me! Now you've been a gracious host—nay, a *captor*—to this point, but I can no longer tolerate your egomania. I don't know what your purposes really are for stealing me and my work, but I deem they are more nefarious than anything else—despite what you say about wanting to bring democracy to your country. I doubt you have little if any influence left there, which probably explains why you're here." Dratshev gestured to indicate their surroundings.

"What I do believe is that you have no interest in keeping me alive unless I'm willing to unconditionally acquiesce to your wishes. I am not. Whatever else you may be, Mr. Madari—a gentleman or a patriot or perhaps merely an opportunist out to make as much money and a name for yourself as possible—you are a scoundrel. A wolf in sheep's clothing. So let us not pretend that your benevolence doesn't have some ulterior purpose. I am not so easily won over, despite whatever you might *think* about what motivates the scientific mind."

For a long time Madari didn't say anything, and Dratshev was convinced he'd finally called Madari's bluff. Then the man grabbed the second EMP rifle being held by the other armory guard, aimed the weapon downrange and squeezed the trigger. At first nothing happened, but then a moment later the weapon bucked hard against Madari's shoulder, hard enough for him to cry out with pain, and then the air in front of the barrel shimmered as if under heat. A moment passed and a massive box made of what appeared to be steel or iron blew apart as if had been packed with high explosives.

Dratshev ducked reflexively and then turned his gaze slowly to Madari, who was handing the rifle back to the guard while rubbing his right shoulder.

Madari whirled to face Dratshev, a gleam in his eye. "That is just a small demonstration of what your genius has accomplished, Doctor. It is my intention to sell this technology to whoever will bid the most. In fact, I released the details of the public auction this morning to five countries. We should be hearing from them very shortly."

"Clearly, I was wrong about you, Mr. Madari," Dratshev replied. "You're neither a fake nor an opportunist. You are, quite simply, a lunatic."

"Perhaps," Madari said. "But there are other lunatics throughout history who were able to achieve much more than I ever subsume I may. And for now, Dr. Dratshev, I will do this whether I have your cooperation or not. Think about it. You can *profit* by this—I will provide you the most advanced facilities at your disposal. Even after we auction this current technology, nothing says we have to stop there. With you by my side, we can develop weapons even more powerful and advanced—weapons I can use to equip those in my country who want to see the same thing as I can. Together, we can build the most powerful army on earth!"

"I...I can't," Dratshev said even as he knew that he would. Madari *had* been right about him. "And yet, I must!"

Ishaq Madari smile. "Excellent. Most excellent."

CHAPTER SIX

Minsk, Belarus

"Mr. McMasters, welcome to Minsk."

David McCarter shook the hand the woman offered him while the remaining Phoenix Force members looked on.

To have called her anything other than beautiful would've been absurd. She had short dark hair, cut pixie-style, liquid-blue eyes and full red lips. The high cheekbones arched gracefully and dipped to soft cheeks with just a hint of dimples at her mouth.

"Pleasure's mine, Miss—"

"Mariam," she replied, "but I prefer if you simply call me Mishka. My cover name."

Just one of her many cover names, actually, although she probably assumed McCarter knew little about her. In the interest of keeping her friendly, the Phoenix Force leader opted not to let on that nothing could be further from the truth.

Muriel Annabel Stanish, age thirty-four, had been a CIA case officer for six years. She'd spent the first two operating Stateside with the documents section specialized in European forgeries. After distinguished service and at least half a dozen requests for transfer, she'd finally been assigned to Minsk, Belarus, to fill a vacancy—one that had occurred under rather dubious circumstances.

"You look rather surprised to see me," Mishka observed. "I suppose they neglected to tell you I was a woman."

"Not at all," McCarter replied.

"Um, I think we're just surprised," T. J. Hawkins interjected with a disarming grin, "that we wouldn't be meeting such a breathtaking young woman as yourself, miss."

McCarter, teeth clenched and looking out of the corner of his eye, said quickly, "You'll have to forgive my associate, but he thinks he's bloody charming when he's really just being annoying."

Mishka chuckled and waved it away. "No worries, McMasters. I get that a lot."

"Do tell," Encizo said, eyebrows rising.

"More than might you think," Mishka replied with a grin of her own. She clapped her hands together for emphasis. "But I'm certain you're tired and would like to go to your hotel. I've arranged an entire floor of rooms for you at one of the local hotels. It's in the downtown area with easy access to all the other areas, but still out of the way of the regular tourist flow. If you'll follow me?"

As the warriors fell into step behind McCarter, who kept pace at her side, the Phoenix Force leader said, "Seems you thought of everything."

"Meaning?" she asked.

"Your choice of hotels was…*interesting*. Just seems you've more experience than we were led to believe."

She shrugged. "It only makes sense, really. I was certain from what I'd been told that you would want to remain inconspicuous and my…experience with the proprietors is that they are discreet."

"And what do you know of our mission?" McCarter asked as they reached a sporty European-made coupe parked a fair distance from the hangar.

"Not out here," she said, shaking her head. She pointed to a large custom van nearby. "You can ride with me. The rest will ride with Carnes in the van with your equipment."

McCarter nodded and gestured for his team to do as instructed. He then squeezed his muscular frame into the small sports car that was fully loaded and boasted genuine leather interior. "Pretty nice ride the Company offers these days."

"It's my own," she said. "Bought and paid for during my layover in Italy. I had it shipped here."

"Seems like some serious dough to lay out for a CIA case officer."

If the comment offended Mishka, she didn't show it—cool under pressure and relatively unemotional. McCarter filed the information for future reference.

"My father ran his own company," she replied. "Physicist for a defense contractor. That's partly why they transferred me here."

"So you were going to tell me how much you knew about our purpose here."

"Enough that it might surprise you," Mishka said. "You're here at my request. Imagine my surprise when the Agency replied less than twenty-four hours later to let me know they were sending you."

"We don't work for the CIA."

Mishka offered a light laugh. "I knew *that* the moment you stepped off the plane."

"How?"

"You're not the typical crew. I've been in this business

long enough to know the difference between a standard tactical unit and black ops. You're obviously trouble-shooters of a different breed, and that's fine by me."

"Glad to hear it," McCarter replied. "Because we were promised we'd have your full cooperation."

"And you will."

"So give me the rundown on what you know to this point."

Mishka blew out a sigh through pursed lips. "Unfortunately, I don't have much more intelligence outside of what you probably know."

"No worries. I'll start with whatever you give me."

"Well, I think it goes without saying this city's crawling with Russian heavies—mostly FSB and maybe a few contacts that were already in-country."

McCarter nodded. "Agreed. Our people informed us they showed up in force as soon as Dratshev disappeared."

"Right. From what I've heard, his abduction was most likely an inside job."

"We were told that, as well, but we had a little trouble buying it."

"Because?"

"Something just doesn't bloody wash," McCarter replied with a shrug. "There's no logic behind staging an abduction of one of their own and then publicizing it."

"I agree. Although I probably don't have to point out the FSB has always placed great importance on propaganda. It could be they staged this for the purposes of security."

"You mean, take Dratshev off the radar and then divert attention by blaming some outside, mysterious party."

"You have to admit, they've done it before," Mishka said.

"True. But despite their efforts, most competing agencies have been able to see through such attempts with relative ease. This time around the fact an outside party really did manage to kidnap Dratshev has merit."

"I think you're right."

McCarter couldn't resist a grin. "Glad we're on the same level."

"Why?"

"Takes less convincing when I tell you our plan."

"Which is?"

"I'll keep the details close to the vest for now, if you don't mind. But what I will say is that we plan to pick up the FSB's trail and see where it leads us."

"Let them do the legwork for you."

"Right. Plus, if this is a legit snatch, it won't take the grabbers long to touch base with the Russian government."

"Unless they have their own purposes for Dratshev."

"That's another possibility and I wouldn't be so naive as to dismiss the theory out of hand."

"If you—"

"Watch out!"

Mishka had turned to glance at McCarter and missed the dark sedan that rolled alongside the driver's side of her coupe. They were traveling along a four-lane road that led to the Old Town part of the city.

McCarter reached beneath his coat and quick-drew a Browning Hi-Power from shoulder leather. He aimed at the small window behind Mishka's seat as the dark sedan swerved toward the coupe and tried to collide with them in an attempt to force her to crash into the cars parked along the road.

Mishka saw McCarter's reaction and smartly tromped

the accelerator to bring the tail of the vehicle up enough to offer McCarter a clear shot at the vehicle.

"Sorry 'bout the window, love!" he shouted before squeezing the trigger twice.

The first bullet shattered the coupe's window and the second took out the passenger-side window on the sedan. The outline of the man's face was all McCarter could make out in the dark, but he didn't have trouble discerning the surprised whites of his eyes. McCarter fired a third shot and the mask disappeared in a crimson spray. The sedan swerved off its intended course as the driver whipped the wheel hard left and put the sedan into a one-eighty.

McCarter whipped a small walkie-talkie from his belt.

"Gray One to team. You got that?"

"Saw it all, Gray One." Encizo's voice came back immediately. "Should we pursue?"

"Hell, yes," McCarter muttered.

McCarter checked the side mirror and saw the van slow suddenly and then begin to swing to the right so Carnes, the driver, could perform a U-turn.

The next minute seemed to happen in slow motion as another sedan approaching from the oncoming lane swerved straight into their lane and picked up speed.

"Shit!" Mishka double-clutched, popping the gearshift to neutral and then reverse as she put her vehicle into a power slide.

The sedan brushed past them, missing by a margin so narrow it made McCarter shudder to think about it. Despite the ferocious attack, Mishka was performing admirably and McCarter felt staunch confidence with her behind the wheel even as his stomach rolled with the turn of the vehicle. In a car with a higher profile the maneuver would've caused them to roll but the low center of gravity kept all four wheels on the pavement. Mishka jerked something down and McCarter realized he'd not even noticed she'd managed to somehow engage her parking brake at some point.

The Phoenix Force leader heard an interesting hiss as Mishka disengaged the air-powered brake. That didn't come standard in any sports car he knew of, which meant she'd had it installed after market. Without being told, Mishka laid in a pursuit course of the sedan that had tried to ram them head-on but the effort proved futile. The sedan had continued on course and smashed into the back of the van carrying the remaining members of Phoenix Force. McCarter felt a ball of rage form in his gut and ordered her to stop short of the sedan on its right flank.

As she braked to a screeching halt, McCarter bailed from the coupe and made a beeline for the van—it had bounced onto the sidewalk and come to a smashing end in one of the storefronts—while he fired at the sedan on the run.

Four men exited the sedan, unaware McCarter had anticipated their moves. As a champion pistol marksman and veteran combatant, McCarter had never missed from that distance, which the first man out of the enemy sedan learned the hard way. Two 9 mm rounds caught McCarter's target in the chest, puncturing his right lung and driving him backward. The man flopped against the sedan, bounced off and came to rest on the pavement.

The front-seat passenger managed to get clear before McCarter could track him, and opened up with an MP-5K on the run. Bullets buzzed past McCarter's head like angry hornets, but the gunner hadn't led the Briton correctly and none of the shots landed.

McCarter made the cover of the van just as Hawkins and Manning burst from the sliding door, both toting weapons from their equipment bags.

"Anyone hurt?" McCarter inquired.

"Bumps and bruises," Hawkins replied even as Manning was already putting distance between him and his friends.

The Canadian warrior leveled his MP-5 SD6 at the survivors from the sedan and triggered a few bursts from the hip. This variant of the Heckler & Koch SMG had built-in sound suppression so the reports were little more than pops in the muggy night air. Two more of their enemy numbers were reduced, one taking a trio of 9 mm Parabellum rounds to the chest.

Hawkins joined the fray a moment later with his own weapon, identical to Manning's, spraying a high sustained burst that swept across the hood and blew the driver's head apart in a mess of blood, bone and gray matter.

The lone survivor popped over the roof a few times and triggered hasty bursts from his assault rifle before jumping into the driver's seat and tromping the accelerator. The sedan blasted from the scene in a concert of squealing tires and roaring engine accompanied by the smoky aftermath of scorched rubber.

The sounds of battle died away, replaced by the distant two-tone wail of police sirens.

Encizo popped his head out from the open van door. "Driver has a monitor for the secure police bands. He says we're going to have company in short order."

McCarter's expression soured as he looked over the now defunct van. Smoke wisped from the engine compartment and the odor of coolant and oil stung his nostrils. "Looks like your chariot isn't going anywhere, mate."

Mishka's car pulled up before anyone could say more. The young beauty jumped from her coupe. "Store your gear in my trunk. Then split up and rendezvous at the hotel. Carnes can tell you where it's at. I'll meet you there."

McCarter looked at his comrades, who all shrugged.

It was James who said, "Sounds like our best option at this point."

McCarter nodded and his team went into action, daisy-chaining the gear into the open trunk of Mishka's coupe. McCarter took the hotel information from Carnes, which he committed to memory before passing it on to Manning.

Through SOP, they already knew how to split up the assignments. Hawkins with James, Encizo with McCarter, and Manning on his own since he spoke French and could easily pass as a tourist. Carnes would accompany James and Hawkins since McCarter had memorized the hotel info and then given the information to Manning.

"We meet in two hours," McCarter said. "No earlier. That should give all of us enough time to get there and scope it out before we check in. Get into trouble, send the pre-coded distress signal to the Farm. Questions?"

Nobody had any and McCarter nodded. "Good luck, mates. Move out."

By the time the Minsk police arrived on scene, nobody but the dead remained to greet them.

NEARLY THREE HOURS passed before all the men of Phoenix Force were reunited in the small, comfortable hotel in the heart of Minsk's Old Town. The light of dawn spilled around the corners of the heavy drapes drawn across the windows in the room shared by McCarter, Encizo and Hawkins. All team members had arrived without incident, but Mishka had been unexplainably detained—when McCarter questioned her about it she'd simply shrugged him off or changed the subject. Mc-Carter finally gave it a rest and just accepted she'd had her reasons for being late. Mishka had already gone far and above proving her loyalty and McCarter knew he had no cause to mistrust her at this point.

"You brought our weapons?" Encizo asked her.

Mishka shook her head. "Too risky. I decided to leave them at a secure location. At least until the police patrols have thinned."

"We can't be without that equipment, ma'am," Hawkins said.

Mishka blinked. "I promise you, all of your equipment is perfectly safe. The cops are out in force looking for you. It's better to wait. Trust me, I've been here awhile now and I know how things work. You don't. If any of us were caught with even the pistols we carry now, they could land us in some remote prison for life. We'd have to shoot our way out."

"Fine," McCarter agreed. "Let's get to this attack and see if we can't figure out how we got bloody compromised. Mishka, you got any idea who those bastards might've been?"

"If I had to guess, I'd say FSB."

Manning raised an eyebrow. "That sounds a little out of left field."

"I was just thinking the same thing," McCarter said with a grunt. "If we accept her theory then we got big troubles."

"Such as?" Mishka inquired.

"Well, for starters," James said, "someone would've had to leak our arrival to the Russians."

"Right," Encizo agreed. "And for another, they would've had to know who we were, where we'd come in and just about a dozen other details about our mission here. The chances they'd have someone that deep or high inside the CIA is against any odds I'd stake."

"How do you know the leak isn't within your *own* agency?" Mishka asked with a challenging expression.

McCarter snorted. "Nice try, love, but that couldn't happen. There are only three other people who have any details of our mission parameters. They don't even store that information in our computers."

"Which are practically impenetrable, anyway," James added.

"So where does that leave us?" McCarter asked. He looked around the room. "Anybody?"

Manning cleared his throat and when McCarter nodded, he said, "Let's assume for the moment the compromise is in the CIA. Chances are pretty good, Mishka, you've been here long enough that it's *your* cover that's been blown and not anybody higher up or back home. Our mission orders came practically from your lips to our ears."

"What are you saying?" Mishka interjected.

"I'm saying that they probably figured out what was happening by keeping their eyes on you. Your apartment here in Minsk is probably bugged, and maybe even your car."

"Impossible," she replied. "I sweep both of them on a regular schedule."

Hawkins shook his head. "Which could well be part

of the problem. If you sweep on a schedule, they'd be wise to that, too. All they'd have to do is deactivate the bugs, wait until you completed your sweeps and then reactivate them."

"So I'll go sweep them right now," Mishka said.

McCarter shook his head. "Too dangerous. They still know your vehicle and your movements. They might've even traced you here, which means we're compromised, as well."

"Not a chance," she replied. "I didn't bring my car. After I dropped off the weapons, I returned it to the parking lot across from my apartment. I didn't want to drive it around with the damage, in case the police noticed and stopped me. I took the first available bus, took another connection, and then walked the rest of the way to be sure I wasn't followed."

"Smart and beautiful," Hawkins said with a wink.

Mishka smiled. "I try. And you're a player, mister."

"I try."

"Axe the cute stuff," McCarter said. "What we need to do is reevaluate our situation and determine if we're safe here or if we should change venue."

"I think it goes without saying we should get out of here anyway," Manning said. "Just for the sake of caution."

McCarter nodded. "Fair enough, but I want to think about it for a bit. Meanwhile, let's get your side arms cleaned up best you can with what's available while I call the Farm to update them on the situation."

"What do you want me to do?" Mishka asked.

"Why don't you and Carnes go stake out the lobby, just to be safe. And find all of the possible alternate exits just in case we have to beat feet in a hurry."

Mishka nodded before gesturing for Carnes to follow her out.

Once they'd gone, James sidled up next to McCarter and nodded in the direction of the door through which the pair of CIA agents had exited. "Do you trust them?"

McCarter frowned into the secure phone as he dialed the number that would connect them by satellite relay directly to Stony Man Farm using high-speed bursts of heavily encrypted data. "I don't know. I want to, but..."

"But?"

"I just don't know."

CHAPTER SEVEN

Major Riley Braden would never have admitted it to anyone, but he didn't trust David Steinham. He couldn't put his finger on it, but something about the defense contractor just didn't add up. For one thing, he'd managed to find a way to violate his agreement with Cyrus without actually making it look otherwise. Braden had mentioned this to Cyrus, but his friend and CO had dismissed the idea as ludicrous.

Braden suspected it might have something to do with Cyrus's fear of losing their contract with Steinham, along with the money that came with it. Braden firmly believed there were other fish in the sea, easier to catch than holding on to the DCDI contract. At the same time, they'd lost a number of good men in a single operation, something that had never happened to Cyrus since starting the company. Braden had worked with Cyrus long enough to know it was partly a matter of professional pride and partly Cyrus's wish that the deaths of their comrades did not become a vain sacrifice.

It was for this reason Braden agreed to take the mission to Belarus, even though he felt deep down the operation would turn out to be a dud.

Now aboard one of Steinham's corporate jets, Braden sifted through the intelligence that had come from the DCDI contact Steinham claimed to have inside the country. Among the scant intelligence reports, Braden took particular interest in a section that theorized a special ops unit of the United States government might be dispatched to investigate Dratshev's disappearance.

All the rest of it had to do with the EMP research Dratshev had supposedly been working on, most of which went over Braden's head. His specialties were covert military tactics and special operations. He had no expertise in the actual science of such weapons—most of it sounded farfetched and theoretical than anything else. Braden had reached out to his own contacts, as well; who'd informed him those holding the purse strings in Moscow hadn't exactly been smitten with Dratshev's work. Braden thought that a most interesting revelation and filed it as highly important if not outright provocative. It also made him wonder if the chance didn't exist that Dratshev's progress hadn't been sabotaged by other elements within his own government. Hadn't Steinham said he'd procured some of the finest minds on the subject and for five years it had gone nowhere? What did that mean in relationship to Dratshev's research?

Braden finally pushed the question from his mind. He closed the file folder, leaned back in his seat and rubbed his eyes. For now he'd rest on what he knew and let his subconscious push the pieces around on the board until something fell into place.

Sooner or later, the answer would come to him.

"ARE YOU SURE you want to drive back to Washington?" Brognola asked.

"Positive, Hal," Carl Lyons replied.

The Able Team warriors had retrieved all the information they could from Higgs and the data crew at the NSA.

"We could have a private charter on its way to Des Moines within a few hours," Brognola announced.

"It's unnecessary," Lyons replied. "We're not going to get anything more here. We've already crossed the border into Illinois anyway."

Price interjected, "That should put you in D.C. in fifteen hours."

"Or less, the way Ironman drives," Schwarz said, directing his voice to the overhead speaker of their rental.

"What do you need from us?" Brognola asked.

"We'll want Black Betty up and ready for action as soon as we arrive."

"Understood."

"You're sure the weapons track back to this mercenary hit team?" Price asked.

"It's your intelligence," Lyons remarked. "But yeah, given the three dead men who were left behind that we positively identified, there's no question they were all veterans. One had supposedly become a freelancer, but the other two were definitely hired on by a guy named Jack Cyrus."

"Yes, we looked into his record as you asked," Price said. "Aaron, would you care to enlighten us?"

"Be glad to," Kurtzman's booming voice replied over the speaker. "Jack Cyrus was a career officer in the United States Army. He completed his course work at West Point and pre-indoctrination for Ranger School at Fort Benning before being accepted to a SWCC boat team school in California. After that, he led numerous special operations in locations all over the world. He was on the back side of his twenty years when he suffered wounds sustained during an engagement in Afghanistan. He was discharged medically after being highly decorated, but his files remained sealed under the order of a military judge."

"Which of course means nothing to you," Lyons said.

Kurtzman chuckled. "Of course. We managed to come across some of that sealed data. It probably won't come as any surprise to you that Cyrus, among other things, had some psychological issues."

"PTSD?" Blancanales inquired.

"Among other things," Kurtzman replied. "Suffice it to say the good Colonel Cyrus's issues were serious enough for an Army doctor to declare him unfit for further duty. They've become much more serious about this issue after what happened with Nidal Hassan in the shooting at Fort Hood. The Army immediately acted on the recommendation and discharged Cyrus."

"So what happened to him after that?" Schwarz asked.

"He did odd jobs for a while, mostly security consulting and a little bit of desk work. But I guess he couldn't stay away from it and after about a year he walked off his job one day and nobody heard from him for more than eighteen months."

"Let me guess," Lyons interrupted. "He falls off the radar for almost two years and then one day shows up with a brand-new mercenary company and a dozen recruits for sale to the high bidder."

It was Price who answered. "Correct. And the most recent highest bidder on Colonel Cyrus's résumé happens to be a guy named David Steinham."

"What's his story?" Lyons asked.

"Steinham's a piece of work," Price said. "His sanity has been called into question more than once, as well, although nobody's ever been able to touch him. Part of the reason for that is he's extremely private and reclusive.

His headquarters are here in Washington. He's head of a corporation called Dynamic Core Defense Industries, DCDI for short. He's been in the defense contractor game for the past twenty-five years. He's a genius and politically powerful—part of that comes from the fact he has his hand in the pockets of nearly every elected official of note in Wonderland."

"Sounds like a real peach," Schwarz remarked.

Lyons grunted. "And he sounds like a guy who'd be more than interested in information about Dratshev and his research."

"You may be more right than you know." Brognola's voice cut in.

"A moment ago," Brognola said, "I just left a special meeting with the Man. If what he told me is true, this thing is about blow up in our faces.

"I'll try to sum this up as succinctly as possible about why I'm concerned," Brognola continued. "About an hour ago, the leaders of five major countries, including the United States, received an electronic transmission over secure UN channels and using a NATO security code. The source of the transmission is still unknown but NSA analysts are working on it as fast as possible. In the meantime, it's the content of this transmission that has us greatly concerned.

"Apparently, Dr. Dratshev is alive and under the protection of—the sender's way of putting it and not my own—a man named Ishaq Madari. The transmission included some proof of life, video and so forth, so we've verified it's not bogus. Of course, we immediately did some looking into Madari's background. You won't believe this guy."

"Try us," Lyons said.

"Ishaq Madari is a thirty-eight-year-old Libyan and was, until about six years ago, a high-level operative within the military security community of his own country. He was also, by his own admittance, a secret member of the Arab Spring. He alleges to have helped the U.S. and other countries smuggle arms to the rebels so they could overthrow Gadhafi and that he has continued to provide pro-democracy forces with whatever means necessary to see his country become a free state under democratic rule."

"Sounds like he has delusions of hopefully returning one day," Blancanales observed.

"Well…whether delusional or not, he's obviously a man with significant resources at his disposal," Price said.

"That still doesn't explain why he went to the trouble of abducting Dratshev," Lyons noted. "Or what he intends to do with him."

"We already know that," Brognola replied. "Madari has assured us that no harm will come to Dr. Dratshev— at least not by his hand. He also plans to let Dratshev continue his research in comfort and safety. Psych profilers agree right now that Madari sees what he's doing as providing aid and comfort to the enemy of *his* enemies. And for him to continue doing his work and achieving the goals of a truly democratic Libya, he's convinced himself Dratshev's research is the best bargaining chip he has at this point."

"Is he wrong?" Lyons asked.

"Unfortunately…no." A long silence followed before Brognola said, "Besides us, there are four other countries in this bidding war. China, Great Britain, Switzerland and Saudi Arabia."

"Those are some pretty interesting choices," Lyons said.

"Not if you think about it the way a guy like Madari probably would," Price replied.

"What do you mean, Barb?"

"They're all countries with great wealth. And not just some of the richest countries on Earth. Every one of them also has an interest in seeing Libya become an independently free and democratic nation."

"I don't understand why Switzerland would care," Lyons said.

"I do," Brognola said. "Think about it. Despite all of the security and policies in place, there is still a lot of money laundering through their banks."

"Exactly," Blancanales replied. "And who wants to be known as a country that happily handles the blood money of terrorists?"

"Okay," Lyons said. "So here's what it sounds as though we know. Steinham, who already has Cyrus under contract, hires a merc team to break into an NSA data vault. And he knew about this how?"

"He's a government defense contractor," Schwarz replied. "It wouldn't be hard for him to come by the information. Am I right, Barb?"

"He'd still have to jump through some hoops, but…yes. He'd have probably very little trouble learning that there was a data vault inside that facility and maybe some general information on what was being stored in that vault."

"Ah, our tax dollars hard at work to keep us secure," Lyons said with a sigh. "Okay, so he learns about Dratshev's abduction and figures maybe he can get in on the bidding? Doesn't make sense since we didn't even learn about it until a while back."

"Maybe he had something else in mind," Blancanales offered.

"That's interesting, Pol," Price said. "Go on."

Blancanales took a deep breath as if he were still gathering his thoughts, and then replied, "Well, suppose he hears Dratshev's taken and all the details about the abduction are contained within that data vault. The kind of stuff Dratshev was working on, or *is* working on, would be stuff that would certainly interest a guy like him."

"So you're thinking it's possible Steinham saw an op to take Dratshev away from whoever took Dratshev from the Russians," Lyons said.

"Who we now know to be Madari," Price noted.

"Exactly," Blancanales said. "And if Steinham is able to learn of this auction put out by Madari, you can be sure he'll go for broke in trying to take Dratshev. It may become easier, too, given that he was able to even learn of the abduction at practically the same time we learned of it."

"You think he's got somebody in his pockets?" Schwarz asked.

"Guy like that is bound to have *many* people in his pockets, including higher-ups inside the CIA."

"And we have another issue of note," Price said. "David's calling in and asking to join our little powwow."

"More the merrier," Lyons said.

A moment of silence followed and then David McCarter's voice came on the line. The Phoenix Force leader provided an update and concluded his briefing by saying, "Our contact inside the Company tells us she thinks it was FSB, but I'm having a little trouble believing that."

"Well, she could be right," Price said. "She has a lot of experience in that city and her superiors give her nothing but high marks."

"Oh, I think she's plenty smart and experienced. I'm just not sure how much I trust her. And a few others on the team are thinking the same thing."

"Well, if you think she's bad news, I wouldn't let it on yet," Lyons said. "Just a little friendly advice."

Brognola quickly sketched out for McCarter the information regarding Madari.

When he finished, McCarter said, "That's interesting, I'll bloody give you that. And it definitely sounds as though our mission objectives have changed."

"Not really," Price replied. "Until we know exactly where Dratshev's being held, it would be better if you continue moving forward just as originally planned. We don't want to let the cat out of the bag yet, especially not given what you just said about your contact."

"Not to mention, we may be able to use you in another capacity if the President decides to go with my suggestion."

"Uh, and what suggestion would that be?" Lyons asked.

"Well, I was getting to it but the right time didn't seem until now. When the Man laid it out for me, I told him I felt it was a foregone conclusion the Russians would get wind of this soon enough. Especially considering China was one of the countries being allowed to bid on the tech. Our belief is that when it does come out, the FSB will do everything in its power to destroy Dratshev, Madari and all of the alleged research and materials they've collected. We can't let that happen."

"So what's the alternative?" McCarter prompted.

"I suggested that since Phoenix Force was already in Minsk, and because we know the transmission originated from somewhere within the European or Mediterranean hemisphere, that we play along and submit a bid by Madari's terms."

"You don't actually think he'd sell to the U.S.," Lyons said with a snort.

"Possibly...or not. But we won't really know until we actually try it. And since we've nothing to lose at this point, I think it makes sense we at least give it the old college try."

"So you're thinking of using Phoenix Force as a courier for the buy?" McCarter asked.

"Of course not," Price said. "I think Hal's figuring the more contact we have with Madari, the more time it buys us to locate him."

"Your mission parameters will change only in a small sense," Brognola said. "If you are unable to get the technology and Dratshev away from Madari, your orders are to neutralize the entire situation. Quickly and permanently."

"Quickly and permanently we can do," McCarter said.

"In the meantime, David," Lyons said, "we'll be keeping Steinham and his goons off your back. But be watchful. We think he might have people either in Minsk—or the more likely scenario is they're on their way."

"Steinham? Who the hell's Steinham?" McCarter inquired.

"We'll bring you up to snuff on that issue in short order," Price said.

"Actually, I'm beginning to think Ironman could be headed for status as the Farm's newest prophet," Kurtzman interjected.

"Because?" Lyons said.

"As soon as we connected Steinham and Cyrus, I began a full data sweep on him. Background, dossiers of all employees past and present, projects, contracts, everyone he's ever worked with or talked to. Seems that one of his corporate jets filed an overseas flight plan. You'll never guess the destination."

"I'm betting…Minsk?" Price said.

"Aw, you guessed it right away!" Schwarz joked. "That's no fun! You should've made it harder, Bear."

"Listen up, gentlemen," Price said, her voice taking a motherly pitch. "There are a lot of players in this game and there are about to be a lot more. I want both teams to be diligent and to report regularly on your progress. Able Team, we'll have Black Betty ready and willing when you arrive here. And, David, you and Phoenix Force pay attention to *everything*. My guess is that you'll have multiple parties inside your AO soon enough, and the lines may get fuzzy quick."

"Yeah, agreed," McCarter replied. "And it wouldn't be the first bloody time, now, would it?"

CHAPTER EIGHT

Greek Isles

While it seemed all was going as planned, Ishaq Madari's years of experience had led him to never assume things would continue to go well. Operations of this magnitude never ran a strictly linear course. There were too many variables and if one expected longevity in life, one had to insert contingencies into any plans when things went awry. According to Mishka, the American force now in Belarus had survived the attack by Madari's team. She'd also informed him the American leader didn't seem convinced by her story about the FSB being responsible for the attack. Fortunately, Madari had been prepared for such an eventuality and advised her not to worry but to proceed as scheduled.

It was a secondary concern, anyway. Madari had finally convinced Oleg Dratshev to work on the EMP weapons and the scientist had appeared to move forward with genuine eagerness. At least for now.

In fact, Dratshev had made considerable progress in just a short time. Madari had invested most of his material resources in a building a lab equal to the task and they were already manufacturing the first of ten prototypes based on Dratshev's material designs. Madari could not resist a smile of great satisfaction as Dratshev presented the first one to him. The barrel of this weapon was half the length of the earlier prototype.

"With good reason," Dratshev replied when Madari remarked on this. "It's made of a much lighter alloy. I also reconfigured the energy chamber so that the pulse is directly cooled by coils carrying the liquid helium. This has created an energy build-up with a shorter half life."

"What about the range?"

Dratshev shrugged and frowned. "Unfortunately, my original modifications of your design did reduce distance and accuracy by about twenty-three percent. However, there is no reduction in force at the peak impact point and it still puts the bearer out of danger. Provided they do not attempt to fire at a target point-blank."

"Of course," Madari said. "Your progress is still remarkable."

"As are your facilities."

Dratshev's remark both impressed and put Madari on guard. He knew demonstrating the progress would have impressed Dratshev enough to elicit the scientist's cooperation but that did not mean he trusted Dratshev, by any means.

"Would you care to test it?" Dratshev asked.

Madari passed the rifle to Dratshev. "I would say the first honor should be yours, Doctor."

Dratshev looked concerned for a moment but then took the offer with indifference. He raised the weapon to his shoulder, aimed downrange and squeezed the trigger. The weapon responded without delay as in the earlier version, and Madari saw no significant recoil effect on Dratshev's short frame. A heartbeat later the massive block of cement blew apart and the energy wave left a hole in the steel plate at the center the size of a volleyball.

Madari nodded but consciously attempted to mask his shock. He said, "Most impressive!"

Dratshev looked at a small gauge on the side of the weapon, something that had not been present on the weapon created by Madari's engineers. "Blast it. The charge has been reduced by half. The lithium ion battery I'd hoped would sustain the energy pulse build is not effective enough."

"Is there any way to recharge it?"

"Not without a significant power source. And even then, the recharge would take time."

"This is not good, Dr. Dratshev," Madari pointed out. "It means your prototype design is only capable of generating two full EM pulses, at most."

Dratshev produced a hiss and shook his head. "I think I fully understand that, Mr. Madari."

"This won't be acceptable to my bidders."

"I beg your pardon?"

Madari had carefully planned when to reveal the information regarding his intent. "I've informed a number of my contacts that you are currently under my... protection."

"A foul term to use in consideration of the truth."

Madari allowed a little smile. "Do tell."

"Despite your hospitality, I still consider myself a captive."

"And you do well on that count, sir. But you must admit that I've intrigued you beyond your wildest aspirations. This is more, much more I'm afraid, than your comrades at the Kremlin. I've been led to understand, in fact, that the highest authority in Moscow issued a terminate-on-sight order to the FSB mere hours ago."

"Of course."

"You knew they would do this?"

"It was always the protocol."

Dratshev lit a cigarette and as he did, Madari could see his hands shake. "So then you acknowledge your life is forfeit if they were to find you, but you scorn the idea that while here you are safe."

"Perhaps I'm willing to take my chances," Dratshev replied through a cloud of smoke that wisped around his head in the gentle breeze.

"Hardly," Madari said. "No, you can put up the brave front if you so choose, Dr. Dratshev, but I will continue to offer you my support and assistance in completing your work."

"Only because you stand to gain something by it."

"And your own government did not?" Madari shook his head. He sat on a nearby bench and crossed his legs. "Since you seem intent on bantering the politics of your situation, let me take a moment of your time to explain myself in more detail."

"What makes you think I'll care?"

"Don't do that, Doctor. It's not worthy of you."

"As you wish."

"My only real concern here is that democratic rule be instantiated within Libya. I hope one day to return to my country a free man."

"I was taken to understand the government in power is attempting this. That would mean that you're actually fighting against them. I believe the conventional term for such rebellion is called terrorism."

"The attempts of the current president and so-called elected body are fallacious, at best. And if I'm a terrorist then you must admit I'm the most mild-mannered of any you've ever met. To be sure, terrorists are fanatics and I can assure you I am anything but a fanatic."

"I suppose your ideology helps you sleep better at night."

"On the contrary," Madari countered. "I've not slept well in a very long time, Dr. Dratshev. In fact, my personal physician has told me that my health is not good and that within a few years I will most likely be an invalid. That's if I live that long."

"If you're attempting to appeal to my sympathies, I'm afraid you've wasted your time. I have nothing but loathing for you, Mr. Madari."

"It probably won't interest you to know this but I did quite a careful study of your background before planning this operation."

"Is that right?"

"You were a mediocre student for the majority of your early school years and it was only by the recommendation of a number of influential professors at Yugev Polytechnica that you came to the interest of certain members at the Kremlin. You have no family to speak of—both parents are deceased, no siblings and you never married. In fact your only relation was your ailing grandmother until she passed…um, what was it? Two years ago?"

Dratshev remained impassive, smoking and staring.

"For the past fifteen years, you've thrown yourself fully and completely into your work. You have no attachments and I would assume you never really did. They are a luxury men like you realize they can never afford, a distraction from your real mistress of science."

"What do you know about attachment?"

"Much more than you might believe. I was married

with two daughters. Do you know what happened to them?"

"I don't care."

"Fine," Madari replied, trying not to look stung even though he felt as if a monster had clutched his heart. "But I will tell you. The bastards I worked for killed them when they found out I was supporting the rebellion. That's right. Gadhafi ordered my family killed. That wasn't before the men who did the job took liberties with all of them, of course. My youngest was twelve. Yes, that's right, I can see from the look on your face it disgusts you. Strange for a man who claims not to care.

"But allow me to tell you why I think you do care. As I explained before, you're apolitical and you want only to further your own scientific curiosity. But there was someone you cared about deeply, once. Ah…I see you thought I knew nothing of her, what was her name? Natalia?"

"You have no right to pry into my life," Dratshev said in a cloud of gray-blue smoke. "*No* right! And I will not listen to you any longer!"

"You will listen!" Madari said, jumping to his feet. He'd had enough of this. "You will listen because I know that you do care about other people. You cared for Natalia and they *murdered* her! She didn't die in any car accident. They killed her and they threw her body in a vehicle and pushed it over that bridge and into the cold water."

"You're lying!"

"And you're a fool! Do you honestly think they give a shit about you, Dr. Dratshev? What kinds of men do these things?" Madari sat to calm himself and shook his head. Finally he looked up to find Dratshev staring at him. "What?"

"Is it true? Did they kill her...did they kill my precious Natalia?"

"I have no reason to lie to you," Madari said with a shrug. He looked away and tried not to think about his own family, his sweet girls killed by the bastards who were now ruining his home country. "As I said, if you don't cooperate with me I merely have to let you go and sell what I have outright. It makes no difference to me."

"Or you're suggesting I stay."

"Yes."

"To what would it profit me?" Dratshev asked.

Madari felt suspicious at first but he could see something new and hard had come into Dratshev's face. The revelation of Natalia's death, which he didn't know to be completely true but for which he had strong evidence and suspicions, had shaken Dratshev's resolve. The scientist would cooperate fully now; of that much Madari felt certain. What he couldn't help but wonder was at what price.

Minsk, Belarus

MCCARTER HAD REACHED the point of intolerability as he paced the floor of their hotel room.

"Frankly, I don't see what you're getting so worked up about," said Rafael Encizo, the ever-present voice of reason. He sat on the edge of the coffee table with a Tanto fighting knife in one hand and a sharpening stone propped on his knee.

"I'm not worked up," McCarter said. He fished into his shirt pocket, removed a cigarette and lit it. "I'm mulling."

Nearby on one of the overstuffed chairs, Gary Manning asked, "You think Mishka's a traitor?"

"I think she's as dirty as a two-dollar whore," Mc-

Carter replied. "But that's not what has me concerned. We've dealt with more than our share of bloody turncoats and we know how to handle them. What has me rethinking this is that bit about this new party of American mercs. What we don't need right now is to start a war on the streets of this city."

"Maybe it won't come to that," Encizo said.

"I have the feeling it may be unavoidable," McCarter said. "And I really don't like this plan the Farm cooked up. We're being asked to play by the rules of the game."

Manning shrugged. "Then change the rules."

"Such as?" McCarter stopped pacing and cocked his head.

"Well, we're pretty sure we know who the enemy is and we have a perfectly good information source," the big Canadian replied. "Instead of sitting here collecting dust, let's take the fight to them."

"You're talking about a shakeup play."

"I am."

"That's the best bloody idea I've heard all day," McCarter replied. He called James and Hawkins to join them, and began, "Okay, Gary's made a pretty good point and I've come to a decision. We're going to turn this around."

"How?" Hawkins asked.

"By going on the offensive," McCarter replied. "If our local spook's right and this is the FSB on us, I don't see any point sitting here and waiting for them to try again."

"Okay," James interjected. "But how do you propose to find them?"

A rap at the door brought a smile and a wink in way of reply. Manning rose and went to the door. He opened it to admit Mishka and Carnes.

"Were your ears burning?" Hawkins asked as they entered.

She gave him a queer look and then put her attention on McCarter. "Hope we're not intruding."

"No," McCarter replied. "As a matter of fact, you're right on time."

"Right on time for what?"

"We were just discussing our next move. I have it in mind that to wait here for the FSB to attack us again is stupid. We need to take the fight to them."

"You're talking about going on the offensive."

"I am."

Mishka shook her head. "That wouldn't be a good idea."

"And why's that?" Encizo queried.

"For one, we can't be sure it was even the FSB who attacked us."

"You seemed convinced earlier," McCarter said.

"Well…" Mishka looked at Carnes, who nodded, before saying, "I'm not so sure it is now. And I know after what happened on the way from the airport you have no reason to trust me. But I can assure you that I had nothing to do with it. And neither did Carnes. We're on *your* side."

"Nobody said we mistrusted you."

"Oh, come on! I didn't graduate from Langley last week." Mishka shook her head. "Don't treat us like we're stupid, gentlemen. You're above that. And let's face it, you got blown fast. But I think I have an explanation."

"We're listening," Encizo said.

"We hear the Russian government has received word a third party has come forward to claim responsibility for Dratshev's kidnapping. At least, that's what they claim."

"And who's the third party?" McCarter asserted, already confident he knew what she'd say.

"We don't know yet," Mishka replied.

A shift of his eyes to the rest of the team made it clear they knew she was lying. Apparently she had no idea that they'd already had word from the Farm about the same claim having been made to the United States. That was damning enough, even if Mishka had neglected to mention that the EMP weapons schematics had been put on the international auction block.

"What we do know," Mishka said, "is that the transmission originated right here in the Belarus. Just outside the city, in fact."

"So you're thinking we should hit this target?"

"I think so," Mishka said. "Before we lose the option."

"Only one problem—you still have our equipment," James pointed out.

"We got a new mode of transportation," Carnes revealed. "New wheels."

"And it's clean?" McCarter asked.

Carnes nodded. "Completely."

"Um, we may now have new transportation but I don't think that's our biggest worry," Hawkins said.

All eyes looked at the Phoenix Force warrior, who had at some point in the conversation managed to go to the window in the main room of one of the two suites. Hawkins had parted just one of the curtains slightly and had his face practically pressed to the glass as he looked out onto the street.

"What you got?"

"Two vehicles, late-model sedans."

"Same as the ones this morning?"

Hawkins shook his head and after another moment locked eyes with McCarter.

"What the hell," James said. "How did they find us so easily?"

"They might be tracking one of these two," McCarter said, jerking a thumb in the direction of their CIA cohorts.

"Whatever they're up to, it doesn't sound friendly," Encizo pointed out.

McCarter nodded and then turned toward Mishka. "You want to take us to where you've stored our weapons?"

"Of course," she said. "It's safe now that we have a clean vehicle."

"Good." He turned to Encizo. "We'll need a diversion."

Encizo flashed him a wicked grin, a glint coming into his eyes. "I was hoping you'd say that. Talk to me."

CHAPTER NINE

When the four armed combatants came through the front door of the hostel, the Phoenix Force warriors were ready for them.

This fact became plainly evident for the enemy hit team but they realized it too late to do much about it. Their offense had suddenly and irrevocably gone defensive, but their attempts to avoid disaster were admirable if totally ineffective.

The first man through the door took a two-round burst in the chest from Encizo's Glock. The impact drove him back so he collided with the gunner behind him. The explosive opening to the battle caused a logjam in the door and tripped up the remaining force.

Hawkins saw his opportunity to snipe the second one with a clean shot through the head. The guy's skull exploded in a messy wash of blood and bone, the remnants of which were consumed by the fiery blast from the grenade Encizo tossed into their midst. Shrapnel whistled through the air in the aftermath and made short work of another man who'd been unable to recover from the two-man pile blocking his entry.

"Let's go!" Encizo called.

The pair retreated up the steps at a good clip. The remainder of Phoenix Force would already be down the back stairwell and making their escape out the rear of the building. It would take about three minutes to catch them—more than enough time for Carnes to get their replacement vehicle in place for pickup. True to McCarter's improvised exit plan, Encizo and Hawkins emerged in time to see the dark panel van roaring up the narrow street that ran parallel to the hostel and surrounding buildings.

As the van came to a screeching halt, the door opened and the two jumped aboard.

"Welcome to Fugitives 'R' Us," James said as he gave a hand to each man.

Once his teammates were secure, Manning gunned the engine as he worked the clutch with the expertise of a practiced high-speed driver. By the time they eased onto a major side street at the end of the block, the automatic van door had slid securely shut.

From his position riding shotgun, McCarter said, "We heard the festivities, mate. Looks like those little jobbers from Cowboy paid off."

"In spades," Encizo replied with a wicked grin.

"So now where?" Hawkins inquired.

"We know the location of the warehouse where Mishka stored our weapons. We need to retrieve them before I decide our next action."

Encizo nodded. "Where's Carnes?"

"After we agreed Gary would drive this time, David politely suggested maybe he should ride with Mishka," James said.

"So it's just us."

McCarter nodded. "Yeah. I'm still not convinced they're playing for our side. Not entirely. If we get blown retrieving our equipment, we'll know the full story. What about the little welcoming party back there?"

Hawkins shook his head. "Definitely not the same crew that we encountered coming from the airport."

"How do you know?"

"They moved differently, for one," Hawkins said.

"And for another, they weren't carrying anything but pistols," Encizo added. "They acted as if this operation would be a cakewalk, like they didn't know what they were up against."

McCarter clucked his tongue. "That sounds jolly odd considering our first encounter. They should've sent a lot more, been prepared."

"Right."

James scratched his chin as he said, "Something doesn't add up here at all."

"Meaning?" McCarter replied.

"Well, first we're not in town ten minutes and we get ambushed on the road to the hostel. That team obviously knew what they were up against and where we were going. Then we get these visitors, half as many as last time and only lightly armed."

"You're thinking two different groups?" Hawkins inquired.

"I am."

"And that's what doesn't add up, eh?" McCarter said. "If one or both of our contacts here are in bed with the enemy, you'd think these little operations to take us out would be more consistent in their execution."

"That is strange," Hawkins remarked.

"I think we've neglected to ask ourselves a key question here," Manning said. "Who stands the most to gain by burning us? Our op here was relatively simple. Get latched into the FSB activities here and wait for them to lead us to Madari."

"That's been eating at me, too," McCarter said. "None of this makes sense. Madari risks kidnapping Dratshev and pissing off the Russians. Then he turns around and instead of ransoming Dratshev, he gets the guy to help him build prototypes of the EMP weapons and put them up on the auction block to very select countries."

"His choice of countries *was* interesting," James said.

"Not really," Encizo countered. "Each of those countries has one thing in common. They're all rich and they all exert major influence in their respective parts of the world."

"And they all bloody well have different and conflicting views toward the political and socioeconomic situation in Libya," McCarter observed.

"Where Ishaq Madari just so happens to hail from," Manning added.

McCarter frowned. "Exactly. And I'm sorry but their getting Dratshev out of Belarus came just a little too easy. I think our friend Mishka could be culpable for that. Playing two ends against the middle."

"Yeah," James replied. "And we're the middle."

"To what end?" Hawkins asked.

"Dunno, mate," McCarter said. "But we sure as hell need to keep our eyes open. She'll make her move soon—that much I'm certain about."

"And when she does?"

"She gets to be the middle."

As soon as Riley Braden's feet touched the tarmac at the small airport in Belarus—the two men assigned for this mission on his heels—he proceeded to a waiting late-model SUV. The trio climbed into the chauffeured vehicle arranged by Steinham's personal assistant at DCDI. Nobody outside of Steinham or Cyrus knew his mission—at least Steinham had assured him and Cyrus of as much and insisted on complete secrecy. Braden didn't buy it. They'd already had one mission compromised—to allow a second breach was personally and professionally unacceptable to him.

The drive to the hotel took only five minutes, and during that time the three men didn't say a word to either the driver or to each other. It was better not to talk about the details of their missions in front of any personnel who hadn't been cleared. This way, if they got blown, they could at least narrow the potential list of suspects. Braden thanked the driver when they arrived at the hotel and then took the keys as previously arranged while another of his men checked them into their rooms.

When they were finally upstairs and comfortable, and the pair of mercenaries in Braden's command had swept the place thoroughly for bugs, they ordered some food and then began to discuss the op. One of the men produced a detailed map of the city and spread it on the table.

Braden pointed to a small area on the edge of Minsk city limits. "According to our sources, this is a probable location where the Russian government planned to keep Dratshev during the testing. It's a known residence used by the FSB because of its security features."

"But why would we go there?" asked the man who went by Muncie.

"That was my question," added Davison, the other team member. "Especially since we figure Dratshev probably isn't even in Belarus anymore. Hell, he's probably not in the country anymore.

"Because the FSB will be there."

"You think they'll still be looking for him?" Davison asked.

Braden nodded. "Look, if there's any chance at all that Dratshev's work has fallen into the hands of a government antagonistic to Russia, you can bet your sweet ass they'll redouble their efforts to find him. They're not just going to stand by and wait to see how this plays out. In fact, if they follow standard procedure and they can't recover Dratshev and his research, they surely have contingency orders to terminate him."

"Easier said than done," Muncie said.

"Why? That's what we're being expected to do."

"I thought we were supposed to try to get Dratshev alive?"

Braden frowned. "That's what we hope to do but it's not a guarantee."

Muncie grunted and his expression betrayed his skepticism.

"What is a foregone conclusion, though," Braden said, "is that we're not the only game in town. The CIA has had people in Belarus since the days of the Cold War."

Davison snorted. "And probably longer than that."

"Right. Which means it isn't going to be that difficult to get inside and see what's what."

"But what if we don't find any information on Dratshev's location? They don't even know where he is, supposedly, so how does it benefit us to go there?"

"Because our CIA contact says the American SOG group here is also looking for Dratshev, and that's where they're going to start."

"I don't get it, sir," Muncie said, scratching his neck. "Are you saying you're trying to hook up with these guys?"

"That's right."

"No, that's crazy!" When Braden offered Muncie a sharp look, he added quickly, "With all due respect, sir."

"Maybe it sounds crazy to you but we don't have time to argue that. And as usual, you'll both keep military discipline at all times. We're being well compensated and I don't plan to do anything that would embarrass the colonel. Not to mention it's my job to make sure you jokers stay alive. You'd both do well to keep it in mind. Is that understood?"

When the two men finished nodding and "yes-siring," Braden returned their attention to the map. "Now, let me give you the op plan."

"WELL?" CALVIN JAMES inquired from the back of the van.

McCarter didn't say anything at first but continued to scan the hard site with his night-vision binoculars. Then he replied, "Quiet as a church mouse, mates."

"I was hoping you wouldn't say that," Encizo retorted.

"Why?" Hawkins asked with a furrowed brow. The warrior was cutting at a piece of jerky with his pocket-knife.

Encizo grimaced as he replied, "Because if it were a beehive of activity, we wouldn't have to worry about being subtle. Now we have to go soft probe and see what we're up against."

Hawkins nodded as he chewed hungrily around the jerky. "Ah. Good point."

"I know," Encizo said with a forced smile.

"Okay, let's not stack up on each other," McCarter said. "We got a job to do and it's time to do it."

Manning inclined his head toward the massive house. "You sure about this, David?"

"I'm not much sure about anything these days, mate," McCarter said. "Why? Something bugger you about this?"

"I don't know," the Canadian replied with a shrug. "Just a gut instinct, I think. Something definitely doesn't sit right with that place. And as you mentioned before, we got no reason to trust Mishka and Carnes's word as reliable."

"Speaking of which, where are those two?" McCarter said, checking his watch. "They should've been here over an hour ago to give us a layout."

"Maybe they're hoping we're dead by now," James said.

"Meaning?"

"Meaning that I think Gary's right. This *does* feel like bad juju."

"We don't have any choice," McCarter countered. "We're just going to have stone up and bloody do this thing. Everyone ready?"

The others grunted assents in varying degrees as slides clacked, magazines tapped and pistols locked and cocked. For this one, they'd all decided to carry H&K MP-5 SD6s. Sporting 3-round burst capacity, the sound-suppressed MP5s were versatile and quiet. McCarter hoped that would serve his teammates well. In the end analysis, this wouldn't be a soft probe anyway.

"Let's do it," McCarter said. "And keep in mind chances are good we're expected."

The five warriors went EVA. They moved across the open ground using the fire-and-maneuver pattern they had deployed hundreds of times before. The situation wasn't ideal, having to traverse this distance without some kind of cover, but McCarter knew this was their only chance to bring an end to this situation.

To the Phoenix Force leader's surprise, they nearly made it to the massive house that served as the FSB hard site before encountering any trouble. That trouble manifested itself in the form of a half dozen armed combatants. They weren't dressed in suits or business casual as Phoenix Force had expected. These men wore urban camouflage and toted semi-automatic machine guns. So it wasn't a FSB safehouse but was instead guarded by military units—an interesting revelation indeed.

McCarter was the first to make contact, swinging his MP-5 SD6 into acquisition mode and triggering a 3-round burst. The 9 mm Parabellum rounds tore through the gut of his target and slammed him onto his back. McCarter glanced to his left when the glint of light on metal caught his eye, realizing he'd made a mistake. The mistake would've been fatal had it not been for the marksmanship of Rafael Encizo, who took down McCarter's would-be assassin with a single well-placed head shot. The man's body crumpled as his skull exploded under the impact.

T. J. Hawkins was the next in line to find a target. Hawkins went prone just as one of the enemy commandos sprayed the space he'd occupied a moment before with a couple short and deadly salvos. Hawkins held his MP-5 rock-steady, undaunted by the proximity of the rounds. He triggered his MP-5 and hit his target with a 3-round burst to the chest. The rounds cut through the commando's heart and lungs before depositing him on the shallow grassy knoll leading to the house.

The remaining trio of enemy gunners realized simultaneously they weren't up against novices but experienced combatants who had obviously been trained to fight like devils. In a move that surprised all five of the Phoenix Force warriors, the remaining three men turned and retreated toward the house. Under other circumstances, none of the men of Phoenix Force would have fired at retreating soldiers, but in this case they could not risk letting the men gain the high ground and cover provided by the house. It would have resulted in their own slaughter, not to mention the fact that they had no idea of the level of resistance they would meet inside the house.

The others followed McCarter's lead as the grim-faced Phoenix Force leader raised his MP-5 and opened fire. Reports from all five MPs echoed through the air like a choppy symphony, the murderous storm of lead cutting a swath through the trio of enemy commandos. As the echo of gunfire died in his ears and the acrid stench of cordite and freshly spilled blood burned his nostrils, McCarter could feel a ball of rage well in his stomach. As he'd suspected, the enemy had known Phoenix Force was coming. They could only have gotten this information one source: Mishka.

McCarter jerked his head as an indication they should proceed toward the house. Manning opened his mouth, almost looking as if to voice a protest, but then quickly shut it and shrugged. Training took over. A hot zone was neither the time nor the place to conduct a conference. There would be plenty of time to evaluate the situation later. Right now, what was in front of them needed the full attention of every man on the team if they were to remain alive.

When they reached the estate-like mansion, McCarter pointed to his eyes and then at Manning.

The big Canadian didn't take long to locate the best

point of attack: a side entrance consisting of two thick doors with heavy paned glass. The others quickly formed on him, fanning out and providing rear guard while Manning retrieved a one-pound block of C-4 from his bag of tricks. With the expertise gathered from years of working with every kind of explosive imaginable, Manning primed the block with a blasting cap and attached it to the door.

All of the men gave the door a respectful distance and Manning shouted a single warning to stand clear.

The C-4 did its work cleanly, blowing the doors apart and leaving a gaping point of entry, charred embers glowing in the cool morning air around its frame. McCarter gestured at James and Hawkins, who took up point and entered the house. He followed with Manning and Encizo bringing up the rear.

They moved as a single fire team through the house, and it took them nearly five minutes just to clear the first floor. They found the ground level deserted and McCarter was beginning to suspect searches of the subsequent floors would reveal more of the same. If Mishka had actually betrayed them, did she honestly think that only six lightly armed soldiers were sufficient to combat five seasoned veterans? McCarter didn't buy that and he didn't think Mishka would have bought it, either—there had to be more to it than that.

They were able to clear the second and third floors in half the time and the results were just as McCarter had predicted. They were in the process of clearing one of the last bedrooms on the third floor when Manning pointed to movement on the grounds visible through the bedroom window. It wasn't an army; of that much they were certain. No country on earth, never mind the Russians, would send a whopping team of three men to eliminate a special operations group such as Phoenix Force.

"What the hell...?" Calvin James began.

"My thoughts exactly," Encizo said with a grin.

"Well," McCarter replied, "let's go find out."

CHAPTER TEN

Washington, D.C.

Able Team stood around the customized van affection-
ately known as Black Betty and admired its sleek lines.
They had reached the special garage arranged by Stony
Man Farm where they kept the vehicle—it was a few a
miles outside of Andrews AFB. With good reason. They
had used the highly specialized van on many missions
prior to this one, although they did so sparingly.

Betty had gone through a number of versions over
the years—each more technically and mechanically advanced than before—along with more lives than a cat.
The many variations had saved the lives of all the Able
Team warriors more times than they could count. Whenever they had a mission that required special capabilities, whether high-tech surveillance or covert probe, they
could call on Black Betty and she'd see them through the
job to the last details.

Much like her adoring operators.

Schwarz sighed. "Ah, always good to see Betty."

"Indeed," Blancanales added with a nod.

Lyons did a check of all the field equipment while
Blancanales got busy with the armory. Schwarz booted
up and ran diagnostics on all of the sensitive electronics
packages aboard the van. This included an entire surveil-

lance and countersurveillance suite, along with a GPS tracking aperture fed by a cluster of short, bristling antennae protruding through the roof. The antennae were normally shielded from the sun and elements by a transparent bubble in the roof, but that bubble could open and the antennae raised or retracted on a hydraulic platform.

When they completed their tasks and Lyons got the all clear, they climbed in and headed into the city night. As they rode, each man was left to his own thoughts while Lyons reviewed the intelligence the Farm had downloaded to their secure on-board computer system. The data made his head itch.

"Hey, listen up," he finally said. "This is from the files on Colonel Jack Cyrus. This guy's been in and out of the worst shit you can imagine." Lyons let out a low whistle. "He's been decorated six separate times for bravery. Service tours include Iraq, Afghanistan, Libya, the Sudan, DRC, and he's been to the hells all over points in the South and Central Americas."

"Sounds tough," Schwarz said.

"Ya think?" Lyons retorted.

"Seems strange a guy like that would be working for someone like Steinham," Blancanales said.

Lyons shook his head. "Meaning?"

Blancanales shrugged. "Steinham's a businessman and a bureaucrat. Cyrus is a hardcore soldier. Those two elements usually don't mix."

"Unless you're running a mercenary operation with your eyes out for the most lucrative contracts," Schwarz observed.

"You have a point," Blancanales said.

"Well, whatever Cyrus's reason for being in cahoots with Steinham, he signed up with the wrong side," Lyons said.

"I hear a 'but' in there somewhere," Blancanales said.

"It's this whole attack on that NSA storage vault in Iowa," Lyons said. "Steinham's obviously got connections in high and very secure places or he wouldn't have known anything about it. And how did he get the intelligence on Dratshev's disappearance? It's almost as if he knew before *we* did. That's no mean feat.

"And what about the fact Cyrus and his bunch knew exactly what they were looking for? They were in there strictly on an intelligence-seeking mission. It was supposed to be a soft op. In and out with the data before anybody knew what happened. But then there's an entire armed force *waiting* for them?"

"It's all strange," Blancanales said. "So we're in agreement on that. We have been from the beginning. But why let it eat at you so intensely?"

"Because somebody's not giving us the straight poop," Lyons said.

"You think the Farm's hiding something?" Schwarz asked.

Lyons turned around and pinned his teammate with an icy stare. "I never said that."

"Then what gives?" Blancanales interjected, determined to head off any problem that might arise between his friends.

"What gives is that Dratshev's disappearance barely hits the airwaves in the intelligence community and Steinham's merc team gets bushwhacked trying to procure information. Clearly a guy with Cyrus's experience would have expected something like that if he had any reason to think it was a trap. He would have had an alternate escape plan, some prearranged signal with his men for getting out of a situation like that. But the fact half his force got killed and they came up empty-handed tells me he wasn't expecting it. There has to be a reason."

"We're open to any suggestions," Blancanales said.

"What happened in Iowa seems highly suggestive of manipulation at the source," Lyons ventured.

"You mean this Ishaq Madari?" Blancanales asked.

"You bet I do," Lyons replied through clenched teeth. "I think this guy masterminded the whole thing. You see up till now, everybody seems to be operating off the assumption that what happened to Steinham's crew and Madari's little public auction have nothing to do with each other. I'm beginning to think just the opposite."

"So you think Madari set up Steinham's people, or at least Cyrus's mercenary group, to take a hard fall?" Schwarz asked.

"Yeah."

"Okay, but to what end?" Blancanales asked with a shrug. "I mean, what's in it for Madari? That scenario suggests Madari has some sort of personal score to settle with Steinham."

"Not necessarily," Lyons said. "Look at how we've reacted to this up until now. We've had to split up our efforts with Phoenix running halfway around the globe to chase some phantom trail. Meanwhile we're jumping around the U.S. like a group of Dead Heads following their last great tour."

"So we're jumping around," Blancanales said. "So what? That's hardly a news flash."

"But *why?*" Lyons said. "Why would Madari do that if he planned to come out publicly anyway? He didn't try to hide the fact he had prototypes on the auction block, nor did he attempt to conceal the fact he was the one who'd engineered Dratshev's kidnapping."

"I think I see where you're going," Schwarz said. "You're thinking Madari purposely leaked this information ahead of time as a way of sweetening the pot."

"Right! Steinham's research has been stagnant the past few years. The guy's a defense contractor and a popular one at that. But frankly his innovation well has run dry. Madari feeds him information first-hand about Dratshev getting snatched. Steinham knows Dratshev's research specialty is EMP weapons, a research specialty Steinham tried to pioneer a few years ago with no success."

"So you think Steinham's looking to find a way to steal the tech himself," Blancanales said.

"I don't know about that," Lyons said. "But it's pretty obvious he knows Dratshev's a catch and maybe he figures he can barter for some small piece of the action."

"Or maybe Madari wants Steinham to *think* he can."

"Exactly."

"But that still doesn't explain how that helps Madari. His stated goal is for a free and democratic Libya. He doesn't care about any of the rest of it."

"No, but think about how far he could press his aims if he was the only one with EMP weapons. Steinham would jump at that bait. He's a businessman, remember? All he knows is defense technology and profit margins. That's how he built a multi-billion-dollar defense contracting empire."

"And how he's held on to it so long," Schwarz noted.

"So how do we find out what Steinham's up to?" Blancanales asked.

"Simple," Lyons said. "We go ask him."

THE DCDI FACILITY would have been the obvious place to start had it been the middle of the business day. This late in the evening, however, Able Team figured Steinham would have left his office and headed home. They didn't know what type of security they would encounter at the house, but they were all carrying credentials as federal agents.

"Shouldn't be all that tough to get access to him," Lyons noted.

"Especially not if we make it look like we're trying to get his cooperation on something important," Schwarz added.

"It, um…*might* be a good idea we don't mention anything about Iowa," Blancanales said. With a look from Lyons he added, "Just saying."

"You're probably right. Why don't we—?"

None of them was sure where the shot had come from, only that it *had* come and that it was meant to kill one of them. Unfortunately for the attacker, the bulletproof glass prevented the round from actually penetrating the cab.

"Gadgets?" Lyons shouted as he reached for the automatic 12-guage shotgun secured in a rack next to his seat.

Schwarz whirled in the rotating seat and flipped a switch. Immediately a screen in the electronic surveillance suite came alive and gave him a 360-degree view of their surroundings. The system was primarily used to detect heat signatures through extensive use of thermal-optic cameras built into the body of the van. It didn't take long for Schwarz to locate the source of the heat. A flash appeared on the screen and for a moment they heard the ping of another round deflected by Betty's external armor composite.

"Lone shooter, second-floor building we just passed," Schwarz announced.

"Coincidence?" Lyons asked.

Blancanales shook his head with a grim expression. "Highly doubtful."

As if in answer to his inquiry, a vehicle swerved into the oncoming lane. Thankfully they were cruising through a secondary commercial area where most businesses were closed so the streets were practically devoid of traffic. Perfect place for an ambush.

"Watch it!" Lyons called.

"I see them!" Blancanales said as he whipped the van to the left and then immediately back to the far right and onto the sidewalk.

The driver of the other vehicle fell for Blancanales's feint and they missed a head-on collision. In other circumstances, and with just about anyone else behind the wheel, it would have appeared like a reckless game of chicken. Lyons knew better. Blancanales was as skilled as they came behind the wheel.

"Flip a bitch and let's handle these worms," Lyons growled.

"Your wish is my command," Blancanales said as he powered into a U-turn and gave pursuit. The maneuver seemed hardly necessary since it appeared the occupants of the dark SUV seemed intent on engaging the Able Team warriors. Whatever the reason they had decided to hit them—and Lyons wasn't near as interested in how as *why*—they obviously weren't up on exactly who it was they were dealing with.

As the SUV came to a halt and the occupants exited, five in all, toting assault rifles, Able Team decided to show them the error in their choice of targets. Lyons was first to go EVA, leaving the shotgun in favor of a Colt SCW. The most compact of all 5.56 mm small arms in the Colt arsenal, the SCW featured a one-piece monolithic upper receiver and collapsible folding butt stock.

Blancanales cleared next, also armed with a Colt—his choice had been the AR-15 A3, a tactical carbine model with a fifteen-inch heavy barrel that sported a 1/9 twist. This gave him flexibility in selection of ammunition, for which the Able Team veteran chose full-blown 5.56 mm NATO rounds.

Lyons and Blancanales opened in concert on the enemy gunners. Blancanales got the first target with a burst to the midsection that doubled the man over as it tore his innards to shreds. He produced a scream as the assault rifle sprang from his hands and clattered to the pavement in front of him, now utterly useless. The screams were cut short by a double tap to the skull.

Lyons got the next one a heartbeat later, cutting a full-auto swathing path from the target's right thigh up to the level of his heart. The unyielding flesh at the thigh was no match for the high-velocity rounds, but something didn't seem quite right. The impact drove him into the vehicle but he didn't fall. It took Lyons a moment to realize that this particular enemy was protected by body armor. Maybe whoever had thrown this murderous detail at Able Team *had* come prepared, after all. Lyons reacquired a sight picture as he brought the SCW to his shoulder and squeezed off another two rounds, rewarded with a crimson spray as the man's head exploded under the impact of the 5.56 mm slugs. The enemy's body did a pirouette before slamming chest first against the quarter panel of the SUV and sliding away, leaving a gory streak in its wake.

"They're armored!" Blancanales shouted as a fresh volley from the survivors burned the air over his head.

"Noted!" Lyons said through clenched teeth, the air rushing from his lungs as he went prone a moment after his friend.

One of the attackers burst from the cover of the SUV and ran out and away in a flanking maneuver. Beneath his assault rifle, Lyons spotted the tubular shape of the 40 mm grenade launcher. It looked to be a civilian variant of the M-203, maybe law-enforcement stock designed for firing tear gas canisters, but that made it no less deadly.

The gunner appeared to have a round chambered and he would have most likely had them dead to rights, but Schwarz, now entering the fray, cut the would-be victory short. Schwarz triggered a full-auto burn from the hip with his MP-5, triggering a steady stream of 9 mm hail that readily found its mark. The grenadier appeared to dance under the rounds as one after another cut through his body and propelled him backward until he stumbled over the edge of the sidewalk. The guy collapsed onto his back, twitched a moment and then lay still.

That reduced the remaining enemy count to just two, but it looked as if it didn't matter much to that pair. They opened with a full salvo from their assault rifles, sweeping the battle zone with as much hot lead as they could afford. It wasn't meant to hit targets as much as to keep Able Team at bay and on that count they did a pretty fine job.

Lyons rolled from the refuge afforded by Betty's armored body and came to one knee with smooth precision. Butt stock locked to his shoulder, Lyons returned the incessant maelstrom with a precision volley of his own, catching one of the men with a round to the shoulder. The impact of a few others seemed to drive him back like the first, but he managed to turn and gain concealment at the rear of the SUV. His partner wasn't quite as lucky, falling under the dual gunfire from Blancanales and Schwarz, the latter having swept out in a flanking motion similar to the grenadier he'd dropped just seconds before.

As the shots died out, Lyons heard the agonized screams of the gunner he'd hit. He climbed to his feet and waved at his teammates to flank the SUV on the passenger side while he made a path that arced far enough out he could take the target with surety if it came to it. He hoped it didn't. This was the sole survivor and they needed information.

The guy seemed prepared and watchful for Lyons. He had his back propped against the bumper but his AR was primed and ready for action. As he swung the barrel, albeit awkwardly, in Lyons's direction, Blancanales came around the opposite side and managed to stomp a boot heel into the man's wrist. A few rounds ricocheted off the cement, the whines of the shots echoing through the air, but the gunner lost control of the rifle—it appeared his hand now dangled at a bad angle where it met his wrist.

Blancanales shoved the barrel of his AR-15 against the injured combatant's neck and said with implicit menace, "That'll do."

Lyons trotted to where they waited and flashed the guy a wicked grin. "Show's over, asshole."

"Not even close," the guy replied. "It's just beginning."

"We'll see about that," Lyons replied.

CHAPTER ELEVEN

Minsk, Belarus

Phoenix Force took the three men approaching the FSB safehouse by total surprise.

The men were obviously experienced soldiers—all had brush-cuts, were in good physical condition and carried themselves like combat veterans. This made David McCarter all the more suspicious about the ease for which they took them unawares. Only one of the three fought back, taking down Calvin James with a surprise leg sweep before Encizo stepped in and delivered a palm strike to the bone just below the guy's right ear, nearly rendering him unconscious.

The apparent leader of the group ordered the two men to make no further resistance and they even allowed Phoenix Force to secure them with riot cuffs. McCarter then pulled the man aside for a private interview.

"You willing to answer some questions?" the Phoenix Force leader began.

"Possibly," the man replied. "As long as we can be civil and you agree to abide by proper etiquette where it regards my men. I presently consider all of us POWs and we expect you'll treat as such."

McCarter grinned. "I'll do you one step better than that, mate. You're obviously American citizens so you're not bound to answer any questions without a lawyer present. And this isn't exactly an *official* battle site."

The guy made a show of looking the place over and then tried for a grin of his own that McCarter found surprisingly disarming. "Could've fooled me."

"So who are you?"

"Braden, Riley R." He rattled off some sort of number and then said, "I'm former U.S. Army, Tenth Special Forces Group. Now currently a part of a PMC called Cyclops."

McCarter said, "Tenth SFG. I know it. Out of Fort Carson?"

"That's right," Braden said, doing nothing to hide his surprise.

"Well then, you're in luck because we're actually a U.S. SOG outfit ourselves," McCarter said. "And I'm afraid that's all I can tell you. So this Cyclops… Wouldn't happen to be headed by a guy named Colonel Jack Cyrus, would it?"

"It is. How did you know?"

"It's part of what we get paid to know. Not to mention the fact that we were told to expect you."

"By who?"

"Our people are in the know about these things. And we had a contact inside the CIA who gave us some information relevant to your proposed mission. We know you're here looking for Oleg Dratshev."

"This contact you mentioned," Braden said. "She a looker goes by the codename Mishka?"

"Maybe."

"No, I don't think you see how this works… What's your name, anyway?"

"You can call me McMasters."

"Fine. McMasters, if you like." Braden cleared his throat and added, "It would seem that this Mishka might be playing two ends against the middle. Maybe even three."

"What makes you think so?"

"Because I happen to know for a fact that she's a CIA agent. This information came straight from the contractor we're working for."

"You mean DCDI," McCarter said.

"I see you *are* informed."

McCarter shrugged. "Goes with the job."

"Anyway, we were put on this assignment even before Dratshev was kidnapped. When we got blown in Iowa, I realized that we had an informant on the inside. Naturally, I didn't suspect either Colonel Cyrus or our boss."

"We know all about David Steinham," McCarter said. "You might as well stop being coy. And you were the ones responsible for killing a bunch of innocent security personnel?"

Braden raised his bound hands with palms facing McCarter. "Before you throw any stones, you should know those security personnel aren't so innocent. All of them are working for Madari."

"Ishaq Madari."

"Right."

"You know about him, too."

"Of course."

"Now you have my interest," McCarter said, folding his arms. "Go on, mate. Might as well spill the rest of it."

Braden shrugged. "Don't see any harm at this point. You know, I never bought into Steinham's plan for us on this mission. When I learned that a U.S. SOG group was involved, I pretty much determined then I wasn't going to get in the way. I didn't sign up with Colonel Cyrus just to fight fellow Americans. We all want the same thing, right?"

"All of us except Mishka, it would seem."

"Yeah, except Mishka."

"So do you have any idea where she might be right now?"

"You mean...*you* don't know?"

McCarter tried his best not to let his indecision show but he knew Braden was a sharp customer and it probably didn't do him much good at this point. "We've had trouble keeping tabs, although we did everything possible to keep her on a short leash."

"We never got the chance to make contact with her."

"Well, she was working with another guy named Carnes. I'm guessing he's probably gone over to whatever side she's gone over to."

"Uh-oh," Braden said. "I don't think so."

"What do you mean?"

"What does this Carnes look like?" Braden asked. After McCarter described him, Braden's face paled. "There's no question about it. That's the guy we found parked just off the perimeter of this place. And I can assure you he's in no shape to play turncoat with anyone. Found him in a sedan with his throat cut. We figured you guys did it."

McCarter looked grim. "Not our style, mate. We don't murder our allies solely on suspicion, and we're certainly not messy or stupid enough to leave bodies around where they can be discovered by other potential sentries."

"So Mishka killed him?"

"I'd say that's a safe assumption," McCarter said. "And worse, now she's completely in the wind."

"Yeah, but if she's not in bed with the Russians and she's obviously turned against her own government, who's left?"

"The one player in all of this who'd have the most to gain from her services."

Braden scratched his chin and looked puzzled for a minute. Finally the realization dawned on his face and he looked askance at McCarter. "You mean she's working for Madari?"

McCarter nodded. "That's only a guess, mind you."

"But it's a good guess."

"Seems reasonable. Only *she* was in a position to keep eyes on Dratshev. All this businesses about the FSB—" McCarter waved in the direction of the house "—was probably just a cover to keep us occupied while she made her plans to get out of Belarus."

"She was providing the distraction for Madari."

"Who else?" McCarter's brow furrowed. "Only thing I can't figure is motive."

"How about money?"

"Possible," McCarter said. "But she doesn't seem the type."

"Maybe she has some other relationship with him," Braden said. "Something you don't know about."

"Maybe," McCarter replied. "We'll have to get our people to dig deeper into her background to see what they can come up with."

"I almost hate to ask," Braden said, "but what about us?"

McCarter produced a combat knife and gestured toward Braden's wrists. The mercenary held them up in front of his face and McCarter released them from the riot cuffs with one quick slash. He then turned to his teammates and ordered them to cut the other pair loose, as well. They did so without question.

"You're letting us go?"

"Hardly," McCarter said. "But I can't very well lock you up here in Belarus, even if my people could get it arranged. And I don't want to take the chance of just cutting you free and clear where you might get in our way down the line. Not to mention that you've been cooperative so I see no reason to be punitive."

"So what're you going to do to us?"

"For now, you'll stick with my team. But I'm in charge, see? You do what I say and when I say, and you don't do anything else without my say. Understood?"

"I guess," Braden said.

"Come again?"

"I mean 'yes, sir.'"

"That's better." McCarter smiled. "You see, I figure you'll probably strike out on your own and continue your mission to find Oleg Dratshev."

"How do you figure that?"

"You seem to have a work ethic. You wouldn't just deviate from or drop a mission unless it was either absolutely necessary or compromised the safety of your team. Therefore, I figure it's better to keep you nearby where I have eyes on you rather than risk us ending up on opposite sides next time we meet."

"I wouldn't want that, either," Braden said as he rubbed his wrist.

"So, truce?" McCarter stuck out his hand and Braden took it with a nod. McCarter turned to the rest. "We're all working together now. I expect everyone to get along and play nice, just like the professionals I know you are. Now that we got that dispensed, we need to figure out our next move. It's obvious that 'Mishka' has betrayed us all. I think she's connected with Madari somehow, so if we get eyes on her then she *should* lead us right to him."

"And if we find him," Manning interjected, "then we find Dratshev."

Encizo nodded. "And the EMP prototypes."

"Wait a minute, hold on," Braden said. "You're telling me these blasted things are…they're *live?*"

"Near as we know," McCarter replied.

"Of course, we only have the word of a former terrorist on that account," Encizo said.

"Madari?" Braden shook his head. "He's a lot of things, pal, but not a terrorist."

"You're kidding, right?" Calvin James countered. "Let's see, we have kidnapping, extortion, murder and auction of stolen and untested property to multiple countries. I think that qualifies."

Manning added, "To make no mention the guy's a former a security expert for the Libyan government."

"That's the whole thing of it, though," Braden noted. "Madari was ousted from Libya because of his democratic views. They raped his wife and daughter and then killed them. Madari tried to keep his position quiet but when the regime found out about his collusion with the rebels, they murdered his family and exiled him from the country."

"Just figures that there are more problems and complications now than before," Encizo said.

"Possibly," McCarter agreed. He jerked his thumb at Braden. "But the major here does have a good point. If Madari's doing this to help bring a fully democratic government into Libya, you can hardly fault the guy."

"Except for the fact he's been colluding with our enemies and paying our own intelligence people to betray us," Hawkins said with a snort.

"So what?" Braden said. "Look, guys, I'm not saying I agree with what he's done but you got to admit that Madari isn't a U.S. citizen. He has no reason to be loyal to America—or any of the other countries he's exploited up to this point, for that matter. The guy's only going to look out for his own interests. He couldn't care less about the rest of it."

"Regardless of his motives," McCarter said, "he's a threat and we need to neutralize that threat. We're going off point anyway, mates. We'll carry out our original mission thoroughly and professionally. Let the politicians debate the good or bad, the moral or amoral—we're *not* in that business. Now, does anybody have any ideas about how we reconnect with Mishka?"

Braden raised his hand slowly. "Uh, we may be able to help with that."

McCarter nodded. "How so?"

"Well, Mishka still thinks she's got Steinham fooled. And she wouldn't have any reason to think we'd be able to put it together exactly what she's been up to. If anything, she strikes me as pretty cocky."

"Agreed. But how does that help us locate her?"

"All I have to do is reach out to Steinham. He knows how to track her every move."

"And how exactly did he manage that?" James inquired.

"Dunno," Braden replied with a shrug. "But I *do* know he's got eyes on her twenty-four-seven. I'm betting if we contact him and tell him she didn't make the rendezvous at the scheduled time that I could get him to tell me where she is."

"Well what are we waiting for then?" McCarter said. "Make the call."

"With pleasure."

Washington, D.C.

IF THEIR ENCOUNTER with the terrorists had done anything, it was to put Carl Lyons in a fouler mood than the previous one. The guy they'd taken alive refused to talk, immediately citing his rights when the cops arrived and demanding legal representation. Lyons had thought about overriding his protests and taking him into personal custody, but to do so would have raised a lot of eyebrows and spurred a lot of uncomfortable questions he didn't want to answer right now. Worse, it would have required the Farm to jump through hoops and maybe even required the Oval Office to run interference.

Able Team didn't need that kind of distraction so they turned the guy over to the local authorities with a story and the backing of their credentials enough to hold the guy until federal authorities could take over. The weapons charges alone would take the guy out of the picture long enough for Stony Man to get the rest of the situation wrapped up.

However, none of it set well with Brognola and Price. They'd been working in the dark on most of this, and at the moment Harold Brognola wasn't having any difficulties expressing his frustration to Price and Kurtzman. They sat in the War Room, having moved there for a dinner break from the Annex. The conversation had started pleasantly neutral enough, but as happened with far more frequency, it inevitably turned to shop talk.

Brognola wolfed down the last few bites of his open-faced hot turkey sandwich before launching a tirade. "You know what burns my ass?"

"A flame about three feet high?" Kurtzman joked.

"You've been hanging around Gadgets too much," Price quipped.

"What burns," Brognola said, "is the fact we can't seem to pick out the good guys from the bad. It's like we're fighting this thing on six different fronts."

"Pray tell," Price said.

Brognola ticked the points off on his fingers. "We got Phoenix Force up against a surgical team sent by Steinham. They, in turn, have also had to fight FSB operatives—which from what McCarter has told us may not have been FSB at all. At this end of the globe, Able Team is up against more of Steinham's people, or maybe *not,* and then there's Steinham himself."

"None of which adds up when you consider the predicament of Dr. Dratshev and this bold move by Madari," Price concluded.

Brognola produced a heavy sigh. "Right."

"We've been operating off some assumptions, though," Price said.

"Such as?"

"Well, we know—or at least we're confident—Mishka is a traitor."

"Ah, yes," Brognola said. "The elusive Muriel Stanish."

"Not that elusive," Kurtzman said around a mouthful of macaroni and cheese. "I did some digging after we spoke to McCarter. Stanish thinks she's smart, but she was hardly experienced at covering her tracks. But I'll get into that in a minute. We should let Barb finish."

"Thanks, Bear," Price said with a sweet smile. She returned her gaze to Brognola and said, "There's also no logical tie we can place between Madari and Steinham. It would appear for all practical intents and purposes that David Steinham might have obtained some of his DoD contracts through less than legitimate means, but then what contractor do you know who hasn't greased a senatorial palm now and again?"

"Yeah, it's tough enough we have to fight the terrorists of the world without also having to watch our backs with the criminal element right there in Wonderland," Brognola said. "But go on."

"It actually appears as if David Steinham is more interested in acquiring the EMP technology in the interests of the United States government. Our profile tells us Steinham is a staunch patriot. His company has developed a lot of promising technology for the military over the years, and it's his tenacity in pursuing better weapons and electronics that has saved the lives of many service personnel."

"That doesn't mean he couldn't be bought?"

Price laughed. "By whom, Hal? Steinham is already a *very* rich man. He has a family and there's nothing in his background, social or educational, that would suggest tendencies toward radicalism. He's also a former serviceman with an impeccable record. The guy has never even had so much as a parking ticket."

Brognola sighed. "So what I hear you trying to say is you think he's on our side."

"Yes. I think he truly is."

"Then how did he know about Dratshev's disappearance? And if he has no affiliation with Madari, why would he be digging up information from an NSA vault in Iowa, the location of which was supposed to be—at least allegedly—a national secret. And what about his apparent affiliation with our CIA friend, Mishka?"

"That's where I think Bear can help us." Price looked at him. "Aaron, you want to fill him in on what you dug up?"

"My pleasure!" Kurtzman took a long drink of ice water before diving into his report. "I did a very thorough background check on Muriel Stanish. It would seem she's had a long-term, sexual relationship with Madari. Although, she filed the relationship with her CIA contacts as being one Iradam Qahsi, who she claimed was a businessman from Dubai. The cover checked out—probably all of it put in place by her in the first place—so the CIA never went further with their investigation. A month ago, in her last major report to her case officer, she claimed the relationship had ended on good terms and she never planned to see him again."

"But apparently that was all bullshit," Brognola said.

"Exactamundo."

The Stony Man chief sighed again. "Okay, so it looks like we have some reason to believe that maybe we're not up against the odds I originally thought. But none of what you've discovered, and I should insert here I think you've both done an excellent job researching this, but... none of what you've said explains who attacked Able Team and why."

"Could have been someone sent by Madari," Kurtzman said.

It was Price who countered him. "No. They knew nothing of Able Team or their mission. And there wouldn't have been any point."

"What about Jack Cyrus and his mercenaries?" Brognola asked

Price shook her head. "Same thing, again. Not to mention that they've have no motive other than protecting Steinham."

"Which means?" Kurtzman asked.

"Which means—" Price tapped her fingernails on the tabletop. "I don't know what it means. And I don't know how to answer that question. At least, not *yet*."

"Well, we'd better come up with some answers soon before whoever attacked them tries again," Brognola said.

CHAPTER TWELVE

Greek Isles

A balmy Mediterranean breeze whipped at Mishka's hair as she stepped off the special jet Ishaq Madari had sent to the airport in Athens. She moved easily across the make-shift tarmac, weekend bag slung over her arm.

Madari met her halfway across the field.

She threw her arms around his neck and delivered a fierce, impassioned kiss. Her hands ran along his shoulders and back as his dipped from her waist to her ass. Then they broke and continued across the tarmac, her arm laced tightly inside his.

"You look well," he said.

"I missed you," she replied. "But thank you."

He nodded. "You traveled light, I see."

"I knew you had a full wardrobe here for me." She smiled. "And one more suited to the climate. These thick pants and sweater are fine for Minsk this time of year, but hardly suited to the Mediterranean."

"What of the, eh...*other* business?"

"It's been taken care of," she said. "I don't really wish to talk about it."

"I'm sure it was difficult."

"It was."

They arrived at Madari's luxury sedan, a foreign job

Mishka didn't recognize, and he followed after her into the spacious backseat. They sat close despite the room as the driver silently drove from the airfield to the estate.

Mishka had always wondered where Madari got his money after being ousted, allegedly penniless, from Libya, but she had not pressed him for the information. She doubted he would have told her the truth anyway. However he'd acquired the wealth, she knew he'd spent most of it trying to bring democracy to the country that had shunned him, civility to a government that hated him. Despite the fact he'd lost everything, Madari hadn't given up on his ideals and for that she'd come to admire and love him.

Their meeting, she found out much later, had not been completely by accident. While Madari had originally approached her due to her position in the CIA, he'd eventually fallen in love with her just as she had fallen for him. They had at first looked to work with each other for mutual advantage, neither of them really having expected their relationship to transform into a passionate affair.

When Madari asked her why she'd chosen to help him execute his plans, she answered, "I do it for love."

Mishka was convinced that Madari's love for her was as genuine as hers for him. He'd now proved it by not only protecting her cover but arranging to get her out of the country.

"You were able to leave Belarus undetected, yes?" he asked.

She nodded.

"You're positive?"

"Absolutely," she said. "There was no way for them to track me. And I had the location chip injected by the CIA surgically removed some weeks back. I kept it with me so it would not arouse suspicion until the American detachment arrived. That's when I destroyed it and left it with…with my partner."

"I am sorry you had to terminate his life."

"I know. But it was more important that your plans succeed."

"It sounds as if you were diligent."

"I was."

"What of these American commandos? Do you have any idea who sent them?"

"My CIA handlers didn't tell me much," she replied with a tired sigh. "Frankly, I doubt they're from any official agency. I suppose they could be Delta Force but I highly doubt it. Military types don't tend to work that closely with civilian espionage personnel, my darling. They go more for the defense intelligence circles. Not to mention these men were…*different*."

Madari's brow furrowed. "In what way?"

"They were older…seasoned. I don't know, I can't put my finger on it, but they weren't your average special operators. Something about them just struck me as unique."

"Well, they are certainly of no threat to you now." Madari chuckled. "In fact, I would imagine that they have their hands quite full with Steinham's mercenaries."

Mishka couldn't suppress a schoolgirl giggle. "I would imagine so. Your involving him in this was a masterful stroke."

"Thank you." Madari's expression changed to smug satisfaction. "I knew if we fed him just enough rope, he would hang himself."

"You realize he isn't going to give up so easily?"

"I do. In fact, I wouldn't expect anything less. He's an interesting man. For an American."

"As am I?" Mishka said, putting a purposeful baiting in her tone. It was her way of flirting with him and he knew it.

"I do not despise Americans," Madari said. "You know this about me. I just don't hold to all the policies of your home country, my sweet."

"It's not my home country anymore. I'm an outcast and a fugitive. An exile much like you, Ishaq. They would go to great lengths to extradite me back to the United States. They may even put out a hit. I'm a much bigger threat to them while I remain alive."

"I've taken care of the security, Mishka. Don't worry. You are utterly safe here." He reached out and stroked her hair. "I will allow no one to hurt you."

They rode the remaining distance to the estate. As they left the sedan and proceeded up the crush-refined walk to the flagstone patio, Mishka asked, "How's your work proceeding with the prototypes?"

"Nearly complete."

She looked at him in surprise. "Dratshev is actually cooperating with you?"

"He is. In fact, we've made excellent progress since he agreed to help us."

"That's amazing, Ishaq!"

Madari waved it away although she could tell her praise of his efforts greatly pleased him. "It was nothing. He is a scientist with a scientist's mind. I understand him. He wanted to see his life's pursuits reach fruition as much as I."

"Do you think you'll be able to mass produce them?"

"Undoubtedly! The ship-based systems have already been tested and proved quite effective. In fact, as soon as construction is completed—which I suspect will be sometime late tonight or early tomorrow—I will have them shipped straight to my yacht. Which reminds me, we will be leaving in the next day or two."

"But I just got here!"

"It's for the *cause,* Mishka. We must be certain before we supply the rebels in Libya that Dr. Dratshev's design is viable. I feel the best demonstration of that test will be in America."

"But that's sending us straight into the lions' den. Please, Ishaq…please, I don't want to go back to America. I don't want to go anywhere near it." She stopped in midstride and grabbed his hands, clasping them in hers and holding them to her cheek. "I'm afraid."

Madari's eyes narrowed and at first she thought he'd be angry with her. But then he smiled, detaching one of his hands and stroking her gorgeous hair. He'd always remarked how dark and lovely it was, bragged how her beauty surpassed that of even the most lovely women in his own country. She'd never believed him but Madari had also not given her any reason to mistrust his intentions. He *was* a good man.

"Very well, my dearest. You can remain here. But I must go and lead this fight, and I cannot have any arguments on that count. It's too important to the liberation of my nation."

She kissed his neck and cheek and then hugged him. "Thank you, darling."

"Now," he said, steering her toward the house by the arm. "Let's retire to my private quarters."

"Oh? And exactly what did you have in mind?"

"Nothing too extravagant. A private dinner and I'm sure you wish to clean up. Perhaps a long bath. And then I intend to show you just how I've missed you so."

"Sounds nice," she replied. "But why wait for dinner? I'm sure you would enjoy a bath yourself."

"I'm sure I would," Madari said with an almost predatory grin. "Most definitely."

Minsk, Belarus

"Greece?" said McCarter. "You mean, as in the Greek Isles?"

"That's the skinny," Price said. "We need you there ASAP. We'll have more intelligence with an exact location well before you reach Greek airspace."

"Mission objectives?"

"The U.S. has a representative buyer who's supposed to be meeting with Madari's front man. He's been told to expect you and give you whatever support."

"A buyer. You mean CIA?"

"No, actually someone from the Greek embassy. And don't worry, he's been fully checked out."

"That's what they told you about Mishka."

Price sighed. "I know and we're sorry about that. Nothing we could do—it was out of our hands."

"I understand, Barb." McCarter cleared his throat uncomfortably and said, "Just stings a little. I had my suspicions—we *all* did really—but I didn't act on them."

"Every so often one or two are going to get buy us. Name of the game."

"Acknowledged. Anything else?"

"Your orders are to connect with the buyer from the embassy, learn what you can and then act on what you learn. Hal's opened the floodgates wide with the Man. Either we win this auction or we take the goods. Barring either of those two outcomes, you're to see to it that neither the prototypes nor Dratshev falls into the hands of competitors."

"And naturally we get to mop the floor with Madari."

It almost sounded to McCarter as if Price were smiling when she replied, "Naturally."

"Check. And what about our friends with Cyrus's mercenary group?"

"Let them go. They're no longer in this."

"Understood. We'll be airborne within thirty mikes."

"Acknowledged. Good hunting, David."

McCarter clicked off the phone and then left the small room at the private hangar and joined his companions. They were ranged around a table drinking coffee.

"Braden, you and your crew are free to leave. You can have the vehicle out there to get back to wherever it is you got your transportation stored."

Braden looked sharply at McCarter. "What do you mean?"

"Just what I said, mate. You're done and finished with the op. Bosses say cut you loose, we cut you loose."

"What kind of shit is that?" Muncie asked.

"The kind that shouldn't surprise you if you've been doing this for a while," Calvin James replied.

"Stand down, Muncie," Braden said, his gaze fixed on McCarter.

"But—"

"I said *stand down*." Muncie closed his trap and then Braden said, "I thought we had an agreement, McMasters?"

"My orders supersede the agreement," McCarter replied. "Besides the fact, you no longer have any stake in this. We know where Madari is and we know how to handle him. He's well equipped and we have it on good authority that he's got a small army at his disposal. He also has significant resources."

"So does DCDI."

McCarter shook his head. "Listen, Braden, my team is fighting for the survival of our country."

"As are we," Braden sad.

"You fight for profit."

"It may come as some surprise to you, sir, but Cyclops and Colonel Cyrus…we believe in America. And so does Steinham. Sure, maybe now and again we're overzealous. And we only engaged those combatants in Iowa because they engaged us *first*."

"You were trying to steal national secrets!" Encizo snapped.

Braden shook his head. "But *not* for personal profit! And I was operating under orders from Colonel Cyrus, who in turn was operating under the mission objectives given to us by David Steinham."

"Look, friend, Steinham's a defense contractor," Manning said. "Nothing more, nothing less—he doesn't have the authority to be dispatching armed mercenaries into a government facility or to pit you against civilian authorities. You guys should've stayed as far away from this mission as possible."

"Okay, that's enough," McCarter said. "We don't have bloody time for this. Major Braden, I understand your concern and I can tell you we all appreciate your love of your country and willingness to serve. But the plain fact of the matter is that our mission objectives don't include working cooperatively with a mercenary outfit. Moreover, I can't risk attaching your people to my team, allies or not."

"Fine," Braden said. "Then we'll do what we can on our own."

McCarter nodded. "I wouldn't expect less, mate. And if it makes any difference I admire the hell out of you for sticking to your ideals. But let me be clear that if you attempt to follow us or in any way interfere with our mission, neither I nor my men will hesitate to take you out. Are we clear?"

Braden's face reddened slightly, but he nodded in way of affirmation. "Crystal."

The mercenary turned to his men and nodded. They rose and headed for the exit while Braden got the keys to the SUV Phoenix Force had been using. Braden looked at each of the faces staring back at them.

For just a moment McCarter wondered if Braden's expression wasn't one of respect and admiration. But he turned so quickly and left the hangar that he couldn't be completely sure.

"Okay," McCarter said. "Now that we've got that out of the way, let's talk about what's going to happen now. I just got off the horn with Barb. Able Team managed to detect transmissions coming from an electronics suite at Steinham's residence. Bear got all over it and apparently they figured out it was a trace on Mishka."

"Where's she off to?" Hawkins asked.

"She took a civilian flight to Athens, Greece—probably under a cover. Not important. The big news is she's finally come to nest at a place in the Greek Isles. Coincidentally, that's where the buyer for Madari's auction just happens to be."

"So she's with Madari, too?" James asked. "Holy cripes…is there anybody she *isn't* working for?"

McCarter shrugged. "The problem is we don't really

have a clue what she's up to. It's entirely possible she had nothing to do with Carnes getting his throat cut."

"Who else would've done it?"

"Maybe the FSB caught on to what they were doing and killed him?" Manning suggested.

"That dog won't hunt," Hawkins said. "Forgive me for pointing out the obvious, gents, but we know the whole FSB scouring Minsk was a farce to begin with. The FSB knows Madari has Dratshev. They knew it as soon as he put the good doctor's work up for auction. They wouldn't be combing Belarus to find him. Mishka placed us all for suckers."

"So what do we do about it?" James asked McCarter.

"The plan is that we're to get to Greece and connect with this bidder waiting in Athens. Barb tells me he has strict instructions to cooperate with us."

"Another CIA contact?" Manning asked.

McCarter shook his head. "He's attached to the embassy. Strictly a bureaucrat, so we won't have to worry about his interference."

"Then what?" James said.

"Once we get the details from our contact in Athens, we hit the location transmitter from Mishka's beacon and we act on whatever we find there. Hal made no bones that we've got a free hand in this, mates. If we can't acquire the prototypes and Dratshev securely, our orders are to stomp them out."

"So it's secure or destroy time," Hawkins remarked.

"That's what I'm taken to understand from my conversation with Barb."

"And what about Mishka?"

"She's another story. If we can take her alive and return her to the States, that'd be my preference." McCarter frowned. "She's a liability, yeah, but she may know quite a bloody lot about Madari and his true intentions."

"What would prompt a woman like that to work with someone like Madari?" Encizo asked almost absently.

"Guess when we catch up with her we can ask her," McCarter replied.

"Yeah, I suppose." Encizo shook his head and exchanged glances with his teammates. "But aren't *any* of you guys curious about that? I mean...*think* about it, men. She had a perfect gig here. Young field operative, plenty of opportunities in front of her. Didn't take her any time to move from a cushy, boring office into a field officer position—a position that many in the CIA would die for, by the way. Why the hell throw it all away and risk the anger of your country for a Libyan exile that just may be crazy enough to want to blow up the whole world?"

"Money," McCarter said matter-of-factly.

"No, not the type," Manning replied with thoughtful ease. "I think Rafe's got a point. There's no sense in what she did here. I think we're going to have to accept the possibility she's working for us. Maybe she saw an opportunity and she took it."

"Then why not just tell us about it?" Hawkins asked. "Why send us on a wild-goose chase?"

"That may not be so easy to answer," McCarter said. "And I do have to admit that our weapons were right where she said they would be. If she'd planned to set us up, she wouldn't have made it so easy."

"Unless she wasn't trying to make it look as though she was setting us up," James noted.

"That's also a consideration," Manning agreed.

"Look, it doesn't really matter now," McCarter said.

"Let's gear up and get ready to go. I'm going to go let Jack know he can start warming up the engines."

"Ah, Greece," Hawkins said with a fond tone of recollection. "I've not been there in such a long time. Beautiful women, fine spirits, balmy weather."

"And let's not forget the good eats," James added.

"We're not going there for a vacation," McCarter replied with mock grumpiness. "So don't get your hopes up."

CHAPTER THIRTEEN

Washington, D.C.

"We have to make something happen," Lyons said.

"Hmm. You already mentioned that," Blancanales replied.

"Did I? Well, I'm mentioning it again. We've been halfway across the country and we're getting no place fast."

"It's interesting those weapons used by Cyrus's group were black market types," Schwarz said.

"That's true," Blancanales agreed. "And that's not something you would expect from a legitimate PMC."

Lyons scratched the stubble at his jaw, irritated he hadn't even had the chance to shave yet. "Part of me isn't really surprised. Cyrus and his crew weren't supposed to be there and they knew it. They came well armed, almost as if they were sensing they'd run into trouble."

"What I don't get is why Steinham's protecting them. Why wouldn't he just give up Cyrus if he suspected it might lead back to him?"

"Loyalty, maybe?" Schwarz said.

"Doubt it," Lyons replied. "We've all had our fair share of dealing with guys like Steinham. He's a typical defense contractor. It's all about the profit margin. He wouldn't rat out Cyrus unless he stood to bank some serious coin in the process. News that he was running his mouth and sold a mercenary group he'd contracted would spread fast. He wouldn't risk alienating his position that way."

"Still, it doesn't seem logical he'd be in bed with some-one like Madari," Schwarz said.

"So now the question is, where do we make our next move? Suggestions?"

"We have the address of the place where the weapons at the scene were stolen from," Blancanales said. "I'd venture that place is as good as any to start."

"Where is it again?" Lyons asked.

"About a two-hour drive from here."

Lyons looked at his watch. "That would put us there well after 0100 if we leave now."

"Place won't be open."

"Since when has that ever stopped us?" Lyons said.

"Yup."

The overhead alarm signaling an incoming call buzzed for attention. Schwarz mumbled it was the Farm and then picked up and reverted immediately to speakerphone so all three could hear.

It was Barbara Price. "Listen, we just got a bead on the possible whereabouts of Jack Cyrus."

"Finally," Lyons replied. "Some good news for a change."

The mission controller continued. "Cyrus has a large amount of acreage purchased under his name, and not registered as belonging to Cyclops. That's why we didn't catch it at first."

"Where?"

"It's an unimproved deed outside Norfolk, Virginia."

"So about three hours," Blancanales observed.

"Exactly."

"Okay. Do we know what we're looking for?" Lyons asked.

"It's hard to tell. We're trying to get satellite position but right now it's overcast in that area and we've had to commit a bit of processing time to staying on top of what Phoenix Force has going in Greece."

"I take it we're not supposed to shoot first and ask questions later."

"It wouldn't be preferential," Price said. "The better option here would be to just talk to Colonel Cyrus. We don't really know for certain yet that he had any inkling that what happened in Iowa would turn into such a tragedy."

"Understood." Lyons paused. "What about the ones who attacked us? Any idea where they came from?"

"They're not with Cyclops—we know that much for certain. In fact, we're pretty sure they're working for Madari. The one you captured is refusing to say a word. I understand they've even threatened to ship him straight to Gitmo and he still won't budge."

"All right. We'll beat feet to Norfolk and let you know what we find," Lyons said.

"Good hunting, boys. And be very cautious. We're still dealing with a lot of unknowns."

"That's where the fun is at," Carl Lyons said.

COLONEL JACK CYRUS couldn't quell the nervous murmur in his gut. The enemy was close—he could sense it. It was a sense he'd gained from years in some of the most unforgivable terrain on the planet.

"Jeepers, Colonel. You're more fidgety than a bomb tech on an IED. Why don't you sit down and take a load off?"

Cyrus stopped pacing and whirled on his communications specialist, Jess Shedline, but he clenched his teeth and bit back the scathing retort he'd conjured. There was no sense railing at the guy. Shedline hadn't done anything wrong and he meant well.

Cyrus had first met the communications expert during a mission in the Congo. Shedline had been a top-shelf contribution in support of their unit during a special op. The two had kept in contact and when Shedline finally ETS'd, Cyrus had offered him a job. Shedline had been young but with plenty of experience. He had a good head on his shoulders and knew how to be a team player. Those were qualities Cyrus found rare to that breed, and he'd been glad when Shedline had accepted the offer.

"I can't relax, Jess. You know that."

"I know," Shedline said with a shrug. "But it was worth a try."

"Any news?"

Shedline shook his head. "Nothing since you asked me ten minutes ago."

Cyrus clucked his tongue. "It's this damn waiting that's getting to me."

"Don't sweat it, Colonel. We'll get to the bottom of whoever compromised the mission in Iowa. And when we do, we'll pin them down and bring things to a swift close. Just like we did in the Congo, see?"

"Yeah," Cyrus muttered. "Just like we did in the Congo."

"Wait a minute!"

"What's up?"

"Call coming through."

"From?"

"Braden."

"*Major* Braden, Shedline." Cyrus didn't wait for an apology but instead snatched the spare headset off the nearby desk and donned it. He nodded at Shedline, who then patched the call to that station.

"This is Cyclops. Go, Raven."

"Cyclops, this is Raven. We've had to scrub our present mission."

"Reason?"

"Chiefly, our friends that were dispatched here wouldn't cooperate. They initially took us in but then were directed to cut us loose."

"What about Mishka?"

"I no longer believe she's in this AO. In fact, we have good evidence to think she may have cut loose her one tie here and fled the country."

"You have a possible destination?"

"Negative. We would need you to tell us that."

"It'll take me some time to acquire the information. Foxglove is not being very cooperative at present. But I think I can persuade him to assist if he knows the mission parameters have been compromised."

"Understood. We'll wait for your transmission."

"Expect return contact in thirty mikes. Cyclops out."

Cyrus ripped the headset off and slammed it onto the desk with a curse and wheeze of disgust. "Get me Steinham on the phone. ASAP!"

HARDLY A CAR passed by Black Betty as Able Team sped toward their new destination.

Lyons could feel the tension build in his neck and shoulders—a telltale sign of where he bottled his stress according to his massage therapist—while he considered what they might encounter. The events that had transpired to this point made no sense to him, and this information about Cyrus and his mercs holed up in some remote retreat made even *less*.

Why would they retreat? A guy with Colonel Jack Cyrus's reputation didn't just tuck tail between his legs and run for no reason. Was he trying to protect Steinham or was it actually Steinham who'd left Cyrus with no other options? And why would Cyrus ally himself with the likes of a nutcase like Madari? It was pretty clear that Madari had been responsible for blowing the op in Iowa and killing several of Cyrus's people.

None of it jelled for the Able Team leader. Lyons had been convinced Cyrus was behind the attack on them in Washington, but Stony Man had provided all sorts of incontrovertible evidence to the contrary. So if Cyclops wasn't working for the enemy and wasn't behind the attack on Able Team, then exactly how did they play into it?

Blancanales's voice broke through Lyons's ruminations. "Ironman? I think we've got more trouble."

"What's up?"

"Two pairs of headlights, one in each lane, coming up behind us. Fast."

"Gadgets?" Lyons called.

"Yes, boss."

"Turn on some of those high-fangled instruments back there and sweep Betty's interior."

"On it."

"What do you want me to do?" Blancanales inquired.

"Just hold position for a moment. We don't know if they're hostiles yet, although the chances are good given this road has been devoid of traffic for the most part."

Lyons watched in his side mirror, keeping vigil with Blancanales while Schwarz activated the internal countersurveillance suite built into the sensitive electronics package. The headlights gained and Blancanales wisely kept a steady speed. If they were hostiles, Able Team had plenty of countermeasures to prevent being overtaken, countermeasures that involved more than ass-kicking and firepower. Although Lyons always hoped that was part of the equation—from where he sat it looked as if the new arrivals were about to oblige.

"Ironman?" Schwarz called.

"Yeah."

"Um, was your ass burning?"

"What are you talking about?"

"Your suggestion to sweep the interior of Betty was some sort of intuition."

"Why?"

"Because we're definitely giving off a homing signal. And it's coming from your AO."

Lyons turned in his seat, feeling the rush of heat come to his face. "Are you trying to tell me that—?"

"Yeah. Somebody's got you bugged."

"Who would've been able to do that?" Blancanales cut in. "We're the only ones you've been near. Other than Steinham."

"Yeah, and that was after the first attack."

Lyons ran through it in his mind. Where had he come into contact with anybody? It wouldn't have been mere sleight of hand—all the Stony Man warriors were trained to counteract pickpocket attempts. Had he let his guard down? It took a little time but then he remembered something. He reached into his pocket and withdrew the small business card.

"Winger!" Lyons exclaimed. "That bastard, Nick Winger. The guy we ran into back in Iowa."

"The assistant to Higgs?" Schwarz asked.

"Yeah. He's the only one that could have done this. And I think it was in the contact card he gave me." Lyons handed it to Schwarz. "Here, check that out when you get a chance."

"Why would some guy you don't even know want to keep tabs on us?" Blancanales asked.

"So they can send a hit team to kill us, *dumpfkopf*," Schwarz replied as he took the card carefully from Lyons. He grabbed a microscanner and swept the card, receiving an immediate confirmation. "Yeah. It's definitely wired."

"Destroy that thing. Now."

"Your wish is my command."

The vehicles were practically on top of them now. "Our friends are now in blackout mode."

"I'll give 'em blackout mode," Lyons growled as he yanked his pistol clear and double-checked the action. "Gadgets, we still got those side-mounted launchers with the tire snares?"

"But of course."

"I think it's time to send these punks a message."

"Roger that," Schwarz said as he flipped a switch that would activate the tire snares.

While it might have seemed to the observer that this was more like something out of a James Bond movie, the tire snare was actually a simple device. Constructed from tungsten steel and launched by a small propellant black-powder charge from the base of Betty's frame, the tire snares were designed to entangle a moving tire and shred the rubber from the rim. They were highly effective but not terribly accurate, and rare were the times when Able Team actually opted to use them. This was one of these times.

Schwarz waited until the first vehicle had come parallel with the van on the inside lane—letting the infrared cameras do the work of ensuring the arrivals were in position—before launching the first pair of tire snares. They hit on target and immediately went to work, cutting the super-heated rubber to tatters in a few seconds and causing the vehicle to veer off the road and ride down the embankment into the center ditch where it spun out.

"That did it!" Lyons called out.

The occupants of the second sedan, which had now gained a position on Betty's tail, opened up with automatic weapons. The bullets whined as they struck the composite-armor shell of the van. Blancanales shouted for his friends to hold on and then tromped the brake pedal, edging the wheel right to left to keep the van from spinning out of control.

The driver in the sedan wasn't so adept and he braked hard to avoid slamming into the rear of Black Betty, causing his vehicle to fishtail before finally reaching the inevitable slide. The sedan veered off the road, tires unable to find purchase on the slick gravel of the shoulder, and then it whizzed down the embankment and finally flipped several times before coming to a stop, its roof crunched.

"Scratch that crew," Schwarz muttered.

"Don't assume," Lyons said.

Lyons went EVA as soon as Blancanales got Betty stopped alongside the road. He charged down the embankment toward the crashed vehicle of his enemy, the MP-5K machine pistol clutched in his hands and ready for action. Only one man emerged from the wreck, and in the unmistakable glow of a fire building from under the bent hood Lyons could see another body lying some distance away, obviously ejected during the rollover.

The apparent lone survivor had gathered his marbles enough to see Lyons approach and reached around on the ground until he found what he sought. Lyons caught the profile of the weapon in the glow from the engine just a moment before he steadied the muzzle of the MP-5K and triggered a short burst that blew the gunner's head off his shoulders. Lyons heard something pop and felt an increase in heat, his gut telling him it would be better to hit the ground at that point.

The nagging urge saved his life as the leaking gas tank caught and the vehicle exploded, sending shards of glass and superheated metal whooshing mere inches over his head. A few flaming bits came down directly on him, but Lyons immediately rolled to his left to get them off before they could do any real damage or burn his skin severely.

The concussion from the explosion had shaken Lyons a little, but not as much as the sound of rounds whizzing past, burning the air around him with angry resolve. Lyons looked up and from his position he barely saw the tops of the heads of four gunners that emerged from the other sedan and were approaching on an intercept course. Their intent was obvious—to fully engage and destroy their enemy if at all possible. They made no apologies for it and their resolve seemed obvious given the wink of the muzzle-flashes.

What they hadn't banked on was the resolve of the three Able Team warriors. For all intents, the crew from the second vehicle had the drop on Lyons and pinned him down. If he dared try to take any of them under the current circumstances, he knew he was sure to get killed, a prospect he felt strongly against.

Blancanales and Schwarz had come to the rescue,

however. Seeing their friend pinned down, they joined the fray by splitting up and triggering their own weapons on the move. Blancanales had chosen a SIG 551 for this engagement. He blasted one of the attackers with a double-burst salvo of 5.56 × 45 mm. The impact drove the man backward, his weapon clattering from numb figures as the shots tore open his gut.

Schwarz got the next two with his M-16 A3, sweeping the muzzle in a corkscrew pattern. At this point they were on a road without traffic and there were no residences in sight. This meant they had some leeway in discriminating a fire zone. The first man danced under the impact of so many high-velocity rounds striking his body simultaneously. They shredded flesh, cracked bone and punctured vital organs in a gory spray that was visible only in the illumination provided by the headlamps of the enemy vehicle. The other man took several rounds to the gut before a stray punched through his left eye. His head rocked and then lolled on his body a moment before it crumpled to the pavement.

The survivor realized his predicament and managed to gain a pretty good position of cover from the natural defilade provided by the embankment. He dropped to his belly and set up position sniper-style. His fire was short, controlled and tended toward deadly accuracy—causing all three Able Team warriors to rethink their status.

Schwarz and Blancanales took cover behind Black Betty but realized it wouldn't do much good.

Another vehicle appeared to be fast approaching, its outline taking shape as it passed under the occasional highway lights. It was a panel truck, much larger and probably carrying reinforcements—definitely not something for which Able Team had planned.

Lyons waited for a break in the firing from the lone enemy near the sedan, and then flashed a signal for his comrades to provide cover fire while he made for the relative safety of Betty's armored body.

"Maybe if we can't outgun them," he said, breathing heavy as he arrived unscathed, "we can outrun them."

Blancanales shrugged. "Make our stand here, make it somewhere else."

"Okay," Lyons said. "But how do we keep the by-standers out of it?"

"Call for reinforcements?" Schwarz proposed.

Lyons shook his head as he heard the roar of the panel truck engine for the first time. "Wouldn't get here in time."

"Looks like we're out of options," Blancanales said.

Lyons removed the magazine from his weapon and slammed home a fresh one, his last, as he replied, "It looks like."

CHAPTER FOURTEEN

Athens, Greece

Alan Demopolis had been in-country with the U.S. State Department less than two years.

For a low-ranking assistant in the diplomatic corps to act as a buyer for U.S. technical interests wouldn't have been the normal course of things, but in this instance it only made sense. The American government couldn't risk using anybody from high up in the ranks in case Madari's play turned out to be a pretext to a more nefarious plan. So they were stuck with Demopolis, which forced Phoenix Force to work with him, as well.

McCarter, determined to the make the best of the political situation, made contact with Demopolis as soon as they reached Athens and scheduled to meet him at a place of the diplomatic assistant's choosing.

McCarter had initially planned to meet him alone while the rest of Phoenix Force provided perimeter security, but then thought better of it and opted to take Encizo along for backup. There wasn't any reason to think Madari knew Phoenix Force was in Greece, or that he meant harm to Demopolis. But after everything that had happened in Belarus, McCarter didn't plan to take chances, and it never hurt to have a second team member who knew the play in case the team leader fell.

McCarter and Encizo found Demopolis at the time and place specified; a café on one of the secondary roads in an older, nondescript section of the city. Demopolis was enjoying a strong cup of coffee and midway through a rather generous helping of baklava when they arrived. He gestured for them to take seats at the little four-top across from him. McCarter and Encizo studied their surroundings from behind sunglasses, watchful for anyone who might be taking other than casual notice of the trio.

Demopolis fit right into the local crowd, the Greek roots obvious in his dark hair and eyes. He didn't have the swarthy complexion bronzed by many years in the Mediterranean sun, but that didn't mean anything. From where McCarter sat, the guy could easily have passed as a native and he could see why the state department had chosen Demopolis for this post, if not the reasons for his selection to act as buyer.

As if reading McCarter's thoughts, he opened the conversation with a smile. "I'm not what you expected."

"Not really," McCarter admitted.

"It's not an insult. You're McMasters?"

McCarter nodded and gestured to Encizo. "This is Mr. Castiano."

Demopolis extended his hand to shake theirs in turn, and then cut into a fresh helping of the flaky, gooey dessert. "Can't get enough of this," he said around a mouthful. After offering to order some for the pair, who declined, and washing it down with the coffee, Demopolis dabbed at his mouth with the napkin and said, "So I assume you've been briefed?"

McCarter confirmed with nod.

Demopolis continued. "It probably goes without saying I know exactly what this is about. I've been read in and I can tell you I'm pretty stoked they picked me to do this."

"First time?"

Demopolis nodded. "Yeah, but we're all trained for this. In fact, I took some additional classes with the DSS at Quantico."

That bit of news impressed McCarter. Not every assistant went through the rigors of training with the diplomatic security service. While Demopolis was still a novice, for him to have even chosen to take the training marked him as a reliable asset—much more reliable than most men in his position. The choice to have him serve as bidder for the U.S. interests was beginning to make sense.

Not that it would matter, as McCarter pointed out when he said, "I assume you also know why *we're* here."

Demopolis nodded. "Make sure we get what we came for."

"And?" Encizo prompted.

"If we don't get what we came for, then you guys are here to take it and I'm just supposed to duck."

"So we understand each other," McCarter said.

Demopolis's smile lacked warmth. "Like I say, McMasters, I may still be a rookie to the diplomatic game but this isn't exactly my first day on the job. The only thing they didn't tell me is exactly what sort of technology we were bidding on. They told me the other players, though, so it wasn't too far of a stretch to gather it was important. Between that and the cross chatter on the other channels, I'm sure it has something to do with electromagnetic pulse weapons—"

"EMPs?" Encizo cut in. "What makes you think so?"

"Come on!"

"Shh!" McCarter said, beginning to feel snappish.

There were things about Demopolis that irritated him. "Damp down, will you? We don't need to take out a bloody ad."

"Sorry," Demopolis said, lowering his voice immediately. "But the word's out all over the place about Oleg Dratshev's abduction. The entire European theater is crawling with Russian FSB."

"That's not good," Encizo said, jerking a thumb in Demopolis's direction. "If *he* knows about that…"

Encizo's voice trailed off and McCarter just nodded. His friend didn't have to finish the thought because he already knew what it meant. Word had gotten out about Dratshev through all of the official channels now. That meant if the governments bidding on the technology knew about it, and the diplomatic community knew about it, then David Steinham's people definitely knew about it. All the players would now be in the game, and their choice to let Steinham's mercenary team off the hook and send them packing had just become a critical error in judgment. There was little doubt in McCarter's mind that might go against them sooner rather than later.

The Phoenix Force leader said to Demopolis, "Whether you're right about what you're bidding on, I can't confirm. What I can say is that it's our job to make sure it doesn't fall into the hands of a competitor. We're authorized to destroy it in that eventuality."

"And we take our job pretty seriously," Encizo added.

"Which means," McCarter said, "that when the moment comes and we tell you to get out of the way it would be a *really* good idea for you to listen to us."

"Sounds fair enough," Demopolis said. "But until that time comes I've been informed I'm in charge and nobody has the authority to override me."

McCarter splayed his hands. "Look, mate, we don't have any intention of—"

A squelch in McCarter's ear followed by Hawkins's voice cut him short. "Heads up, boss. We got big trouble right here in River City."

McCarter keyed the transmitter clipped on his belt. "You want to be more specific?"

"Get *down!*"

McCarter and Encizo went toward the fancy tile patio of the café, each grabbing a lapel on Demopolis's jacket on the way down. Had the warning come any later, all three of them would've been ventilated by the autofire that burned the air around them. One poor bystander who'd just been lifting a cup to his lips couldn't escape the odds and his skull split open under the impact of several high-velocity slugs.

McCarter winced as he saw the guy's body flop in the seat, but there wasn't much he could do about it. Fortunately the brick facade took most of the brunt, and those inside the café were spared the fate of this man. McCarter pushed it from his mind as he whipped his Browning Hi-Power 9 mm from shoulder leather and turned to assess individual target locations.

That's when he realized the assault had been swift because the attackers were on motorcycles.

THEY RODE A pair to each motorcycle for a total of twelve enemy combatants, the front positions driving while the back sprayed the café and courtyard area around it with bullets.

The gunners were utterly indiscriminate, careless of who or what they shot up as long as they managed to bring down McCarter, Encizo and Demopolis. Phoenix

Force wasn't going to let that happen. Hawkins had no idea where they'd come from or who they worked for, but obviously their attempts at secrecy had been frustrated once more. Immediately after he'd shouted the warning to McCarter and Encizo, the trio answered the call to action.

James broke his concealment behind a high stand of rosebushes in a planter in front of a clothing store across the small plaza from the café, his Beretta 93R ready for action. He took up position near a stone fountain, braced his forearms against a pillar and sighted to lead one of the motorcycles as he thumbed the safety to triburst mode.

James stroked the trigger, maintaining a rock-steady hold on his pistol as it bucked with the release of three successive 9 mm Parabellum rounds. The hits were on target, two catching the gunner on the back of the motorcycle in the torso and the third cracking his helmet. The impact flung the gunner's body, upsetting the delicate balance of the motorcycle and sending it to a skidding halt.

MANNING HAD BEEN watching the action from the high point of a restroom window on a second floor. He immediately whipped the compact sniper rifle from his bag and assembled it in under ten seconds—a new record for the Canadian marksman—completing the assembly by hammering home a magazine with capacity for eight rounds of 7.62 mm.

Manning eased the rifle barrel out the window, having to put his booted feet on the toilet seat to gain a clear view. James had brought down one motorcycle team from his position and as Manning put his eye to the scope he watched as Hawkins neatly dispatched a second.

The Phoenix Force warriors on perimeter watch had been able to take down the attackers with some success because of their distance, and because the enemy hadn't expected such a response. McCarter and Encizo, however, were pinned down by a constant barrage of enemy bullets and a well-coordinated attack. Manning knew he'd have to equalize the situation if his friends stood a chance of coming out the other end of it.

Manning put his cheek to the cool, polished stock, engaged the scope and acquired his first target. Given windage and lead time, and the relative speed of the motorcycles, Manning held no delusions his skills would need to be above par. The next few minutes would likely prove some of the most challenging of his career. Manning pushed nagging doubts about being up to the task from his mind as his finger rested on the trigger.

A moment later the first round left the barrel of the rifle at a muzzle velocity of nearly 1600 fps. The bullet cut into the fuel line and sparked off the tank. A moment of eerie quiet went by, at least quiet from Manning's position, before the motorcycle burst into a flaming rocket on a path that terminated with a storefront wall.

Manning had already rocked the bolt on the rifle and chambered a live round before the first enemy motorcycle completed its fiery path. He sighted on the next target, took a deep breath and let half out before squeezing the trigger. It looked like a miss but when the motorcycle kept on a forward path instead of turning to avoid one of the walls containing a fountain pool, and the wheel struck the wall and sent the two riders flying into the unyielding marble with a bone-crunching splash, Manning felt merely grim satisfaction with the results.

THOMAS JACKSON HAWKINS engaged his own attackers just a moment after James took the first pair. He produced a

SIG P-239 and burst out the door of the boutique where he'd occupied a corner table with a perfect view of the café. The swiftness of the attack might have taken a lesser observer by surprise, but not a Delta Force combat veteran like Hawkins. The Texan had a keen eye and honed reflexes and his warning had unarguably saved the lives of his teammates.

Now they were pinned down and he would have to step it up one more level—or maybe by a factor of ten. In any case, their enemies knew they were up against determination and experience, and Hawkins was about to reinforce that point for them. He raised the P-239 and squeezed the trigger twice on the motorcycle crew as they passed by, their attention focused entirely on their targets.

The pair of rounds was delivered in a way that made perfect sense from a tactical perspective. The first caught the driver in the torso between a pair of ribs. It continued into a lung and forced a bloody spray from his mouth, completely obscuring the visor. The second round, despite its intended target, smashed through the gap between the helmet and right shoulder of the rider with enough force to drive him off the bike entirely just before it rolled onto its side and came to a smashing stop—now uncontrolled with a lifeless operator—by the plate-glass window of a sewing shop.

IN LESS THAN a minute the vicious assault by a half dozen motorcycles had been cut to just a third of the original force. That did much to bolster the confidence of McCarter and Encizo, who had been pinned down by a fiery metal storm.

McCarter, Hi-Power in play along with Encizo's Glock 21, took cover behind the low stone wall of the patio of the café. The two put their focus on the closest threat, a pair of intent gunners that had dismounted their motorized steed and were foolishly charging their position, oblivious to the disasters that had befallen their ranks.

McCarter and Encizo opened up simultaneously, pumping a punishingly accurate volley at the charging gunners. The first one fell under several 9 mm zingers to the gut—a testament to Encizo's resolve and skill—the rounds burning through the man and tearing at the critical coverings of his vital organs. He produced a half shout of pain before drowning in his own blood and skidding chin-first into the pavement.

McCarter got the other with a double-tap to the head that blew the man's faceplate open. Plastic and fiberglass shattered and his skull, having no place to go, imploded and produced a grisly mess from every available orifice, the result of applying great force to a self-contained entity.

A flash in his peripheral vision caused McCarter to turn to see Demopolis leave the relative safety of the table and patio wall. "Wait!"

It did no good. Demopolis immediately collapsed under the blast of autofire triggered by the surviving pair. These men had seen the demise of their comrades and decided to get off their motorcycle and find the best cover available. They knew the enemy had at least one sniper, placed high and with a pretty good if not somewhat limited field of fire. They also had two more on the ground but not within range. Still, their situation was tenuous and they at least knew they had to do what damage they could before beating it the hell out of there.

McCarter cursed and then looked to his right to see James trying for a better position. The last pair of attackers had managed to settle in and it would prove a pretty good challenge trying to overcome their position. To attempt to rush them in force would have been pure suicide. McCarter had to admit that the surviving enemy gunners had good position.

It was T. J. Hawkins who came up with the answer they needed. The Phoenix Force warrior had wisely brought along a satchel with ordnance from the Stony Man armory. One included a smoker and Hawkins dropped it dead into the middle of the action, filling the narrow plaza surrounded by the shops with a thick haze of blue-gray smoke.

As soon as the smoke spread sufficiently, Hawkins lobbed a second grenade into the fray. It bounced a couple of times and then a cloud of gas burst from the canister, this time under significant pressure. While the CS gas would have been more effective in a closed space, it was close enough to the enemy position to be effective. The noxious gas would drive them into the open. They immediately burst from their cover in an attempt to escape.

Straight into the unerring fire of James, Hawkins, McCarter and Encizo—all four had been waiting for just such an eventuality. They all squeezed off several rounds and the pair of gunners danced like marionettes under the impact of the rounds. The fusillade of fire from the quartet of Phoenix Force warriors struck at every vital point, shredding flesh, cracking bone and puncturing organs.

As the echo from the gunfire died, McCarter rushed to the unmoving form of Demopolis, knelt and checked for a pulse. He didn't find one, hardly surprising given what appeared to be half a dozen red splotches in the guy's back. James and Hawkins proceeded quickly but cautiously to their position, arriving just as McCarter stood.

"Well?" James inquired.

McCarter shook his head.

Encizo said, "Poor bastard."

The sudden wail of nearby sirens prompted McCarter to say, "Which is exactly what we're going to be, mates, if we hang around here. Where's Gary?"

Hawkins jerked a thumb in his general direction. "Sure he won't try to reconnect with us here given the impending arrival of the cops. We should probably go straight to the rally point."

As they jogged out of the plaza and headed in the opposite direction of the sirens, Encizo told McCarter, "You realize they're going to blame us for Demopolis buying the farm."

"Tough," McCarter replied. "Wasn't a bloody thing we could do about it. It's the CIA who lost control of their agent, not to mention they actually trusted Madari to play fair. They're keeping one step ahead of us and I, for one, am getting bloody damn tired of being a punching bag for Madari."

"What do you want to do?" James asked.

"Take all bets off the table. Now we have one mission and one mission only. Destroy Madari and these weapons. From here forward, we take the offensive."

CHAPTER FIFTEEN

Rural Virginia

The panel truck came to a screeching halt and immediately the Able Team trio aligned the sights of their weapons on the grille between the headlights.

At a signal from Lyons, all three opened up simultaneously and splattered the front of the truck with a hail of destructive hot lead. There was no way they planned to let the enemy escape, especially not one that had bothered to go to such lengths to destroy them. If nothing else, they could gain information and maybe such intelligence would help them peg down exactly who they were up against and why they were having such a hard time keeping this mission out of the public eye.

The sparks, telltale signs of the effective firestorm, were much more evident once the lights of the panel truck succumbed to the metal-smashing effects of 5.56 mm and 7.62 mm fire from the automatic rifles wielded by Able Team.

It seemed to do nothing, however, to deter the seemingly endless parade of armed combatants that disgorged from the back of the panel truck and immediately fanned into formation. These were professionals, sure, that much made obvious by their practiced movements. But being soldiers, whose side were they *really* on? Were these more of Cyrus's mercenaries or additional numbers of hired guns under the employ of Ishaq Madari? Or were they maybe a personal force in the employ of David Steinham? It would be hard to find out if Able Team couldn't survive the encounter.

Rounds bounced and sparked off the pavement or Black Betty's armored body, which were troublesome to be sure—not nearly as troublesome, however, as the unmistakable shapes of the weapons being set up by two separate fire teams. Those were rocket launchers and they definitely put the odds in favor of the enemy.

"Are those—?" Blancanales began.

"Yeah!" Lyons confirmed.

"Ironman," Schwarz said during a lull in the firing while he slapped home a fresh magazine. "Betty's homogenous armor can withstand intense heat and just about every small arm round. But it's no match for rocket-propelled grenades. We need to think about a retreat action."

As a fresh hail of gunfire burned the air over his head, causing Lyons to duck, he replied, "I know, I know! But they have apparently some very *different* ideas. I don't think we can get out of here before they're set up. We need to try to neutralize them."

"Wilco!" Schwarz reached into the van and came away with a stand-alone grenade launcher, a variant of the M-203 that fired 40 mm HE shells. He verified the weapon was already primed with a shell and then sighted on the nearest party and triggered a blast. The grenade fell a bit short of the enemy group, but the resultant explosion seemed enough to divert them from a more prolific course toward ensuring Able Team's destruction.

The second group had managed to gain enough ground

they were now in a position to hit Black Betty head-on, and there was wasn't much the Stony Man warriors could do about it. They were just simply outgunned and out-manned, and not equipped to handle a force of this magnitude with the limited armament inside Black Betty.

Only those precious reinforcements Schwarz had talked about before could help them in their situation, reinforcements that would arrive only in time to find a smoking mass of ruins—the remains of Betty—accompanied by three charred bodies.

Lyons whipped his head to the side, directing his voice toward his compatriots that they should get clear, when the enemy position suddenly exploded in a brilliant flash. Chunks of dirt, stone and highway debris exploded high into the air and the secondary concussion from the blast about rattled the teeth from the three men of Able Team.

They were at a complete loss for explanation until the air above their heads burned with heat and the blast of rotor wash whipped dust and gravel around them. The black chopper streaked low overhead and then zipped out and came around for a second pass. Another pop-flash from its side and the panel truck disappeared a moment later under the powerful rockets being launched from the late-model attack chopper, which looked like a variant of an Apache.

Machine guns from the opposite side of the chopper erupted a moment later, and then a second chopper appeared and joined the battle. This one looked like a refurbished Blackhawk, an assessment confirmed when the chopper came to a hover and turned sideways, its profile now illuminated by the burning hulk in the middle of the roadway. It was all that basically remained of the panel truck.

Lyons and his teammates were so astounded by the sudden ferocity of the attack, coupled with the turn in fortune, they almost forgot there were still enemy combatants on the ground. No longer the point of concern, they turned their precious remaining munitions on the distracted troops, cutting them down with swathing fire while the machine guns from the assault chopper—along with help from manned guns in the Blackhawk conversion, laid down brutal and unforgiving air support.

Within less than a minute after the choppers arrived, the last of the enemy troops fell under the swift and direct assault of the air support. The attack chopper then swung away from the carnage and buzzed out of the area very quickly, while the Blackhawk finally found a safe stretch on the highway upon which to touch down.

At first, the Able Team trio refused to break from the relative safety of Black Betty's shadow, completely unsure of the origins of their saviors. While they were simply grateful to be alive, it didn't mean they were going to trust these new allies at face value. These avenging angels had come out of nowhere, with no reason to be able to differentiate between their friends or foes, and yet they'd come down on Able Team's side.

"Hey, man, I don't get it," Schwarz said. "Did the Farm figure we were in trouble and send help?"

"I don't see how even the Farm could have sent somebody this fast," Lyons said.

"Beware of wolves in sheep's clothing, old friend," Blancanales said.

"Yeah," Lyons replied. It was all he could think to say.

The rotors began to slow to a thrum as two shadowy forms stepped from the chopper and approached Black Betty. One of the men held a sub-gun of some kind but the other appeared unarmed. In fact, he trotted toward them with his hands up—obviously meant to show he meant Able Team no harm and that he was coming without intent of posing a threat.

Lyons had no trouble believing it, really. In spite of Blancanales's warning, the choppers could easily have polished them off after dealing with their enemies. Instead they were now on the ground, vulnerable, and clearly heading into this offering a proverbial white flag.

Something in Lyons's instincts told him that, allies or not, they were at least interested in being heard and he owed them that much. In response to a nagging suspicion, Lyons lowered his weapon and stepped into the open, making himself visible in the single spotlight from the chopper now blanketing the meeting ground in a bright yellow light.

Lyons couldn't make out the face of the man with his arms in the air until he got within touching distance.

Peering over the top of Betty's grill, Schwarz let out a low whistle and looked at Blancanales with utter disbelief. "Cyrus? I don't believe it!"

Colonel Jack Cyrus cast a glance in their direction and then locked eyes with Lyons. "Well, you apparently know who I am. I suspected as much. Unfortunately, I don't know who *you* are."

Lyons said, "I'm sure you can understand that's the way it's supposed to be."

Cyrus nodded. "I didn't believe your bullshit story about being with the Feds when you showed up at my boss's doorstep."

"Yeah, well…your *boss* didn't exactly want to claim you," Schwarz pointed out as he and Blancanales joined the little ad hoc meeting there on the highway turned battleground.

"Thanks, by the way, for saving our asses," Blancanales said with as good-natured a grin as he could manage.

"I was gambling on which side represented the good guys," Cyrus said with a nod as acknowledgment. "Looks like I picked right."

"You did," Schwarz said.

"Only question is how did you know which side to pick?"

"That's a much longer story," Cyrus said. He looked at his watch. "One that I'm afraid I'll have to save for another time and place. Now, it's time for us to go."

Lyons raised his rifle, leveling it at Cyrus's gut. "Afraid we can't let you do that."

"What the hell are doing, Ironman?" Blancanales said.

Directing his voice over his shoulder while keeping his eyes on Cyrus, Lyons replied, "I'm just keeping to the mission plan."

"Your mission was to find me and kill me?" Cyrus asked, his eyes challenging Lyons while he kept his voice and demeanor cool as ice.

"In a matter of speaking."

"Is it possible you could hear me out first?"

"I don't think whatever you have to say would change our minds."

"It might."

Lyons thought about a moment longer, realized that he wasn't listening to his initial instinct, and then he lowered his weapon. "Okay, we owe you that much."

"We can go to my place," Cyrus said. As he turned to leave he added, "It's not far. But then again, you already knew that. Didn't you?"

"Yeah," Lyons muttered. "We already knew that."

USING THE GPS coordinates provided by Cyrus, along with a the chopper as a guide, Able Team reached the wooded acreage outside Norfolk that was listed in different parcels under Cyrus's rather vast personal holdings, but that they knew he used for training the men under his command.

As it turned out, Cyrus was quite a host and granted the Able Team warriors a much warmer reception than they would have otherwise had by penetrating his compound and engaging his men. This caused Cyrus and his immediate command staff a considerable laugh when Blancanales pointed it out. The choice to reveal their original mission objectives to Cyrus soured Lyons at first, but he quickly saw the genius in it.

He also began to realize that Cyrus wasn't the evasive criminal they'd originally made him out to be. Cyrus at least *stood* for something, not like his employer Steinham, who didn't appear to be out for any interests but his own. It was over a ration of tacos and ice-cold beer that Jack Cyrus took exception to Lyons's notion; one that Lyons hadn't been shy about voicing directly.

"On the contrary, Irons," Cyrus said. He wiped the beer suds on his upper lip with the back of his hand before saying, "In fact, I'd wager that Mr. Steinham may well be a bigger patriot than anybody in this room."

"That right?" Blancanales prompted with a disarming smile.

Cyrus nodded. "Right enough. You see, everybody has it in their head that he's merely a businessman, that it's only the next contract he's worried about. But I know a different guy. I've done a lot of jobs for him, and all I've ever seen is a guy who's really passionate about what he does. No, I can't see Steinham ever being in league with a guy like Ishaq Madari."

"Who said anything about him being in league with Madari?" Lyons asked.

"Isn't that why you showed up at his place unannounced? He had you guys pegged from the start. He knew you weren't with any legitimate agency. And it wasn't hard for him to figure it out, especially after the very public encounter you'd had with Madari's people just hours before that."

"So that first team *was* from Madari," Schwarz said.

"Yes."

"How do you know?" Lyons said.

"Because we've been watching him for quite a long time now. You see, Steinham had been keeping one eye on Oleg Dratshev's work from the beginning. DCDI tried to develop EMP weapons quite a number of years ago, but they couldn't get past all the physics. Apparently, from what little I understand of it, a lot of energy must be built up for even one brief pulse. Containing said energy within conventional weapon systems, even if you can produce it, is no easy task."

"Yeah, we get the physics aren't simple," Schwarz interjected. "But that still doesn't explain how Steinham managed to tie Dratshev's work with Madari's interests."

"His little lady friend, the mole that called herself Mishka."

"The one working for the CIA," Lyons said.

"Right…her. She'd been on Steinham's payroll practically from the start. He recruited her while she was still going through her field officer indoctrination and training. Wasn't difficult to recruit her, really—one patriot can recognize another."

"So he saw an opportunity to learn about Dratshev's work by planting her inside Minsk?" Blancanales asked. "How did he make that connection?"

"I don't have all the details," Cyrus said, hands splayed. "I'm not even sure I should be talking about this at all. But you guys seem on the level. And I have it on good authority that we may have mutual friends."

"Is that right?" Lyons asked.

Cyrus nodded as he jammed a toothpick in his mouth. He sat back in his chair and folded his arms. "Seems some of your people overseas could have played hard-ball with some of my guys but chose to cut them loose."

"You're talking about Braden."

"I am. He was over there on a mission from Stein-ham—not really anything I would have sent him on if I'd had a choice. But a contract is a contract and as long as it falls within our code of ethics, we have to honor any mission objectives he hands down."

"And what code of ethics is that?" Lyons asked.

"We won't assassinate noncombatants, such as by-standers, and we won't operate against children. There are *no* acceptable casualties in our ranks. Strictly by the book. Finally, we won't subvert American allies and we *never* operate against our own. Ever."

"Meaning you won't fire on American soldiers."

"Or cops from any federal law-enforcement agency."

"What about Iowa?"

"We didn't know what we were getting into. Riley—er, that is, Major Braden—walked into a bad situation and he was forced to defend himself. Not to mention we lost as many as they did."

"Take it easy," Blancanales said, raising a hand. "We also found out that the guards you killed weren't legitimate security. Turns out they were terrorists working for Madari, as well."

Cyrus looked suddenly relieved as he removed the toothpick from his mouth and let out a long sigh. "I didn't know that. Thanks for the information. That helped."

"Least we could do for pulling our bacon out of the fire," Schwarz said.

"All that aside," Lyons said, "we've made you aware this is an American SOG operation and now we need you to stand down."

"Wish I could," Cyrus said. "I'd like nothing better, actually, but I'm afraid we can't do that."

"And why not?"

"Because we've come into some intelligence that indicates Madari plans to test these weapons. And that he plans to do it against Americans."

"Here?" Schwarz asked.

Cyrus shrugged. "I doubt it. That would be kind of stupid, don't you think? Attempt to turn untested weapons against us in our own country? That would be doomed to fail. No, our intelligence thinks he'll do a demonstration against an American target overseas. Maybe a ship or a plane."

"That sounds like information you'd best turn over to *us*," Lyons replied with a warning smile. "Let us handle it from here out."

"Not as long as I have a contract," Cyrus said.

"Don't go after this, Colonel Cyrus," Lyons said, the warning implicit in his tone. "Stay out of it and let us do what we're best at."

"Look, guys, I have no intention of interfering with you," Cyrus said. "But it stands to reason that if these weapons fall into Madari's hands and he actually intends to use them against American citizens, he could do it anywhere. We have the privacy of our client to protect."

"A privacy that's been compromised," Lyons said.

"Says who?"

"You just told us you were working for Steinham," Blancanales said.

"I did. But I never said it had anything to do with this particular mission," Cyrus replied. "Steinham is a big part of our revenue and we get lots of lucrative contracts. But that isn't meant to imply he's our *only* client. And I can assure you he's not our only client with an interest in energy pulse weapons."

"So you mean you're working for someone else?"

"I mean that I've told you all I can tell you. Now you're free to go as long as you give me your word you won't try to bring a detachment of Army National Guard down on my head here."

"How do you know we won't promise it and then just break our word once we leave?" Lyons asked.

"Because of the very fact you just asked that question," Cyrus said with a cat-ate-the-canary grin. "Not to mention that I know men who keep their word, and you three are definitely cut from the same cloth as we are. You want to see Madari fall just as much as we do. And I know you sure as hell won't stand idly by as long as there's a potential threat to American citizens."

Cyrus shook his head and rose, circling the table with the intensity of a shark trapped in a shallow beach. "Look, you said it yourselves. We're already on the same side. Let's just agree to remain allies on the premise that we want the same thing. We just have different ways of getting there."

"You aren't worried our paths won't cross again?" Blancanales asked.

"Oh, I can almost assure you our paths *will* cross again," Cyrus said. "I just don't want our next meeting to find us on opposite sides of the skirmish line."

"We'd hope for the same thing," Lyons said. "But we can't make any guarantees. As you've said, the safety of the American people is our first priority. We have orders that if these EMP whatchamacallits can't be secured then they *must* be destroyed."

"Along with anyone who might want to possess the technology," Blancanales said with a nod of affirmation. "You understand we can't make any distinctions on that count."

Cyrus stopped and looked at each of the three men in turn. "No, I don't understand. But I understand orders and I understand duty. And I understand you have to do your duty and follow orders, just as I must do the same. It will be too bad if that winds up landing us in a case of opposition with each other."

And even as Cyrus said it, the men of Able Team had to admit they shared such a regret equally.

CHAPTER SIXTEEN

Greek Isles

High winds whipped the faces of the five warriors of Phoenix Force as they moved into jump position. Exactly twelve hundred feet below them lay the island where they had tracked Muriel Annabel Stanish, aka Mishka.

McCarter had insisted on jumping below radar signatures. Although they had no reason to believe Madari's compound boasted any sort of radar station or tracking of air traffic, he didn't care to risk it. So far Madari had managed to keep one step ahead of them, up to and including tracking of the Stony Man teams if what they'd been told about Able Team was accurate. If Madari was sophisticated enough to succor a CIA agent, engineer Dratshev's kidnapping and develop advanced weapons, he was surely capable of tracking the movements of any special operations group.

That didn't mean Phoenix Force didn't have a few tricks up its own proverbial sleeve. First, they were more than experienced enough to execute an assault operation against compounds such as this one. They had acquired the layout of the island, which McCarter understood included a private small-plane airstrip, and a full estate with adjoining underground facility the experts at the Farm believed to be some kind of lab.

McCarter's one concern was the potential for going up against EMP small arms, but he considered it more important to take the fight to Madari on their terms.

The only other detail to be worked out was what to do about Mishka and Dratshev. As far as they could tell at this point, Dratshev was an unwilling party to this game of Madari's and so they would do everything they could to recover him unscathed. Mishka might prove a valuable asset, but given her betrayal of Phoenix Force and the murder of a CIA agent, she was an expendable asset at best.

McCarter wasn't big on killing women, but he hated traitors even worse. He couldn't understand why Mishka would ever ally herself with the likes of Ishaq Madari. She had no ties to Libya; she didn't seem like the type motivated by money, so had she done it for...*love?* Had she really fallen for the nutcase's pitiable story of losing his family to the Libyan government he'd served for so long?

Only time would tell—time in numbers that were running down fast. One way or another, they'd find out what was going on and then they'd do whatever necessary to close it out once and for all.

McCARTER TOUCHED down and shed the parachute pack from his body before Manning touched down, the last on the ground. The five Phoenix Force warriors assembled just short of the makeshift airfield, which they knew boasted a man-made road that led uphill to the estate set higher in some ridges.

While Madari didn't own the entire island, he had apparently acquired a good part of it. None of the intelligence from the Farm had explained exactly how a man like Madari could have possibly arranged to amass such wealth. There were rumors that he had financiers with very deep pockets, maybe even terrorist factions, all bent on possessing the EMP technology he'd promised.

Now it seemed clear that Madari had never intended for anyone to get their hands on Dratshev or his brain-child, and if there were outside organizations that had backed Madari, his life wouldn't be worth two bits inside of a week once they discovered they had been betrayed. Then again, maybe that had been Madari's plan all the time. It didn't make a lot of sense, really, given Madari's stated goals.

McCarter ran the various scenarios through his mind time and again as Phoenix Force made their way toward an almost inevitable showdown with Madari's personal security force. He was hoping if he could understand Madari and what motivated him; it would make it much easier to predict the guy's next move.

As they neared the perimeter of the estate—having wound their way this far through the trees and tall brush that lined the makeshift road that led from the airstrip— McCarter signaled for his men to spread out. He wasn't certain the numbers or kinds of resistance they would encounter; only that it was sure to come.

McCarter's insight was proved a minute later when the first of the resistance materialized in the form of a sniper bullet that burned past his ear close enough for him to hear its path.

NOTHING HAD HAPPENED as Mishka foresaw it. She'd been an intelligence officer long enough to know that things didn't always go as planned. She'd hoped since arriving here she would be safe—that she would have time to spend with Ishaq and then some to spare. Instead, after a lovely evening of food, wine and plenty of sex, he'd left her to her own devices while heading to the launch on the far side of the island.

According to what she'd learned from him, along with things she'd overheard the past day, he'd modified his yacht with prototypes of the EMP weapons. They were preparing to cruise from the islands into the open sea and make all possible speed toward the United States. This troubled Mishka on many accounts, not the least of which had to do with her understanding that her fellow Americans wouldn't be hurt by his plans.

Now it was all coming apart. Not only had he left her alone—in part she came to realize this was as much *her* decision not to accompany him—but also that he now seemed like a different man. Or maybe it was more…indifferent. He was worried about all of it coming together to achieve his political ends in Libya, while Mishka had done everything for him in the name of passion. She loved him so much it hurt and yet he'd seemed to cast that aside for his own ends.

This reality came crashing down on her in a way she could never have seen in her mind's eye. Mishka didn't know what she'd really envisioned, but what she did know was that it wasn't to have anything to do with Libya or America or these infernal weapons. Madari had obviously abandoned his pursuits of her, perhaps having felt he'd already conquered her affections and now cared only for completing whatever mission he had in mind in America.

Two armed men entered their private suite, unbidden, while she was still in the process of getting dressed after a long bath—a bath intended to wash away their night of spent passion.

"What do you want?" she asked of the man she recognized as head of Madari's house guard.

The man, whose name was Iman Jachan, didn't reply. Instead he went to her closet, opened it and immediately removed a light jacket. "A strike team of commandos has entered the perimeter. We have instructions to take you to the bunker."

"I'm not leaving until I speak with Ishaq."

"That will be quite impossible," Jachan said with a frown. "The ship left more than three hours ago."

"What? But he wasn't scheduled to leave until tomorrow."

Jachan's smile could have been described as anything but ingratiating. "I'm afraid plans have changed, Mishka. Now please, there isn't much time. I am personally responsible for your safety. You will need to put that on—" he gestured to the jacket "—and then accompany us to the bunker."

"I already told you, I'm not leaving."

Jachan produced a pistol and aimed it at her. "You have no choice. You will come with us now, please."

Mishka thought of her bag on the far side of the room that contained her pistol and a small dagger, but she knew it wouldn't do any good. She'd never get to it in time. So she tried another tack. "This is now my home. And I will not cower in some dank, dusty hole while Ishaq is risking his own life. I will fight for what is mine, Mr. Jachan. And if this strike team is the men I believe they are, you can be assured when I tell you that you will need my help to defeat them."

Jachan looked conflicted, and he paused in seeming consideration of her words. "How do you know?"

"Because they have probably tracked me here."

"How?"

"I don't know how. Do you have video of them?"

Jachan nodded.

"Then lower your pistol and let me see it. If they are the American special operators, I may be able to help you because I've dealt with them. I've seen them in action. Your course will not be easy."

Jachan stood there a moment longer and then holstered his pistol. "Then put on the jacket and follow me."

Mishka did as instructed and then sauntered casually across the room and retrieved her bag of tricks.

"What's that?"

"Just some personal things I don't wish to leave behind."

"Leave them. The bunker has everything you need should we not be victorious this day."

"They could be used to identify me," she said. "Or perhaps compromise Ishaq's mission. I will not leave them behind."

Jachan hesitated again and then nodded. "Fine. Then let's go."

She slung the bag onto her shoulder, nodded and then gestured for them to lead her out. As they left the suite and headed down the stairs to what Mishka knew was probably in the direction of the control room, she reached surreptitiously into the bag and located her .380-caliber pistol. She palmed it as they crossed through a shadowy section of the downstairs, and slipped it into the pocket of her slacks. It wasn't that comfortable a fit but she knew she could always transfer it to the holster in the bag later.

When they got to the control room, Jachan directed her to an unobstructed view of one of the monitors and pointed to a man dressed head-to-toe in camouflage fatigues. The brown hair and intent, fox-faced expression left no doubt in her mind. It was McMasters.

Mishka nodded. "That's the group of Americans I thought it was. This one is the leader."

"Then let's try to take him out first," Jachan said as he raised a radio to his lips. "It will have a great psychological effect on the others, I'm sure."

"I'm sure," Mishka whispered.

But even as she looked at the monitor, content she knew what would happen next, she couldn't shake the cold feeling in her gut.

McCARTER DROPPED AND rolled as soon as he heard the bullet. He came up behind a thick tree and brought his MP-5 SD6 to bear. He keyed up his mike. "Omega One to Omega Team. Spread out and find cover. Sniper. Probably on the roof."

Encizo's voice replied a moment later. "Copy, Omega One. You sure?"

"He just tried to fit me for a toe tag, mate. I'm sure."

"Roger."

McCarter let his weapon dangle from the sling over his shoulder as he whipped a pair of binoculars from his load-bearing harness and dashed to the next tree some ten yards away. Two more rounds chopped the air in his wake and McCarter cursed. It would be difficult to get an exact location on the target as long as he had the Phoenix Force leader's scent. He might have to continue working as the bait until Manning could get his sniper rifle in play. This would make coordination more diffi-

cult but McCarter didn't sweat it. Every one of his teammates was a professional and had been trained to operate
in tandem if McCarter found himself pinned down and
unable to give tactical direction.

McCarter took a glance and saw the opening in the
trees that gave him a view of the roofline. He pulled
back in time to avoid a bullet that hit the tree he was
using as concealment with a sickening thwack. Yeah,
no doubts the sniper had his mark and he wasn't going
to let it go easily. The other troublesome aspect was that
their being detected this soon probably meant electronic
security had taken stealth as their advantage. The security force assigned to the residence would be on high
alert by now and prepared to defend their position until
the bitter end.

McCarter meant to ensure that end meant confining
losses to the enemy.

First, though, they had to take care of the sniper who
McCarter had no doubt could reduce their numbers and
thereby increase the odds significantly. McCarter keyed
his transmitter. "Omega One to Omega Two. Do you have
position on our birdie?"

"Not yet," Manning replied. "I have no joy from this
spot."

"Can you get to my position?"

"Working on that now."

"Roger. Out."

MISHKA WATCHED WITH fascination, something she
wouldn't have admitted to Jachan. There was little doubt
in her mind that if her countrymen reached the house the
situation would definitely fall to their favor. She'd seen
them beat the odds several times. They didn't fight like

normal men—they fought like devils with a purpose. They were almost fanatical about it, really, and yet she knew firsthand from having met them they were anything but fanatic.

"You cannot let these men through, Jachan."

"It's not my intention."

"But your sniper on the roof missed. You might think about someone better."

Jachan's face visibly reddened despite his swarthy complexion. "I believe you've done all the good you can here. It's time for you to retreat to the bunker as originally planned."

"I told you I wouldn't do that."

"It's no longer a request." He turned to his lieutenant and gestured at Mishka.

The man immediately stepped forward and grabbed her elbow, none to gently, steering her away from the console and out of the control room. They were through the manor in less than a minute and headed for a rear door when Mishka reached into her pocket, drew the pistol and aimed it at the head of her escort.

He didn't react in time and Mishka grit her teeth with a mixture of malice and satisfaction as the .380-caliber round punched through the man's temple and blew out a significant chunk of his skull. His eyes rolled upward as his body dropped to the carpeted floor. Whether the shot was heard at this point didn't make much difference— Mishka didn't plan to wait around.

She reached to the body and lifted the man's weapon and assorted ammunition packs and other equipment that would prove useful. She would find some way out of this on her own—she didn't need any help. If all went well, the Americans would provide Jachan's men with the distraction needed to make her escape. They had been quite accommodating in that role before and they would do so again.

Mishka was counting on it.

CHAPTER SEVENTEEN

Through a bit of stealth and whole lot of good luck, Gary Manning managed to reach a position close enough to McCarter to get a vantage point on their sniper. McCarter tossed the binoculars to him and Manning caught them one-handed.

The Canadian lifted the binoculars to his eyes and swept the roofline twice before he spotted their quarry. The sniper was set back in one of the dormer-style windows, just out of the light, but a glint of sunlight on metal gave away his position.

"I can rectify this pretty quickly," Manning said, tossing the binoculars back to McCarter.

They'd been keeping low and speaking quietly, tossing the binoculars so low that the sniper couldn't see the interaction.

"Go for it," McCarter replied.

Manning nodded, rose, and made his way through a blind spot provided by the overhead foliage. The Canadian positioned the rifle and took aim, sighting the scope on the right location. At that angle he wouldn't have a direct shot, so he would need to concentrate his fire just to the right. If he played his cards right, the rounds would penetrate the thin siding of the house and strike the target. It would take a few shots, but at least it would remove the threat long enough for him and his teammates to make for the house proper.

Manning waited only a moment before locking the stock to his shoulder and squeezing the trigger three times. All three rounds hit where he'd intended, but it was just a matter of taking the risk of breaking cover to see if he could make the house. He thought he'd seen the flutter of the enemy sniper's rifle, so it was possible he'd landed a hit.

"Go," Manning practically whispered.

He counted the seconds, reaching four before Mc-Carter and Encizo broke through the tree line and dashed toward the house. The sniper rifle remained silent on their approach and Manning grinned, helpless not to enjoy a moment of satisfaction. His plan to take the sniper from that angle had obviously worked despite the risks involved.

Now, if our luck can just hold out a little longer, he thought.

IMAN JACHAN SAW the commandos approach the house and knew immediately they had somehow managed to neutralize the sniper he'd placed in a dormer on the second floor. With his only sniper dead, the battle would now be joined at the estate.

Jachan considered himself neither a freedom fighter nor a crusader. He was more of a privateer—a solider-for-profit that took whatever assignments he chose, when and where he chose them. His work had always been on his terms and he intended to keep it that way. However, he'd taken this assignment on the condition he could run the show when it came to the operations, and Madari had left him to it. He wouldn't now abandon his post. They would defend the estate to the last man, even if the estate was not occupied by its master.

As the minutes ticked by, Jachan became more anxious. Something was definitely wrong. Aburam should have returned by now. The bunker was only a couple hundred meters from the house.

"Stay here and keep me apprised by radio of the enemy's movements," he said before leaving the control room.

It took him less than a minute to find his lieutenant lying facedown on the expensive tile floor, his lifeblood seeping from a fairly large head wound. On closer inspection, Jachan realized the wound had been caused by a small-caliber handgun.

"You murderous bitch!" he swore. To the ceiling he let out an agonized howl and added, "I'm going to find you! And when I do, I'm going to *kill* you!"

The last echoes of his outrage were drowned by the blast of the front door being blown off its hinges. The American commandos had finally made entry to the house.

HAWKINS AND JAMES were the first through the smoking hole blasted out by the HE charges they'd placed against the front entrance door.

They fanned out, moving inside the darkened foyer and keeping low. Those profiles saved their lives as a cacophony of gunfire overtook them as house security behind furniture opened up on them. Hawkins dived and rolled, coming to a stop on one knee and triggering his M-16 A3. The weapon chattered ceaselessly as Hawkins sprayed his would-be assassins with a storm of responsive fire. The ferocity of his counteroffensive forced them to seek shelter, scattered as they were with the two moving targets they were trying to hit.

Several rounds cut through the flimsy wood of an antique sofa and found the flesh of one man's thigh. He let out a scream, his weapon leaving his grasp as he rushed both hands to plug the burning holes and staunch the flow of blood. In so doing, he'd exposed enough of his head that Hawkins managed to sweep the other direction and catch him on the second pass. Two more runs busted the man's skull wide open and his body flopped onto the floor.

James had barely escaped being cut to ribbons. One of the rounds clipped the flesh just above his right ankle but he assessed it only as a graze after a quick inspection. Even as he looked at it he was spraying rounds in the direction of his enemies to keep their heads down. He didn't score any lucky hits but it didn't matter because a moment later Encizo primed an HE grenade and lobbed it into the room.

The shooters were busy reloading, charging their batteries as it were for the kill, when they heard the grenade land between their respective positions. They only had a moment to look at each other in terror before the thing went off. Superheated gas and flame decimated the area around them, the concussive effects coupled with the shrapnel whistling through the terrorists like BB pellets through rice paper.

McCarter and Encizo immediately followed inside and began to lay down cover fire, swathing the area with 9 mm Parabellum rounds while James and Hawkins got clear of their positions. They didn't dare stay in one place or they would make prime targets, just as they nearly had a moment before. They fanned through the room, moving in a fire-and-maneuver pattern.

Two more enemy gunners appeared on Encizo's left

flank. One passed by a front window. Glass exploded and a round sheared neatly through his right skull and blew off the left part of his face. His body teetered only a moment before collapsing to the ground, neatly dispatched by the marksmanship of Gary Manning. The Canadian had taken up an outside support sniper role while the remainder of his teammates made entry.

The other man didn't let the death of his comrade distract him. He lined up his weapon and prepared to cut down his enemy. Instead he was the one who got cut down with a double blast to the gut from Encizo and McCarter.

James had decided he'd had enough of trying to dodge his enemies and opted for a more permanent if highly volatile solution in CQB. He popped the pin on a thermite grenade and tossed it through the open door that looked as if it led onto a kitchen where two gunners had taken up firing positions. The clattering of the grenade along the expensively tiled kitchen floor was followed by heat. Fragments of molten metal, heated to several thousand degrees in just a second, rained onto the two gunners. It instantly transformed them into human torches and James put out mercy rounds—they were staggering around, awash in flames—to end their suffering.

The sounds of battle fell away and left only the eerie silence and persistent ringing in the ears of the four Phoenix Force warriors.

McCarter keyed up his mike and announced to Manning, "We're clear."

"You want me to join you?"

"No, hold your position and wait for instructions. We're going to sweep and clear the rest of the house."

"Acknowledged."

McCarter clicked off and then told his men, "I don't want to split us up but I don't think we have a choice. This place is just too big for us to waste the time searching in pairs. Keep in constant radio contact and report anything you find and where you find it."

"What about Madari and Stanish?" James asked.

"Take them alive if you can," McCarter said.

"If we can?" Hawkins queried, brow furrowed.

Something went flinty in McCarter's expression. "If they leave you no choice, then do the needful."

The men nodded and then McCarter doled out the assignments. The place was only two floors so two would search upstairs and two would remain on the first floor. McCarter doubted the upper rooms would be heavily defended. Obviously their approach had been detected and so any key personnel had already been evacuated, if McCarter didn't miss his guess. But they still had to go through the motions, whether or not it just gave the enemy more time to escape wasn't something he could be concerned with. They first had to secure their AO.

But McCarter also couldn't help but wonder where Muriel Stanish might be headed. Or whether "Mishka" was truly on their side.

HER HEART THUDDED in her chest, perspiration a glistening sheen on her cheeks and cleavage in the midday sun, as Stanish emerged from the brush. She'd been running for nearly half an hour along the trail that would take her out to the launch. She had changed her mind, determined to accompany Ishaq as he'd originally requested. She no longer saw the wisdom in staying behind. Whatever he had planned—and she knew he'd not told the truth about not testing the weapons in America—she had to be with him.

Some part of her also knew she was running out of time. The American SOG team had somehow managed to track her here. Of this she had little doubt. She checked first to make sure that someone wasn't waiting to ambush her and then dashed across the clearing. A million things seemed to run through her mind as she ran. How had they found her so quickly? Had Madari been tracking her? Had she somehow betrayed herself or her plans, maybe left some clue behind?

The only other man who would have had some idea of her operations was David Steinham. She'd taken his money, sure—it had allowed her to live a bit better while in Belarus. Besides, he'd never pumped her for any particularly classified information, but rather just to keep him informed of Oleg Dratshev's movements. It had turned out to be rather fortuitous when she'd met Ishaq Madari and she'd mentioned it in passing after a little too much wine. That's when it had all changed between them.

So if it wasn't Madari who'd been tracking her, that meant Steinham had somehow found a way to keep tabs on her. It wasn't until she made it across the clearing unscathed that she realized what it was. The phone he'd given her! There must have been a tracking device inside it. Probably routed to the GPS so that when she turned it off—something he would have expected her to do under any circumstances—it activated some other internal chip that he used to monitor her location. After all, he was a government defense contractor and had the most advanced and sensitive electronics at his disposal. The guy made guidance systems for weapons.

The yacht was gone but there remained a small launch,

the water lapping gently against its sleek sides. Stanish considered her options and then realized that in truth she didn't have any. She didn't know when the yacht had departed but she *did* know it was to have been earlier this morning. Could the launch catch it? Could she navigate into the open sea, braving the waves of the Aegean and eventually into the Mediterranean?

Even as she pushed on and made her way toward the launch, Stanish wondered if she would have the fuel. The launch had actually been a part of her lover's massive yacht, one he'd special-ordered and christened *Amra'a* not just a few short months after they were together. She remembered how that had impressed her—simply and cleanly, its closest translation meant "woman."

Stanish sensed something wasn't right as she approached the launch and when she got within fifty yards she figured out what that something was. Jachan stepped out of the shadows of the small boathouse at the end of the dock. She could see the pistol in his hand but she didn't halt her approach. If she could get close enough to the oversize launch—a launch she secretly wondered if Ishaq had left behind in the event she changed her mind—she might be able to overcome Jachan. It was risky but Stanish didn't really see that she had much choice.

"That's far enough," he said. As she stopped he added, "Quite far."

"Not even close," Stanish replied. The tone in her voice thinly veiled her challenge.

"I don't understand it," Jachan said. "Why have you betrayed us? Betrayed Ishaq?"

"I haven't betrayed him," she replied. "*You* have betrayed him. You thought to keep me a prisoner. I'm no man's prisoner."

"Enough talk!" Jachan barked. "Take your hand out of that bag. I will not let you murder me in cold blood like you did Aburam."

Stanish eased her hand out of the bag and, along with it, held it high in her fist just enough to expose the head of a fragmentation grenade. "I have no intention of shooting you. But I also plan to make sure that you never have the opportunity to come between me and Ishaq."

She released her grip and the spoon flipped away with an audible clang. She was committed now and she felt a smug sense of satisfaction as she watched Jachan's eyes light up.

Stanish tossed the grenade overhand and Jachan instinctively turned and dived off the side of the pier and into the safety of the water. The grenade followed him, just as she'd planned. She knew he would be stunned by the underwater explosion, so she waited until he surfaced, disoriented and helpless. The pistol reported twice, the first bullet crashing through Jachan's chest while the second punctured his throat. Jachan's eyes remained wide open in shock and his last couple of breaths were garbled and bloody.

Stanish dived in and swam to the launch, climbing aboard and pausing to catch her breath Then she rose and went to the control panel of the launch. She found it had a GPS and she set the control to the specific signal of the *Amra'a,* the one she knew that Madari had registered with the government so as not to appear as anything but a valid businessman.

Then she fired up the engine, cleared the mooring lines and within a minute headed for open water in pursuit of her lover.

CHAPTER EIGHTEEN

The several technicians in the control room were anything but diligent at sticking by their posts.

Rafael Encizo had found the place abandoned and was still attempting to tap into the system when McCarter joined him. He was trying to crack the codes to get into the system and getting no place fast.

McCarter made a suggestion. "Let's load one of those cracking dongles into the system and see if Bear can't get in."

Encizo nodded. He reached into his pocket and withdrew what looked like a simple flash drive while McCarter transmitted a secure code via satellite uplink from his phone.

The flash drive contained a special program that would receive additional instructions once Kurtzman interfaced with it. Without Stony Man receiving such a code, in a certain amount of time the program on the flash drive would be activated. If the device was not removed, the program launched a self-destruct sequence that would send out a destructive virus and then activate an overload to its sensitive circuitry. That overload would not only turn the device to slag but make any information on it unreadable.

All the computer owner would know was that somebody had inserted a device that had melted and fused itself to the computer. That, and they would no longer have access to their information. The computer virus was extremely pervasive and could replicate itself if necessary, completely wiping any physical or electronic trace of Stony Man off the map. And since the code had never before been encountered, and was set to destroy itself after the damage had been done, no current security countermeasure in existence could deter it.

It was just one more way Stony Man's SOG stayed one step ahead of its enemies.

"Okay, the code was received," McCarter said. "Now it's just a waiting game."

After barely a minute, all the screens that had just been blue with silver text that read SYSTEMS OFFLINE flashed into life.

McCarter grinned. "Well, bless your heart, Bear."

His teammates arrived a minute later and reported the all-clear.

Manning said, "I see you've been busy."

"Not really," McCarter said. "We're waiting on Bear to find something interesting. Until then—"

McCarter's cell phone warbled for attention and he picked up midway through the third signal. "Go."

"We've found something of interest," Price said. "Or, well, more like several 'somethings' of interest but the biggest one is that we think we know how they're getting the EMP prototypes out of the country."

"Any way we can stop them?"

"Not at this point," Price said. "Apparently they've gone out by boat and they're too far out for any reasonable chance of catching up. At least by water."

"So how do you want to handle this?"

"We've used our diplomatic channels to alert the Hellenic navy. They've agreed to send a patrol interceptor to look for Madari's yacht."

"Yacht?" McCarter was puzzled. "I don't get it? How did he actually expect to get a yacht into U.S. waters without being intercepted by USCG? Or even out of here for that matter. And a trans-oceanic voyage in a small yacht? Seems a bit bold."

"You won't think so once I tell you that *yacht* isn't really so much a yacht as a converted freighter."

"How did you find that out?"

"The computer systems we tapped didn't have much in the way of information on the EMPs. In fact, mostly all we found were mathematical computations and some other data. Looks like most of those computers were there just to store camera footage, run the house security, and so forth."

"Mostly used for security, then," McCarter interjected.

"Pretty much. However, because it was for security it also monitored all electronic communications in and out. There are all sorts of emails between Madari and the maritime fabrication and construction firm he used to make the conversion. All the holds were left intact. It would also appear as if he ordered materials that by themselves are not odd, but when put together by one of Bear's algorithms, looks as if they planned to build some sort of gun platform."

"Well, we did think that they might have some EMP capabilities," McCarter said.

"Right," Price replied. "Which makes any such attempt to intercept them very dangerous. You guys aren't really equipped with anything large enough to take them out so we told the Hellenic navy we believe the boat may be attempting to smuggle rare artifacts from the country, artifacts we believe might belong to the Greek government."

"And what if Madari does have one of those weapons active and decides to test it out on a live target?"

"We considered that possibility. But you must also realize that despite Dr. Dratshev's considerable advancements in this field, we still don't think the technology is advanced enough to be of any real effect. And even if it is, it's still no match against the speed and surety of conventional onboard naval weaponry. I have little doubt the Hellenic navy is quite up to the task of defending itself against one lone freighter-turned-yacht if it comes down to it."

"Let's hope so," McCarter said. "In the meantime, what's our next step?"

"You still have to deal with Madari's people. There's a bunker with a full testing range not more than a hundred yards south of the estate. You'll want to check that out. There may very well be some sort of material evidence left behind that will give us a much better clue as to what we're up against."

"There may also be some personnel we can take alive," McCarter pointed out. "A live body says a whole lot more than a dead one."

"Very astute observation. Just do what you think is best on that count. As soon as you've gotten all you can there, I'd recommend you pack it in and come home. There's really very little more you can do at this point. We're convinced the government in Athens won't give up Madari once he's been taken alive."

"Because?"

"We let them know they were in on the attack in Athens. They deal *very* severely with anyone who employs such terrorist methods. And they're especially not happy about several Greek citizens being killed. Between that and the complaints they're fielding from our folks about the death of a member of the U.S. embassy, you can bet they'll go out of their way to deal with Madari."

"And then maybe we get Dratshev as a consolation prize."

"You're catching on."

"All right. We'll touch base again once we've cleared the island."

"Good luck."

McCarter disconnected the call and turned to his teammates.

"All right, lads, it's a-hunting we will go."

ISHAQ MADARI WATCHED with immense satisfaction as his men loaded the cargo plane at the small-business terminal of the airport in Athens.

Even as he waited for them to complete their work, he thought of his yacht heading out to sea. The authorities would be in for a very terrible surprise if, or when, they intercepted his yacht.

Meanwhile, he'd be well on his way soon, bound for the United States, where he planned to demonstrate and test the weapons, not only to prove their effectiveness but also as a matter of recourse for their interference.

And then there was the American defense contractor to consider. Steinham. Madari had a very personal grudge to settle with that bastard. Steinham had been the one to provide technology under the table to officials within the Libyan government, technology that ultimately resulted in the demise of Madari's family and defeat of the Libyan fighters bent on democracy. This was Madari's way of making a statement while simultaneously verifying the efficacy of his plans. If the weapons worked as Oleg Dratshev promised, Madari could then transport them into Libya and bring down the government dictatorship once and for all.

What nobody in American seemed to understand was that Madari really wanted what *they* wanted in Libya. Madari had no personal aspirations for power. His was simply a mission of revenge.

"You're quiet," a voice said.

Madari jumped in spite of himself and then turned to see Dratshev had come alongside him. "Just thinking of the past."

"I've done my best to always put the past behind me."

"You're a philosopher now?"

Dratshev shrugged and took a drag from his cigarette. "Not a philosopher. Realistic. A pragmatist, perhaps."

"I'd consider that a reasonable description based on our short time together," Madari said. He sighed and nodded toward the equipment being lifted by hydraulics into the undercarriage of the plane. "Are you sure these prototypes are ready for testing?"

"You didn't give me a lot of time," Dratshev said. "But, yes. I think they will perform suitably."

"They still seem to require a considerable amount of liquid helium to keep them cool. I don't know how practical that is."

"It's totally impractical!" Dratshev exclaimed, crushing his cigarette underfoot. "At least for the small arms. As I said, you will only have two shots from each of the twenty-five prototypes. Assuming they were constructed to my exact specifications."

"You oversaw the building and testing yourself. You know they are."

"It hardly matters, really. Because of the destructive power of an EMP beam, their real-world applications are as a mass-damage weapon. There is little maintenance required, and the actual ability to maintain nominal temperature during charging is a much more practical matter for the larger weaponry. The small arms is another matter and still largely unpredictable."

"So you're saying there could be some danger to my men using them?"

"Not as long as they follow the instructions."

Madari sighed. "And that boils down to waiting between shots for the liquid helium to provide sufficient cooling."

"Not just sufficient," Dratshev reminded him, lighting another cigarette. "*Optimal* cooling must be achieved."

"Or the weapon will melt down and become unusable," Madari said. "Yes, I remember."

"Do you really think these tests are necessary? Wouldn't it be a sounder plan to simply smuggle them directly into your country?"

"That's exactly what the American government is expecting me to do. I cannot afford to be predictable. I've stalled these plans as long as I can, and now there's no turning back. I've committed nearly all my resources to this effort. Which brings me to another point. I couldn't have done this without you. I shall always be grateful."

"Is this your way of telling me I'm free to go?"

Madari chuckled. "I said I was grateful, not insane. You must accompany us. Surely you knew that."

"I half expected as much. And, frankly, I must admit that I'm very intrigued to see how they perform under real battle conditions." Dratshev took a drag from his cigarette and in a gust of smoke he added, "Yet, I don't see how I can be of more use to you."

"On the contrary. We have a very limited supply of weapons." He gestured toward the last of the crates being loaded. "Once we've expended that supply, or if we encounter any difficulties, I will need your expertise to figure out how to manufacture more."

"But you've left all your equipment at the lab."

"Not at all. Most of the equipment at the bunker was transferred to the yacht."

"You've just said that yacht is a decoy. That it claims to be sailing for the United States."

"Exactly. But once at open sea, there will be an emergency—" Madari made quote signs in mid-air "—and the closest port at the time of that emergency will be Derna. As to the equipment, it's been disassembled and to the unpracticed and uninformed eye, it would look merely like spare parts for the yacht. Remember, I converted that yacht from the hull of freighter. It is quite capable of holding more than it would appear. There are plenty of smuggling compartments aboard. Once the captain corrects course and gets permission to dock, it can be easily off-loaded and transported into waiting trucks."

"Won't they be intercepted as soon as they attempt to enter Libyan waters?"

"It's possible, although if they declare an emergency it's most likely they will be permitted to dock at Derna." Madari shrugged. "There is always the risk the equipment may be discovered and identified for what it is. But I have made very extensive arrangements for said emergency to keep them in port long enough to offload the equipment while repairs are made."

"And then?"

"Then whatever happens to the boat and its crew will be of little to no consequence."

"They are your sacrificial lambs."

"Nothing of the sort," Madari countered. "They are merely a resource, nothing more."

"So again, I'm left to ask—why not simply move forward with your plans directly? Why this detour to the United States?"

"I don't just need to test the weapons, Doctor. I need a way to make a statement to the Americans so they understand that *any* interference would yield catastrophic results. And finally, there is a man in America who is partly to blame for what happened to me and my family. He must pay the price for what he did."

"So you're doing this not to test the weapons," Dratshev interjected. "You have a personal vendetta to settle."

Madari fixed the scientist with an icy stare. "And if I do?"

"It's nothing to me. But you are being a bit hypocritical."

"An opinion."

"No, it's much more than opinion. I've observed that you're patriotic and sympathetic to the plight of your country only when it seems to suit your personal ambitions."

"Then you're poorly uninformed," Madari replied. "And not nearly as insightful as I had first judged you. You see, my paying back this American defense contractor has nothing to do with a personal ambition. The things he did led to the destabilization of my government. We wanted to put a diplomatic power into place, to hold free elections, to remove the dictators that had long occupied the central seats of government.

"We were very close to doing that until the American CIA stepped in. They used technology created by this American defense contractor to undermine our efforts and ensure the current regime stayed in power. They did this to my people, the common people and freedom fighters, while doing exactly the opposite in Syria. The weapons that should have gone to us went to them instead."

"That's because the Libyan government wasn't using chemical weapons against the rebels in your country."

"No! That's utter propaganda. I was at all of the secret meetings in Benghazi. I spoke personally with the so-called U.S. diplomats. They lied to us and then they betrayed us! And we've been unable to trust them ever since."

"I believe some of your people got their revenge," Dratshev said. "The Americans paid with the lives of several."

"Ha! What several? A few low-ranking pawns? My people have died by the thousands! There can be no repayment for that on such a small scale. No, this operation will make a much bigger statement. And now we are at an end to our discussion, as much as I have enjoyed our debate. The equipment is loaded and our time has come. Soon, very soon, we shall strike a new victory for Libya."

CHAPTER NINETEEN

There was a small team guarding the bunker, and they were prepared for the arrival of Phoenix Force. After the first volley of mortar shells was lobbed in their direction, McCarter ordered a tactical retreat to discuss their alternatives.

"Obviously there's something they don't want us to see down there," Hawkins said.

McCarter nodded. "And then again, maybe this is a stall tactic."

"What do you mean?" Encizo asked.

"We already know that neither Madari nor Stanish was to be found anywhere at the house. We're already assuming they've moved into the project bunker that's now being heavily defended, but there's no way for us to prove that. Could be just another dead end."

"We still can't take that chance," Manning replied.

"Nope, we bloody well can't. So let's rethink this. I believe there may be another way into that bunker."

McCarter scratched a rough layout of the testing grounds in the mud with a stick. "Okay, so here's the bunker complex. According to the plans Bear extracted from the security computers, there's nothing but a beachhead on the western side. Pretty good chance they won't have a mortar defense for that area."

"There could be some other type of defense, then," Hawkins said. "Worse than mortars."

"Worse than mortars?" Manning asked. "What the hell could be worse than mortars?"

"Mines."

They fell silent at Hawkins's revelation. It was something McCarter had considered but hadn't really wanted to bring up. "Okay, it's a good point to consider. Could be mined or booby-trapped in some other way. But I saw a pretty good-size dock across that beach line. That's probably how they brought in supplies and other materials by boat."

"Or shipped them out," Encizo pointed out.

McCarter nodded. "The EMP weapons. Right. We'll just have to go into it and keep our eyes wide open. We'll proceed using normal hostile target approach tactics. Understood?"

The men nodded in unison.

"Good. Let's move out."

They formed up and headed out single-file, with adequate distance between them and Encizo on point.

Mediterranean Sea

As soon as Stanish got within range of the yacht—something she considered fortunate given the circumstances—she fired a signal flare. To her surprise, they spotted the flare and must have recognized it as one of their own, because they heaved to and powered down to allow her to catch up. It still took another ten minutes before she reached them.

She approached port side to the yacht, where she spotted twin locks for craft-to-craft mooring. She tossed the large rope mounted to the front of the powerboat and two men on the deck of the yacht tied her off. They then used a winch to pull her gently into position until the power-boat clips locked into the mounting locks with a clang. Then she scaled the rope-ladder they dropped to her and within a few minutes she was on the bridge.

The captain introduced himself as Jabir Nero and he spoke passable, if halted, English. "You are Despinis Mishka?"

She nodded. "Where's Ishaq?"

Nero looked puzzled and then shook his head, replying matter-of-factly, "He's not here."

"What do you mean he's not here?" Stanish demanded, doing her best to keep her tone in check. After all, this was Nero's ship and he'd kindly granted her permission to board when, as they both well knew, he could just as easily have blown her out of the water.

"He's not here. He's on his plane to America."

"Plane?" she repeated. "What plane?"

Nero shook his head and shrugged. "I'm sorry, miss, he no on this boat."

"A decoy," she whispered more to herself than Nero. Then she asked, "So if this ship isn't bound for America, where *is* it going?"

"I cannot say our destination. Kyrios Madari, he ordered me not to talk until we are ready."

"Ready to do what?"

Nero looked hesitant at first.

Stanish had never met him personally until now, but she knew of him. He'd been born in Libya, where he'd lived until about ten, when his family was forced to flee to Greece. She didn't know the details, but Nero had ended up in the Greek foster care system. With no attachments and no known family to speak of, Nero had been the perfect choice to serve as captain of this vessel, and Madari had once told her that Nero was fiercely loyal.

"I asked a question!" Stanish snapped. "Ready to do what?"

Nero gestured for her to follow. They left the bridge and walked down the starboard side until reaching some steps that descended to what Stanish guessed was Nero's cabin.

"So what's the big secret?" she asked once they were alone in the cabin.

Nero dropped a map of the entire region on the table and pointed at a spot she immediately recognized as the port city of Derna, despite the fact the entire map was labeled in Greek.

"We are to change course here—" he pointed to a marked latitudinal-longitudinal coordinate "—and then radio to the Derna port. We are to declare trouble with our engine and advise them that our attempts to raise our port of call were unsuccessful."

"And then what? They permit you an emergency dock?"

"Yes." Nero sighed and wiped his big palm across his face. "Then we will unload the equipment under cover of darkness and transport it to those waiting inside Libya."

"A grand plan," Stanish said. "Unfortunately, it's not likely to work."

"Why?"

"You realize that at this very moment both the Russian and American governments are probably tracking this vessel. The chances are good you won't make it to Derna."

"We have defenses."

"Defenses, yes, but defenses that are untested. You would be better to put about and return to the island."

"I cannot do that."

"Can't or won't?"

"Despinis Mishka, I cannot. I *cannot!* This would betray Kyrios Madari."

Stanish chewed her lower lip in contemplation. She didn't want to do anything to curtail Madari's plans. But part of her was still furious at him for lying to her. Why had he told her he was going to be on the boat, and even tried to convince her to go, if he'd known he'd never be on it to begin with? Had he known she'd flat-out turn him down when he suggested she come along, or merely changed his plans when she refused to go?

It didn't matter. She couldn't turn back now. The powerboat didn't have enough fuel to get her back to the island, and she dared not attempt to head to Athens. She'd be detained immediately by coastal authorities, if not intercepted by a Hellenic naval warship. And then there was the issue of Nero. She couldn't very well tell him what to do. This was his ship and she didn't have any authority. A boatload of sailors certainly wouldn't respect her.

What if she threatened Nero? Would he cave? Probably not—she didn't see that would solve anything anyway.

A klaxon sounded, interrupting her rumination and startling Nero so severely he upset the small table near his bedside as he jumped to his feet. He squeezed past her, whipped open the cabin door and scrambled up the steps for what passed as the bridge.

Stanish kept on his heels, impressed by the efficiency of the men on the boat. Pockets of men crisscrossed the deck, each on a different but important mission. When they reached the bridge, Nero immediately found the field glasses and raised them to his eyes. On the shimmering, blue-white horizon of water she could make out the bristling outline of another ship.

Nero grunted and then handed the field glasses to her. "Hellenic navy. Looks like a patrol boat."

Stanish, surprised at Nero's action, took the glasses hesitantly at first but then put them to her eyes for a look. They actually provided a decent magnification, and even from this distance she could tell Nero had called the play exactly.

As she swung them across the ship, stopping when she saw the various weapons emplacements, Nero spoke to her as if he could see what she saw. It was almost as though he was taking her on a guided tour. "It's an HSY-56A gunboat-class patrol boat. Looks like a newer version."

"Is it armed?" she asked.

"Not heavily," he replied. "But we're not armored and would be no match."

"Why all the concern?" she asked, lowering the field glasses. She glanced at him. "Isn't it better to just act normal—keep a low profile? I'm sure they're just on routine maneuvers."

Nero seemed to ponder this a moment and then jabbered something at a man who, she assumed, was probably the equivalent of his first officer. The guy barked something back and Nero grimaced. "They wouldn't have approved our course if it brought us that close to a naval vessel on maneuvers. No, this encounter was no accident."

"So you're saying…"

"They're on an intercept course."

Stanish said, "You realize that you can't allow them to detain or search this ship."

"We may have no choice."

"You have a choice. You have weapons aboard?"

"Just the one prototype on the top deck." He pointed out the bridge window to the foremast where a rather large boxy structure protruded. "We were to use it for protection against pirates."

"Well, now it looks like you'll have to use it for other purposes."

Nero's face tightened. "We cannot! We are no match for a warship, *despinis*."

"Well, you'd better change your thinking quick. You're running out of time."

PHOENIX FORCE MADE their circuitous route in no time and arrived at the beach unchallenged.

Encizo peered from the dense foliage and pointed at the charred, smoking remains of the dock edge.

"What in the bloody hell...?" McCarter began.

"Looks like the handiwork of a grenade," Encizo replied. He glanced over his shoulder at Manning. "Maybe a rocket, Gary?"

Manning pushed forward to get a better look and then shook his head. "No, definitely a localized explosion. I'd say your first guess was correct."

James squinted. "Looks like a body floating. There."

All looked toward where he pointed.

McCarter said, "All right, enough sightseeing. Let's shag our butts and get this done. Rafe?"

Encizo nodded and after one last check he emerged from cover and sprinted across the uneven terrain of wet sand. Tides had been high the past three days so there wasn't a dry spot to be found. Despite the squashing underfoot, Encizo managed to glide across the ground in a whisper-quiet fashion. Years of training in maritime combat had made him the weapon of choice for situations just like this one.

Hawkins came next, prompted by a gesture from Encizo, who had settled near where the trees gave way to a path leading from the dock up to what served as the back door into the bunker complex. At least according to the layout Kurtzman had provided.

McCarter had insisted on a two-pronged attack this time, letting Encizo and Hawkins clear a path before the other three would bring up the rear in a support role. Once they were assured that an ambush didn't await them on the path, the pair nodded to each other and burst from cover. McCarter waited for James and Manning to go before leaving his spot. They had just barely reached the same point from which Encizo and Hawkins had just left when they heard weapons fire coming from up the path.

"About twenty yards," James said. "Give or take."

"Let's do it," McCarter ordered.

The three charged up the path and crashed through a narrow point before it opened onto the production facility housed inside the bunker area. The range was visible just to the left, as was the roof of the main facility. The trio spotted Encizo and Hawkins as they picked their way toward one point of the bunker where muzzle-flashes were visible.

All three men grabbed the nearest cover, raised their weapons and began to trigger alternating volleys at the muzzle-flashes. They may not have hit anything but the suppression technique worked well all the same. Hawkins and Encizo pressed forward, moving with the cautious ease of practiced professionals.

Encizo reached the enemy emplacement first. He pressed his back to the part of the bunker protruding from the ground, primed a fragmentation grenade and tossed it through an opening. He then moved off and away at an angle in time to avoid the blast, which followed just microseconds after the shouts of surprise coming from the enemy within. The shrapnel did its work, the blast in the confined space even powerful enough to send a human arm, or what remained of it, rocketing from the opening. Phoenix Force had succeeded in their mission.

I only hope we find something to make it bloody well worth it, David McCarter thought.

CHAPTER TWENTY

The battle to take the bunker had only just begun.

Although Phoenix Force managed to breach the perimeter, there were still the mortar emplacements to contend with, as well as personnel that might be waiting to ambush the warriors. McCarter decided the best way to deal with that situation was to split his team into two groups, one to handle the exterior resistance while the second did an interior search to clear any remaining enemy occupants.

Manning and James were lucky enough to get handpicked to take out the mortars, a job they were itching to do since it would mean securing the rest of their teammates from any further light artillery attacks.

Manning, having been wounded during their initial breach, felt especially committed to taking them out once and forever. He demonstrated his relish for the job by being the first one to engage a pair of mortar men. Madari's engineers had cut a shallow trench on the perimeter of the proving grounds where they'd lined the same with mortar emplacements. It seemed almost like old-fashioned trench warfare, but in this case the enemy didn't seem all that aware its position had been overrun.

Manning explained it with two controlled bursts from his MP-5 SD6. The impact of 9 mm rounds was close enough to lift the first of the two targets onto his toes. He teetered backward and slammed into his comrade, who took the first two-thirds of a 3-round burst to the shoulder and the last slug through the side of his neck. The man emitted a queer, blood gurgle before dropping like a stone onto the corpse of his partner.

Two more enemy gunners saw the battle and rushed up the trench from the opposite direction, drawing side arms, revenge evident in their expressions. James knew it wouldn't stand. He raised the M-16 A3 to his shoulder, the weapon in single-shot mode, and triggered one successive round after another. The 5.5 6mm high-velocity bullets made short work of the pair. The first caught a round just below his nose. It smashed bone in his face, crunching the upper palette before continuing onward until it sheared his brain stem. The second gunner received two shots to the chest but that didn't stop his forward motion. Even dead on his feet, he managed to trip over his deceased comrade before his lifeless body landed in the mushy sand floor of the trench face-first.

"Blast those emplacements downrange!" Manning shouted to James. "I'll take care of these!"

James nodded, whirled and dashed in the direction from which their would-be ambushers had come. His AR had an M-203 mounted beneath it and was already primed with a 40 mm HE grenade. Manning didn't have a grenade launcher but James knew it wouldn't be a problem. He had his bag of tricks with him, and destroying the emplacements at the other end would pose no difficulty to the Canadian explosives expert.

James stopped when he got within firing distance, took a knee and brought the M-16 A3 to his shoulder. He free-sighted, disengaged the flip-down safety and stroked the trigger. The weapon bucked against his shoulder with the kick of a shotgun, and a moment later the mortar emplacement disappeared in a fireball of high explosive that whooshed eighty-two feet into the air. James grinned, nodded with self-satisfaction and then rose and headed back to cover his partner.

ONCE RAFAEL ENCIZO used det cord to make short work of the door, he, McCarter and Hawkins proceeded inside. They staggered themselves with plenty of space between as they came through the makeshift entrance and moved down the corridor, weapons at the ready. Once more, Encizo had point with McCarter and then Hawkins on rear guard.

They reached the end of the corridor unchallenged and encountered a snag. The heavy steel door was secured by an electronic lock mechanism, one only accessible by a swipe card.

Hawkins suggested blowing this one, too, but Encizo shook his head. "Out of ordnance."

"And we can't risk taking the time to go find Gary," McCarter said

Hawkins's face brightened. "Wait a minute…"

He turned and trotted down the corridor, disappearing from view. McCarter and Encizo backed off the door a few feet and crouched in the dim light.

"You think there's anyone inside waiting for us?" Encizo asked.

McCarter shrugged. "Who knows? Could be. Madari's people have been able to stay one step ahead of us so far. This is actually the first time we've managed to do our bloody jobs with any effect."

Noise at the entrance demanded their attention and Hawkins returned holding a computerized swipe card with a grin. "May we be needing this?"

"Where'd you get it?" Encizo asked.

"Picked it off one of those sentries we took out back on the path."

"That's good thinking, T.J."

Encizo reached out and Hawkins transferred the card to him. The Cuban inspected it a moment and then rose, shuffled the door and swiped it downward. The lights next to the control pad changed from red to amber, and then after a soft double beep went green with a hiss.

As Encizo pocketed the card and pulled the handle to open the door, he muttered, "Interesting—sounds almost like it was hermetically sealed."

"Hold it," McCarter ordered, putting his hand on Encizo's arm. "You think it's a good idea to go in there unprotected? They might have been experimenting with chemical weapons."

It was Hawkins who replied. "Doubtful, boss. While they may be dealing with some basic industrial chemicals like helium and such, there wouldn't be any danger of biologicals."

Encizo nodded. "He's right. Not to mention that nobody we've encountered up to this point appears to have been wearing hazmat suits. I think it's safe."

McCarter exchanged glances with the two and then slowly nodded at Encizo to proceed as he removed his hand of restraint.

The trio went through the door, McCarter and Hawkins following well after Encizo made entry and signaled he'd cleared the immediate area with a twirling sign. They continued in the same staggered formation up the hall, generous space between them, their target a well-lit doorway. The hallway terminated at a flight of steps that descended to a landing. Beyond the landing they emerged in a massive production area. Odd-looking machines of every type dotted the lab-like facility. There were computer monitors and testing equipment scattered along stainless-steel tables, but all of them were dark. Bright, sterile lights overhead provided the only illumination.

Hawkins emitted a long whistle. "Holy guacamole."

"You said it," Encizo agreed.

"Well, obviously this is where they were producing the EMP prototypes," McCarter observed.

"You think Madari really was cranking out weapons here?" Encizo inquired.

McCarter nodded. "I'm no specialist but I'd say this is awfully intricate to be sheer window dressing. It looks to me as though he was using Dratshev to conduct the real deal."

Hawkins pointed across the room to cylinders lined against a far wall. "Those are helium tanks. I recognize the chemical symbols painted on them."

"Why helium?" Encizo asked.

"Probably acts as some sort of cooling mechanism," Hawkins replied. "Like McCarter, I'm no physicist. But I know enough to tell you with certainty that building an electromagnetic pulse strong enough to be used as a weapon would generate massive amounts of heat. Liquid helium or frozen CO_2 are about the only two substances I know of capable of reducing that heat."

McCarter nodded. "He's right. Water-soluble oils or glycols wouldn't cut it. We're talking massive heat."

"And the CO_2 probably isn't practical because it would take so much," Encizo said with a nod.

"Sounds like you know a bit more about it than you let on, Rafe," Hawkins said with a playful punch.

"Not really. I was a maritime accidents investigator at

one time. Remember? Large quantities of carbon dioxide are very common aboard marine vessels."

"Of course," McCarter said. "Use them for fire suppression."

Encizo nodded. "Among other things."

Their earbuds signaled for attention followed by Manning with his call sign. McCarter said, "Go ahead."

"We're clear here. Heading on your position now."

"Roger that."

"Um, my comp shows you're underground?"

"Yeah. Just follow the breadcrumbs." McCarter grinned at his comrades as he added, "You'll find us. And keep a watch on your six. Looks the facility's been abandoned but no telling if there are stragglers."

"Understood. See you in two mikes."

"Out," McCarter replied. "Okay, we'll wait until they get here and then start combing this place for any intelligence. Hawkins, see if you can get these computer systems turned on. Rafe, you start scraping for any evidence of what they might have been up to here. No detail is too small. If they really do have active weaponry, even prototypes, we're going to need to know everything we can about what we might face."

"What about Madari and friends?" Hawkins asked. "We can't let them get to wherever they might be going if those things are hot."

"Won't matter if we don't know how to fight him."

"Agreed," Encizo said. "Those computer models Bear ran for us indicated a single EMP weapon could fire a beam with a magnitude sufficient to pulverize all of us in a moment. It's like a midair earthquake."

"Either way, it's not how I plan to go," McCarter said.

"So let's get to work and figure out how to combat this threat. It's time to put Madari to bloody rest."

THANKFULLY, NERO finally ordered the klaxons off now that his men were in position. The HSY had closed the gap considerably, despite Nero's instructions to his pilot and navigator to keep the boat on course and make best possible speed toward the port city of Derna.

"Technically," Nero told Stanish, "we've cleared the nautical boundaries of the Aegean. However, that wouldn't seem to matter to this interdiction patrol."

She nodded. "Our good Hellenic captain aboard that patrol boat apparently got his directives from on high. I'd say he plans to follow them to the letter."

"As I've said, we're no match for a military vessel."

Stanish whirled on Nero. "Captain Nero, this is your ship but it is the property of Ishaq Madari. You will *not* surrender the ship under any circumstances."

Nero splayed his hands. "But I have no choice."

"I do," she said. She yanked her pistol from its place of concealment and pointed it at Nero's head. "Now either you resist them with every tool at your disposal or I'll be forced to take over and do it for you."

Nero's eyes grew wide. While he might have been a seasoned sailor, he was no means an experienced combatant.

Technically, what Stanish was doing could be considered mutiny and would most possibly buy her a bullet in the back when she wasn't looking. But that didn't mean she'd give up without a fight. She'd always been a fighter according to her father, who she was sure had secretly wanted a son but instead got a bouncing baby girl.

Oh, her father had always loved her. She didn't have

a daddy complex, something she'd been certain to rid from her psyche so she could pass the psychological batteries the CIA had thrown against her during the early recruitment period. Unfortunately her father's attitude toward her had been more aloof and her mother hadn't been around long enough to figure out she'd been missing love. Stanish wondered if that's why she'd clung so desperately to her love for Ishaq Madari—or at least the idea of loving him. Now, after what he'd done and how he had lied to her, she had to wonder what it had all been about. She didn't believe anymore that he really cared about her.

Either way, Stanish needed to protect her own interests now, whatever the costs. She would use Nero for such purposes and, failing that, she would kill him and take her chances with the Hellenic navy. After all, she could convince them she'd been kidnapped and brought aboard against her will, and request the protection of the Greek government. She already had the proper documents with any number of new identities. "Mishka" and Muriel Stanish would simply disappear.

"Decide, Captain Nero. *Now*."

Nero nodded finally and Stanish lowered the pistol to her side. She wasn't about to put it away. A new relationship had been created between them and it wasn't one she preferred. She looked to the foredeck, where the massive square fixture covered the EMP weapon—or so that's what Nero had told her. She had no reason to doubt him, since at that point he'd not had any reason to mistrust her.

"Order your men to put that thing into action," she said. Nero nodded and reached hesitantly for the radio. She added, "Do it slowly."

When he'd finished giving the orders, Stanish watched

at least a half dozen men go into action. They rushed across the deck and got busy disassembling the shell covering the weapon. When they'd completed the work, the weapon stood gleaming in the midday sun. The HSY-56A had now come within firing distance. The radio squawked to life the next instant, and Stanish knew it had to be the commander of the Hellenic navy vessel.

"They're ordering us to heave to," Nero said.

She shook her head. "Ignore them. They'll next fire a warning shot across the bow. Get that thing prepared to fire."

"But—"

Stanish raised the pistol once more. "Do it *now!* Don't make me ask again!"

"Yes, *despinis!*" He grabbed the radio and barked some more orders.

She watched with satisfaction as the octagonal body swerved into position. The oddest thing about the weapon was that it didn't have any barrels, and thus no profile to indicate it was a weapon. In fact, to Stanish it looked like little more than a spotlight. The exterior coating was painted matte white with no other distinguishing marks, and the main firing port was rectangular in shape. To look at it head-on would have left nearly anyone with the impression of a gigantic flash bulb, similar to the fancy cameras of decades past.

The only odd accoutrements on the device were the massive, high-pressure coils that rippled from its sides. She didn't know much about EMPs but she'd heard enough talk from guys like Steinham and Dratshev to know they were filled with liquid helium. This served as a cooling agent to the device as the EMP charge built up, moving the liquid helium through high-pressure chambers at supersonic speeds.

"It's much like the same system used by the CERN large hadron collider," Dratshev had once explained, "but on a microcosmic scale by any reasonable comparison."

The men aboard the ship shifted nervously as the EMP finally locked into position. Stanish looked at Nero, who watched her with nervous eyes, and then she nodded. Nero seemed hesitant at first, but a few flicks of his eyes at the pistol she held casually at her side seemed to serve as a sufficient reminder of her threat. Finally, Nero reached for a button atop the main console of the bridge controls and pressed it.

At first she thought it was the actual firing mechanism but then realized it was nothing more than a signal to the men below to engage the weapon. Stanish's eyes traveled to the weapon with fascination. She'd never seen anything like it. Sonar disruptions and laser beams in small laboratory tests, yes. Once she'd even been invited to watch surface-to-air defense systems aboard a U.S. Navy cruiser. But this? No, nothing like *this*—a weapon that boasted such power it could easily destroy whole vessels if applied well and able to build a sufficient amount of energy.

In the case of this one, however, Stanish knew it was a prototype and a hastily built one at that. There was little chance it could do the kind of damage on the scale she'd been told was possible by Madari, but she could just barely imagine.

A minute went by as the HSY-56A came within firing distance. Stanish had hardly paid attention to the radio where the voice of the officer aboard the Hellenic gunboat became more urgent with each attempt to raise the yacht. Hellenic navy or not, she knew their only chance would be to get in the first strike. Suddenly she heard the echo of a boom and massive arcs of light whipped across the bow of the ship. The volley had come from a very large anti-surface gun mounted at the aft, an OTO Melara 76/62C. Sea-water cooled, it could fire 120 rounds a minute utilizing a 440-volt, 3-phase main circuit.

The volley burned the air, a testament to the firepower and capability of even this small military vessel.

"Get that thing *going,* Nero!"

Nero shrugged and splayed his palms, indicating that at this point the situation was completely out of his control. Stanish returned her attention to the EMP gun—at this point she knew there was little chance the thing would even work—just in time to see something disturb the air waves immediately in front of the main rectangular firing point. The air shimmered like a highway in desert heat but there also appeared to be something else in the beam. It was… Stanish sucked in a breath. The multihued arc of a rainbow was just visible within that brief moment, an electric charge that quickly turned blue-white.

Then the spectacular display disappeared as suddenly as it had appeared, and Stanish realized she'd missed the initial results. She turned to see the better half of the aft deck of the patrol boat erupt into a gaseous ball of molten metal and fragments. The intense heat and subsequent burst from the magnetic pulse had apparently done damage to the magazine stores, as well, and secondary explosions began to erupt through the under-decking where the 67/62C had once sat.

Spectacular, she thought. Utterly spectacular.

The HSY-56A came hard around and began to move

away from the yacht as fast as her engines could carry her. The gun on the foredeck was an antiaircraft weapon and wouldn't have done her any good in this case. Men were now clustering on the starboard side, which was now the side facing the yacht, armed to the teeth with every kind of personalized and crew weapon probably available in their armory. They weren't about to take any more chances.

She could see crewmen running around the deck wearing fire-suppression suits and attempting to maintain control of the smoldering, thick black smoke that roiled from the aft deck. Dozens of men had been employed to attempt to put the fires out before they consumed the entire ship. If they didn't get it under control quickly they would start taking on water and eventually the ship would plunge her way beneath the surface and head straight to the bottom of the Mediterranean Sea.

"Well done, Capta—"

Stanish never got the last of her compliment off as she felt a forearm snake around her throat and yank hard in a back and downward direction. Stupid! She'd left herself vulnerable and now Nero was trying to take her out while he had the chance. Unfortunately for him, she had quite a bit of experience in hand-to-hand combat and she immediately reached to the boot knife she'd donned while on the stolen powerboat.

She twisted her head to the right, the action threatening to tear the muscles in her neck. Nero was strong but he wasn't experienced and he really wasn't in good physical condition. She managed to drive the knife into his thigh right at the point where it met his knee and slightly toward the rear. He emitted a scream as the now useless leg buckled beneath his weight and caused him to release his hold.

Stanish had dropped her pistol but managed to recover it before she dashed from Nero on hands and knees. When she was out of reach, she climbed to her feet and whirled on the captain. His dark eyes stared at her, burning with a mixture of hate and fear, his expression defiant. She raised her pistol and shot that look off his face. She whirled to face any additional challengers but the pilot navigator and first officer had been too busy avoiding the HSY to deal with what had just transpired. Apparently they figured Nero would be able to handle her alone. They were wrong.

"You speak English?" she asked, and they both nodded. "Good. Then you'll understand me when I tell you I'm the captain now."

CHAPTER TWENTY-ONE

Washington, D.C.

David Steinham could hardly believe his ears when he received the news about Madari, the American special operators Major Braden encountered, and the rescue of the three federal agents by what could have only been Cyclops.

Steinham hadn't bought their story about being part of Homeland Security. The lead guy had been especially tense around him during their entire visit. Steinham had been in the defense business long enough to know CIA when he saw them. Hell, those guys might have even been NSA or part of some organization so secret even its name was classified. Steinham didn't doubt they existed—in fact he *knew* they did because he'd developed technologies for their use.

And he'd been well compensated. Damn Madari all to hell anyway! Steinham had funneled millions of dollars at that guy and in the end he'd come up with squat. The EMP prototypes should have been his to barter, to sell or exploit as he chose. Instead, Madari had gone off like some madman and ruined all of Steinham's plans. The only question left for David Steinham was what to do about it.

He had several options. One would be to track Madari and send Cyrus after him, but Steinham wasn't sure how much good that would do him with the U.S. government. Obviously they would be watching him very closely now, and he'd have to be extremely careful what next steps he took. Undoubtedly they would have both his home and DCDI offices and labs under surveillance. All of his activities the past few years would also be closely scrutinized by agents of the CIA. It was possible he'd even be put on no-fly or fly-watch lists, his face splattered across every national and international antiterrorism database.

"Damn it to hell!" Steinham picked up a ceramic frog his wife had given to him as a Christmas gift one year and hurled it across his office.

"Problem?" asked Jack Cyrus, who sat casually in a nearby overstuffed chair.

"You *bet* there's a problem. I still can't believe you helped those undercover agents. You do realize they're watching our every move!"

"Look, Steinham, don't get ugly with me. I told you it wasn't a good idea going into business with these people, and now all it bought you is a lot of bad will. Not to mention the fact Madari's the same guy responsible for killing some of my best people."

Steinham looked horror-struck.

Cyrus continued. "Oh, that's right—I know all about your little affiliation. I haven't forgotten that you sent us out on what was doomed to be a suicide mission."

"I told you before, Colonel, that I had no idea Madari's people would be entrenched there."

"You should've known who you were dealing with! Ever heard the phrase 'keep your friends close but your enemies closer'?'"

"I don't need to be lectured, Colonel Cyrus."

"Apparently you do. If I hadn't pulled those boys out of

the scrape they'd got into, they'd be looking even harder at you right now. You even sent Braden overseas when you knew good and well he might be walking into some sort of trap. Now you have a CIA operative who's turned on you and Madari's in the wind."

"Maybe," Steinham said, a new revelation dawning in his expression.

"What do you mean 'maybe'?"

Steinham rose from his seat and began to pace the room, something Cyrus noticed he did regularly whenever he was scheming.

"I'm beginning to think maybe I know exactly what Madari has planned."

"So what? You going to keep me in suspense for a while?"

"Not at all," Steinham replied, stopping to raise a finger. "In fact, I'm about to rely very heavily upon your knowledge and expertise. We know that Madari has at least the prototypes and we know he has the scientific backing that has allowed him to make them operational. It wouldn't be all that easy for him to get the weapons into Libya and he wouldn't risk attempting it anyway."

"You're saying he'd want some sort of guarantee they were going to work first. He'd want to see them in action."

"Exactly! I have the sneaking suspicious that he will come…*here*."

"What? You mean right here to Washington?"

"Why not? You said it yourself before, Colonel. There's little doubt that Madari will want to ensure the prototypes are effective in combat. He's a user—just as he used me and just as he used my CIA contact there."

"Mishka," Cyrus confirmed with a nod.

"I knew this about Madari, which is why I didn't choose to reveal my relationship with him until you told me about rescuing the American agents, or whoever they are, from some of Madari's people. He's definitely thought this through—no surprise since I always esteemed him to be somewhat of a clever one."

"Smarmy would be a more accurate description, sir."

Steinham offered a stony grin. "If you like. Whatever you might think of him, he's not an idiot. He will consider any action you took against his people as requiring recompense."

"Ridiculous."

"To us, yes. But not to a man like Madari. You see for him it's a matter of honor. He thinks he has me at a disadvantage, and maybe to some degree he does. But what he seems to have forgotten is that much of his efforts were due to my funding him. I would have never thought he'd betray me."

"Well then, what *did* you think?"

"I thought he was a driven man, and so I thought he would do whatever he could to swing Dr. Dratshev around to developing the prototypes. That's why I spent so much time and effort grooming my contact in the CIA."

"Seems like your plan backfired."

"Not really, if my assessment of Madari is accurate."

"I'm still not following."

"As I said, I believe he will come here to Washington, D.C. When he does, he'll bring the prototypes with him."

"Looking for payback while also testing them out to make sure something doesn't backfire on him."

"Or at least to make sure that Dratshev was playing

on the level with him. And if he does as I think he will, he'll play straight into our hands."

"Because you'll be ready for him."

"No, Colonel Cyrus—*you* will be ready for him!"

"We're not going to be any match for EMP weapons, Steinham," Cyrus said, forgetting military or contractual protocol for a moment. "I won't risk any more of my men or send them to be slaughtered like sheep. You want that, you'll have to hire some other sacrificial lambs. There are limits to our contract."

"You're paid to take risks, Colonel."

"I'm also paid to keep my men alive. Cyclops can't do you any good if we're either spread so thin we're ineffective or there aren't enough left of our numbers we can effectively repel an attack against you or your assets. Those are the plain facts in the matter whether you like them or not."

"If you'll do me the courtesy of allowing me to propose a new strategy, I think you'll find the risk to you will be very minimal. And you also seem to forget that if I can lay my hands on those prototypes or even Dratshev, you will stand to benefit, as well. Think of it! Your PMC will be credited with recovering the technology even our own SOGs were unable to acquire, and I will then have the only resources close enough to making EMP a practical reality in modern weaponry. We're talking billions in profits with the added distinction of serving our country! Isn't that why we're in this business, Colonel?"

Cyrus stood and crossed the room to stand in front of Steinham. He folded his arms and let his eyes scan Steinham's face. Finally he said, "Be careful, David. Be *very* careful, because if I didn't know any better I'd say you're starting to sound an awful lot like a fanatic yourself. And I, for one, will risk neither my assets nor my reputation on the ravings of a madman."

"Need I remind you, Jack, that you wouldn't *have* a reputation if it weren't for me? Everything you have I practically gave you! So I'd appreciate it if you'd show a little loyalty."

"Loyalty is a two-way street, Steinham," Cyrus said, turning on his heel and heading for the door.

"Where are you going? Is this your way of terminating our agreement?"

Cyrus stopped in his tracks and turned to look at Steinham once more. "No, you don't get off that easily. You still owe us money and I expect you to honor the debt. And you can be sure I'll hold up my end of the bargain, even going so far as to implement this crazy plan of yours. But so help me, sir, if you cross me again or this mission compromises my men unnecessarily, I'll make it my personal mission in life to hunt you down and kill you myself. Am I being perfectly clear with you?"

Steinham's bottom lip trembled in fear, mostly from the expression of murderous determination he saw in Cyrus's eyes. Yeah, the guy would make good on his threat.

"You are," Steinham replied.

Cyrus nodded and left.

Stony Man Farm, Virginia

"Afraid there's not much left." David McCarter's voice sounded a little tinny through the speakers in the operations center at the Farm.

Normally their communications channels were clear but there was a mother of a storm between them, and the dedicated satellite was having difficulty penetrating the disruption at that particular point in its orbital path. They didn't worry about it. Any garbled transmissions would resolve in the next few minutes once that satellite had cleared the storm perimeter.

"David," Price said, "were you able to determine if the prototypes are legit?"

"Very little doubt of that," McCarter said. "I don't understand most of this bloody stuff but it seems T.J.'s got a handle on it."

"Talk to me."

Hawkins's voice chimed in. "We found at least a dozen supersize tanks of liquid helium inside the bunker. There were no lines connected to them but there were compression fittings on all of the tank outlets."

"God help us," Brognola muttered.

Price looked at him but her voice was directed toward the speakers. "That's not the kind of news we were hoping to hear. We *had* hoped that Madari was just blowing a lot of steam. But if they were cooling the weapons with liquid helium, there's little doubt the prototypes are the real deal."

Kurtzman interjected. "We may have something else to confirm our suspicions."

"What is it?" Brognola asked.

"I just got an alert that a Hellenic patrol boat encountered the yacht we were looking for, which was in position not far from where we lost Muriel Stanish's signal. They attempted to stop the boat per the information we gave them regarding its general size and description. According to our NSA sources, the ship refused to heave to and they fired a warning shot across the bow. One moment they're bearing down on this rather innocent-looking yacht and the next moment their aft-deck gun exploded and a better portion of the upper tiers of the ship hull were melted to slag in just seconds."

"Holy sweet bollocks." It was McCarter's voice.

"Not exactly my sentiments but I think you captured it well, David," Price replied.

"I'd have to say that makes the threat about as real as it gets," Brognola said. "Not to mention it verifies what's had us worried from the beginning. Dratshev has actually managed to crack the code to successful scaling of electromagnetic pulse weapons."

"I think this has gone on long enough, Hal," Price said. "I know that secrecy is our primary mandate, but I think we'd be wise to involve the military at this point. We should at least put the Mediterranean Joint Command on alert."

"Agreed," Brognola replied with a somber nod.

"I also think we should see if they can dispatch the nearest vessel to intercept and destroy that vessel."

"Why involve the Navy?" McCarter said. "We can handle this."

"You *are* going to handle it," Price said. "I want you guys airborne in twenty. Just leave what you have there. I doubt it's in any danger of being discovered until we can send in an appropriate team to clean house."

"Meanwhile," Brognola added, "I'll get the Man on the phone to see if we can't get some cooperation from the Navy. I'm sure they'll be able to tell us the closest ship for intercept."

"Right." Price nodded. "David, you and the rest of Phoenix Force will rendezvous with that ship once we've identified it. They'll be at your disposal to launch a mission with the objective of destroying that yacht at any cost."

"You sure we'll have their full cooperation? Some captains are sticky widgets about giving up control."

"The captain will still be in charge of his vessel, but Phoenix Force will be in charge of the actual operation."

"Don't worry, men," Brognola clarified. "You'll have the authority of the Oval Office behind you. Just be polite and smile a lot. I'm sure you can do that."

"Sure, *I* can," McCarter replied, the grin evident by the tone of his voice. "But I'm not sure about the rest of these savages I'm leading. They didn't attend the same charm school as I did."

"Somehow I'm sure they'll manage under your expert tutelage," Price replied. "I have faith in you. Just get it done and be safe."

"Understood. McCarter, out."

A long silence fell over the room as each got lost in thought for a time. Such a weapon could have devastating consequences if used on any sort of a mass scale.

Brognola finally broke the silence. "I don't know about you two, but I don't like the feel of this at all. We've had what I would deem a significant breach in our own internal security."

"What are you talking about?" Kurtzman said. "We're locked down tighter than a drum."

"Not electronic," Brognola said. "Not even as it relates to the Farm. I'm talking the security of our field teams. So far, Madari's people have been able to keep one step ahead of Able Team by successfully planting electronic surveillance on Lyons. High-tech surveillance, no less."

"Oh, yes, that reminds me…" Price said, reaching for a sheet of paper on the table and sliding it to Brognola.

"This just came back. It's an analysis on that bug. Turns out the internal circuitry is untraceable, bought on the black market. But the design…there's no mistaking—it was created by DCDI."

"Steinham?" Brognola's eyebrows shot together like arrows meeting at a bull's-eye. "Are you saying this equipment was planted on them by Steinham's people?"

Price shrugged. "Not necessarily. I mean, I suppose it's possible but… Aaron?"

"We have another theory," Kurtzman said, taking up the cue. "We think that some part of Madari's financing may have come from David Steinham. Certainly there's no mistaking this circuitry blueprint. It's right from Steinham's personal records, the ones he holds in an electronic vault on site and thinks nobody can get access to."

Price smiled with admiration. "Aaron had that puppy cracked in fifteen minutes."

"Aw, it weren't hardly nothing," Kurtzman replied with mock humility.

"So maybe Steinham was financing Madari's research."

"It would explain a lot," Price replied. "Not only would it explain why our friend Stanish compromised Phoenix Force in her role as their contact, but it would also explain her relationship to Madari. She may well have gotten close to him originally while she was on Steinham's payroll."

"Okay," Brognola observed. "So Madari wants revenge against the Libyan government and joins the Arab Spring movement. Steinham sees an opportunity to play on that and so he makes a deal to help finance Madari."

"Which explains where Madari got a lot of his money,"

Kurtzman added. "He wasn't personally wealthy when he left Libya, and he didn't have a lot of wealthy friends."

"But," Price noted, "he *did* have some people who were willing to invest in his plan for a high-tech platform like EMPs with both large and small-arms applications. Anybody, foreign or domestic, bringing that kind of tech to the table would almost certainly become the most popular defense contractor in the world."

Brognola nodded. "Countries would pay billions for it, including the United States. Steinham was looking to stay on top whatever the costs. So it's a good theory. But it still doesn't explain why he sent Cyrus into that NSA storage facility. Surely he had to know Madari's people were on the place."

"We don't think so," Price said. "In fact, we think that's when Steinham first realized Madari had betrayed him."

"So he used Cyclops as the proverbial sacrificial lamb, acting as though he didn't know Madari but that he had intelligence the guy was behind Dratshev's kidnapping," Brognola said.

"Right!" Price said. "Which, in fact, it was Steinham who had engineered most of this right from the start. Otherwise, how could he have known about Dratshev's kidnapping before anybody else? It wasn't *just* because Muriel Stanish had her ear to the ground. It was because he was the one who started it all."

Brognola shook his head. "What greed will drive men to do."

"It could be that Steinham's motives were genuine," Kurtzman said. "He's held in very high regard among his colleagues and the politicos in Washington."

"True," Price said. "They're even honoring him this

Friday at the annual conference for Private Contributors to American Military Defense."

"If Madari did in fact betray Steinham, and now he's in the wind, wouldn't you think Steinham would do whatever he could to track down Madari?" Brognola asked. "Or at least try to steal the technology or even get his hands on Dratshev."

"It's possible," Price said.

"Why do you ask, Hal?" Kurtzman said.

"Just something that was bothering me about what Cyrus told Able Team," Brognola said. "He said their other clients were interested in the EMPs. But he *also* told them they had intelligence Madari might try to hit an American target abroad."

"What're you getting at, Hal?" Price asked.

"I think Cyrus was being played by Steinham just like he was playing us," Brognola said. "I think Madari has *every* intention of using those weapons on American soil. And I think he's going to use them against Steinham and the Cyclops mercenaries."

"Well, there is the major meeting of the DoD contractors this Friday night," Kurtzman reminded them. "That would be a pretty good opportunity to take out Steinham and Cyrus's people simultaneously."

"Not to mention the crippling blow it would mean against America," Price said. "We'd lose some of the finest minds on the planet."

"Put Able Team on full alert," Brognola ordered. "We're going to crash the party."

CHAPTER TWENTY-TWO

Mediterranean Sea

The USS *Resolute* knifed through the whitecaps of the Mediterranean, its sleek lines a testament to the power of the United States Navy's most modern and powerful Zumwalt-class destroyers. The lead ship in its class, and only one of a handful that had been outfitted with the latest in equipment and modern-warfare capabilities, the *Resolute* boasted the most advanced technology and survivability systems.

In addition to a crew complement requiring fewer than 150 sailors and a composite superstructure to increase speed and maneuverability, the *Resolute* was a formidable and awesome sight on the high seas. Its armament and equipment included Multi-Function Radar and an Advanced Gun System with a 155 mm gun, which, when complemented by its LRLAP—long range land attack projectile—had a range up to 80 nautical miles. The hangars were equipped with a PVLS—peripheral vertical launch system—for a variety of aircraft and air-combat systems such as drones and unmanned combat air vehicles. Finally, at just six hundred feet in length, she could do better than thirty knots and displace just under 15 long tons.

At the helm was one of the most respected destroyer

captains in the modern Navy. Very few people knew about the personal relationship between Captain Samuel Garth and the President of the United States. They had been childhood friends, something neither advertised.

"I wish this conversation didn't have to take place under such grave circumstances, Sam. But for what it's worth, I'm glad it turned out to be you in command and not somebody who was unfamiliar to me."

"Same here, Mr. President."

"I'll be as brief as possible and then I'll let you get to what needs to be done. The short story is that the team that you're about to rendezvous with are some of the finest combatants in our arsenal. They have literally saved this country from destruction on more occasions than I would ever care to count. And they've done this for a number of my predecessors, as well.

"Now, while I'm not at liberty to divulge the nature of their operations to you, I can say that I both consider this a personal favor to the President of the United States by asking your full cooperation with them. They aren't there to step on your toes or to run your crew or ship—the *Resolute* is yours now and it will be after they arrive. But you will take any direction from them relative to this mission."

"I understand, sir. May I ask you to hold one moment?"

"Of course."

Garth turned to the crew and said, "Clear the bridge."

Without hesitation, the men did as ordered under the watchful eye of the XO, who was about to be the last one out when Garth thought better of it and asked him to stay. Garth returned to the conversation. "Permission to speak candidly?"

"Granted."

"Why are they coming here to perform this operation? If this ship poses such a danger, why not just let me neutralize her on site? I could drop an ASROC or SM-2MR right straight down on that puppy from so far away we wouldn't even see the blast."

"We're hoping it won't come to that. In fact, this team's mission is to take the crew and cargo in one piece. There's significant intelligence and equipment aboard this vessel that is of vital interest to the United States military, not to mention its criticality toward maintaining the defensive efficacy and superiority of this nation. Bottom line, Sam, I wouldn't be asking this if it weren't the utmost importance to national security."

"Aye, sir."

"That said, if it comes down to no other choice—particularly if you are told by the leader of the SOG team that it must be done—I authorize you to take whatever action may be necessary to protect your crew, your ship and this nation. In other words, if you're left with no options other than to destroy that vessel than I have no qualms telling you to blow it out of the goddamn water. Is that understood?"

"Aye, Mr. President. My ship is at your command, sir."

"No, Sam. Your ship is at *your* command. I'm merely asking to borrow her for a couple of hours, tops."

"You got it, Mr. President."

Garth hung up the phone and turned to his XO, Commander Derek Jankovich. "Number One, return bridge crew to duties and then prepare the top deck to receive the special operations team. We are to cooperate with them fully."

"Aye, sir. What's our mission?"

"I'll wait for the SOG team to arrive and they can brief both of us at the same time. Head guy is named McMasters."

"This a SEAL team, sir?"

"For now, it's a matter of national security and that's all I'm permitted to divulge. When I know more, you'll know more."

Jankovich aye-ayed a last time with a snappy salute, whirled on his heel and left to perform his duties.

Garth thought about how his day had started off relatively normal that morning. He'd breakfasted with the officers—a standard tradition on Wednesday mornings he'd started after his first ship command and one he'd continued since then—before heading to his cabin to begin writing reports. Again, as was his routine, he'd spent the late part of the morning walking different areas of the ship on an ad hoc inspection, greeting enlisted and officers alike and even stopping here and there to assess ship morale. He'd then headed to the bridge, where he would spend the rest of the day until evening mess. That's when he'd gotten the rather unexpected call from the President.

Well, whatever was going on it sounded important enough he'd need to be on his toes. This was a chance for the brand-new USS *Resolute* and her crew to shine as never before.

The approach of a chopper as reported by a radar officer commanded his attention and pulled him from his reverie.

"Are they transmitting the correct confirmation code, ensign?" Garth asked as he stepped up alongside the radar man.

"Aye, sir. Looks like they have the proper phrase of the day and encryption code."

"Understood, thank you. Operations?"

"Aye, sir," the Ops officer replied, stepping forward smartly.

"Inform the XO the team we're expecting has arrived and to prepare for deck-landing. Also advise him it's my understanding this pilot is highly experienced with ship landings so we shouldn't have to do any hand-holding for this one."

"Aye, sir."

As the Ops officer, a highly experienced lieutenant commander by the name of Tim Lee, turned to execute his orders, Garth reached for his own neck and massaged the new knot that seemed to have formed there. Yeah, the massive knot he detected was all the proof he needed that the morning that had started so simply was about to end as one of hell of day. And Garth, for one, wasn't looking forward to it in the least.

"CAPTAIN GARTH?" MCCARTER said, extending a hand for a firm shake. "I'm McMasters."

"No rank given," the XO observed. "You're not military?"

McCarter smiled. "Not exactly."

Hawkins added, "We're more special operations out of that chapter missing from the playbook."

"I see," Jankovich replied with a nod.

"I think you can appreciate when I tell you, gentlemen," Garth interjected, "that I wasn't given a whole lot of information regarding this mission. Frankly, I'm not happy about that but understand that secrecy is important. All the same, I was wondering if you might do me the courtesy of at least some sort of briefing relative to what we're going up against. Especially since I've been asked to lend you whatever manpower and equipment you need."

"No manpower, sir," Manning said.

McCarter continued. "But we are going to need one of your Seahawks—"

"I thought you'd brought your own chopper," Jankovich cut in.

"We did, but it's a civilian variant. That won't cut it for an air assault operation, and especially not at night."

"Exactly what is your plan, McMasters?" Garth asked. He'd been told to cooperate and he would, but he was also responsible for every man and every piece of military hardware aboard his vessel. He wouldn't just blindly hand over a chopper worth millions of dollars to a team of men he didn't know.

"The details of our exact operation are classified, Captain," McCarter said.

"Maybe so, mister," Garth snapped. "But the fact is this is still my ship and the President told me personally that I was entitled to know everything I was getting into."

"The President called you personally?" James asked, doing nothing to hide his expression.

"That's right." Garth smiled. "*Personally.* I talked to him for several minutes. Now I'm more than happy to cooperate with you guys but you *will* tell me about your operation before I just hand over one of my aircraft, especially if it won't be my men at the stick."

Encizo started to look as though he was about to protest but McCarter raised a hand to cut it short. "Men, start checking our equipment. Maybe the XO here can show you some place where you can do your checks unimpeded."

"Be glad to," Jankovich said, gesturing for them to follow.

When they were gone, McCarter nodded at Garth and said, "Sir, if you don't mind, I'd like to see you in private. This isn't a matter for any other ears but yours and I didn't wish to get into any territorial pissing contest with our side present."

Garth nodded in return and then turned and led him into the ready room. When the door was closed, Garth perched his butt on the edge of desk and said, "Okay, mister. Lay it out for me."

"I don't know how much you know about what's been happening in this theater of operations as of late, but suffice it to say it hasn't been pretty. A man named Ishaq Madari, a former Libyan dissident and member of the Arab Spring revolution, has kidnapped a Russian scientist and coerced him into developing prototypes of electromagnetic pulse weapons."

"Holy shit," was all Garth could apparently think to reply.

"Yes, that was the assessment of our leadership, as well." McCarter shook his head and folded his arms, pinning Garth with a hard stare. "I don't think I need to tell you, Captain, my men have been through hell and back on this mission. Somehow, Madari's managed to stay one step ahead of us. He's also enlisted the aid of a rogue CIA agent, and he's been responsible for the death of at least several U.S. political officials."

"So how did you wind up here?"

McCarter took a deep breath and then sighed. "I'd like to say it was a short story but it really isn't. Let's just say that our mission began in Minsk and eventually landed us in Athens and then on one of the lesser Greek Islands, with a name I still can't bloody pronounce."

"You have been around the block."

"Yes, sir. And now—as I noted before, Madari's managed to keep just out of reach—both Madari and the scientist are in the wind. And we have confirmation from our people, along with what we've personally witnessed, that these weapons are viable."

"How do you know?"

"One was used just several hours ago against a Hellenic patrol boat at the Aegean-Mediterranean water boundaries. The enemy ship appears to be a yacht but does, in fact, have at least one heavy prototype aboard."

Garth rose and began to pace the small area in front of the desk, scratching his chin absently as he thought through what McCarter had just said. Finally he turned and looked at the Briton. "If it was one of their more modern patrol boats, like the HSY variants, their primary weapon would have been a 76 mm rapid-fire anti-surface cannon. You mean to tell me that one small yacht equipped with just a single one of these prototypes managed to outgun a Hellenic naval vessel?"

"That's right, Captain," McCarter replied. "Now everything we know about this weapon would seem to indicate that it's only capable of taking out other watercraft or land-based targets. We have no reason to think it can take out aircraft—at least we don't have any evidence of such capability—so we figure the best way to come at them would be fast-attack helicopter via standard air assault."

"And you want to go in dark," Garth concluded.

"Correct. We've been mandated to take this thing intact if at all possible. We figure if we take out the crew, we'll take out their ability to operate the weapon. That leaves them having to fight us conventionally and on that count we've got them well outclassed."

"That's for sure." Garth grinned a knowing wink at

McCarter, who returned it with a conciliatory grin of his own. "Seems like you've got it worked out, McMasters. I have two of the newest MH-60R multi-mission-capable Seahawks, and one of them just became yours."

"I appreciate that, sir."

"Also, I think it would be wise, based on what you told me, if we had a second one flying backup."

"Putting a lot of your eggs in one basket, Captain Garth?"

"No...no," Garth said, raising a finger. "But I like the way you think. No, my thought is that maybe that ship can just run some interference, create a distraction. We can stay far enough back not to get in the way. But don't you think it would be nice to have a second option available?"

"As long as we don't risk friendly fire."

"I think we can accommodate whatever your mission objectives may be. And give you a margin of safety. Sounds like this Madari has significant resources. Surely you've thought about the fact he might have another vessel nearby to help if things go in the toilet with the first."

"To be honest," McCarter said, mentally kicking himself, "I hadn't thought of it. But now that you say as much, I suppose I should have considered the possibility."

"Probably best, also, that we keep the *Resolute* out of range. This way if you give me the word I can launch missiles to sink the thing. She won't pose any threat if it comes to that—this much I can guarantee."

McCarter nodded. "We're hoping it doesn't come to that, but I appreciate all of your support."

"It's my pleasure. Good luck, McMasters. I wouldn't want to trade places with you even if I could."

"I don't blame you, Captain," McCarter replied.

SIXTY NAUTICAL MILES to the east, Stanish had managed to convince the others that she was in charge and any view to the contrary would most likely be a fatal one.

The Hellenic patrol boat was now rapidly fading to their rear and the sun seemed to race toward setting. The red-orange-purple glow across the beautiful water mesmerized Stanish. It made her want to be someplace else, any place really, and despite her feelings of betrayal she wanted to fold herself into the warm and strong embrace of her lover's arms.

After she had been told of their plans to take the ship to the port in Derna, she considered any alternate possibilities. At this point, it didn't make sense to return to the island estate. There would probably be remnants of the men waiting there with orders to shoot her on sight. Turning around and docking at Athens, while convenient, wouldn't do much good, either. It would attract immediate attention from customs and law enforcement, and perhaps force her into hiding in Athens longer than she wanted. She didn't have any contacts there, either.

By now, she thought, I'm not only out of friends but I have my own government looking for me.

The only thing she could do was to carry out Madari's plan and go to Derna. She'd get herself into the country and wait for him there. Eventually he'd show up and then she could get his explanation for why he'd abandoned her and lied to her. She wanted to look him in the eyes and hear his reasons, and if she didn't believe him then she'd kill him herself.

She had given up *everything* to be with him because she loved him. Or maybe she hadn't loved him; maybe she'd been in love with the *idea* of being in love with him. Either way, he owed her an explanation for his actions, and she would do everything she could to hear that explanation from his own lips. She had nothing else left to her. She'd made herself an enemy of the U.S. government and renounced her citizenship and values for a man. In return, he'd betrayed her.

And she would be avenged.

CHAPTER TWENTY-THREE

The twin MH-60R Seahawk choppers skimmed the waters of the Mediterranean at better than a hundred knots. They were operating in a complete blackout state—the men of Phoenix Force were glad for the cloud cover that had moved in and completely obscured the moonlight. McCarter glanced at the luminous dial of his chronometer and checked the time against their progress. Nearly 2330 and they were only fifteen minutes into the flight.

McCarter keyed up the headset that linked him directly to Grimaldi. "Jack, you read me?"

"Five by five."

"How long to target?"

"Not sure. We don't have any signal so we're going strictly off sonar and last known position."

"Best guess?"

"Estimate, seven minutes. No more."

"It's possible they've changed direction. How will that affect our assault?"

"None, really. We'll still come on the port side, just as you asked. Safest place to hover will be the rear."

"Yeah, I remember you said the Hellenic navy officers reported they thought maybe the weapon was on the foredeck of the yacht. They couldn't fire at us without the risk of hitting their own bridge. Is that our thinking?"

"Pretty much," Grimaldi replied. "Beside the fact the

aft of a ship is always its weakest point. That's where the engine is, too. So if we have to blow out the propellers we at least have a chance."

"Okay, just wait until we're down to the last man on deck and you have my signal before pulling away. Especially since I'm the last one off the line. Hate to get dragged away before I have the chance to participate in some of the bloody fun."

"Understood."

"Roger that, and out." McCarter clicked off and then tapped his helmet to attract the attention of the rest.

They were attired in matte-black fatigues and rigged for full combat. The intense looks on their respective faces told McCarter he didn't have to worry about delivering any speeches.

What McCarter couldn't shake was how Madari had chosen to handle his affairs. He had called attention to himself and then, as if rubbing salt in the wound, had used a device, the very existence of which he was attempting to keep under wraps.

The more McCarter thought about it the more convinced he was that Madari was using the yacht as a decoy. That meant it was not only an unimportant aspect of the game in Madari's eyes, but the chances were good he considered it an expendable asset. Well, Phoenix Force wasn't about to play Madari's game if they could avoid it.

Yeah, McCarter thought. Time for us to start calling the bloody shots.

The five-minute mark passed so quickly McCarter could hardly believe it. Still, all of them saw the diffuse red light come on to indicate they were on approach of the target and the team should prepare for their assault. McCarter gave them a high sign before he gestured at

Encizo. The Cuban nodded and then reached to disengage the latch and open the door.

The salty Mediterranean winds buffeted them in the confined space of the chopper where they had positioned themselves. Encizo checked his safety harness before leaving his seat and taking a knee at the edge of the deck plate. He kept one hand on his MP-5 while the other held tight to the door as Grimaldi made one last bank of the MH-60 before coming to a smooth hover above the rear of the ship.

They waited a few extra seconds for Grimaldi to match speed before the red light flashed. Encizo deployed the rappel lines, attached his carabiner and detached the safety harness. He then flipped on the power switch of the night-vision goggles before lowering them to his eyes and vaulting over the side with the practiced ease of a professional. Of all the Phoenix Force warriors, Encizo was the most comfortable with operations at sea. The guy was a natural swimmer and experienced in maritime combat.

Hawkins followed immediately after him, then James and Manning. As he'd promised Grimaldi, McCarter was the last to go over the side and even as he descended he could see his men were already busy fanning out and engaging the first of their targets. He could make out the muzzle-flashes of their weapons and couldn't help but reward himself with a brief grin and a surge of satisfaction. This time they had brought the fight to the enemy and caught them completely off guard.

To the victor go the spoils, thought David McCarter.

As soon as Rafael Encizo hit the deck of the yacht and disengaged from the harness he went into action.

His sixth sense alerted him to movement up the port

rail and he turned just in time to see two armed sentries come into view. Encizo knelt, swung the MP-5 slung across his right shoulder into action and triggered a salvo with the weapon in burst mode. Triple 9 mm Parabellum rounds punched into the first sentry's gut and drove him back until he smacked the railing. The impact was enough to cause the lifeless guard to lose his balance and flip over the rail to descend into the dark water below, swallowed instantly by the choppy waves of an unforgiving sea.

The second man managed to get off a volley of autofire from his assault rifle before Hawkins dispatched him neatly with a single shot from his M-16 A3. The first two rounds Hawkins triggered didn't quite cut it, as the Phoenix Force warrior was trying to detach and get clear of the rappel rope at the same time as defend Encizo's position. The third round did the trick, though, entering the man's skull just above the bridge of the nose and blowing out the back of his head.

Pandemonium seemed to erupt on the aft deck of the yacht as one Phoenix Force commando after the next descended, cleared and took up an offensive position. McCarter and team had resolved this wouldn't be a holding action—they had a specific set of objectives and they planned to execute their mission plan without hesitation.

Their biggest concern was to identify the EMP weapon and secure it so the crew couldn't use it against any other vessels. They especially didn't want it to threaten American naval assets. While McCarter had been assured the likelihood of it being able to take down aircraft was almost nil, he didn't plan to take *any* chances. Madari had outfoxed them quite enough and McCarter wouldn't permit any repeat performances on that mark.

At present, it didn't appear the crew was all that concerned about attempting to use the EMP gun, wherever the hell the thing was mounted. Instead they were doing their best to get organized and recover from the initial surprise. It wasn't working well for them, mostly because it appeared nobody was really in charge.

Two more gunners charged up the starboard side but McCarter stood ready. He raised his MP-5 and triggered a sustained burst as he swept the muzzle of his weapon at an upward angle. Rounds smashed through the pair, the first of the slugs clipping the hip of one man before cutting a path across his guts. Entrails were shredded as the shearing force of the rounds exposed the man's belly to the outside world. The survivor caught several across the chest while still in motion. He continued forward with his arms wind-milling out of control, but the path was cut short by another round that caught him in the jaw and blew out the left side of his head. His lifeless body crashed into a deck stanchion and slammed him onto his back.

McCarter whipped his head around. Encizo and Hawkins make their way toward the stern along the port side walkway they'd just cleared a moment before. McCarter nodded with satisfaction. Witnesses aboard the Hellenic patrol boat had sworn they'd seen some kind of device atop a gyro pointed at them just prior to their gun exploding. Most agreed the device had been in the stern area of the yacht, so McCarter had made it part of Hawkins and Encizo's primary mission to locate the device and secure it at any cost while the rest of them cleared the ship of any enemy personnel.

The yacht couldn't be that well defended. They had surmised the crew complement at a maximum of twelve.

If true, they'd just neutralized a third of the enemy force. The deck astern looked clear now so McCarter gestured for James and Manning to follow him up the starboard side. All were wearing night-vision goggles, which appeared to have scored a point in combat superiority for Phoenix Force.

McCarter could only hope, however grimly, their luck held out a little longer.

THE ATTACK HAD come swiftly and without warning.

None of the equipment aboard the yacht had detected the approach of the choppers. The whipping of chopper blades against the air had been the only thing to tell Stanish something was afoot. She leaped out of Nero's cot, which she'd commandeered after his demise, and she smacked her head on the plate that hung over its length. She cursed with fury as she rubbed her head.

She reached for the pistol in her holster and then grabbed the satchel of weapons she'd brought along. She went to the cabin door that she'd secured and opened it, poking her head out. She couldn't see anything along the narrow corridor but she heard the shout of the sentries on deck, which was followed by automatic weapons fire a moment later. They only had ten crewmen aboard the yacht, besides the XO, pilot navigator and herself—only about half of those were actually armed with sub-guns designed solely for the purpose of repelling boarders.

It didn't sound from what she heard above as if they were having much success. It had to be special forces of some kind, and they likely weren't from the Hellenic navy. Only American or British naval resources would have had been able to dispatch such a team in this short period of time.

Stanish thought about closing and re-locking the cabin door but she quickly realized the foolishness of such an action. They could easily pin her down and she couldn't position against superior numbers of SOG commandos. Plus, she had no story to tell them they would believe at this point—under the circumstances she didn't doubt every intelligence agency from Europe to Northern America had her face and details. The bastards probably even had orders to kill her on sight.

She secured the satchel to her shoulder, checked the action on her .380-caliber pistol and left the cabin, headed in the direction of the bridge. She made the steps and popped her head out the door. A cool ocean breeze assaulted her face and a blast of salty spray stung her eyes. The shooting was much louder but only for a moment, and then it died. She emerged from the small door and secured it behind her.

Stanish turned to head for the bridge but spotted the approach of shadowy forms on the starboard side walkway. She ducked out of sight and bit her lip, unsure of where to go. If she fought back they would probably take her out before she took down one, maybe two at most. If she remained indecisive, they would surely capture her. Either way didn't hold much appeal. She weighed her options and realized she had no choice—she couldn't afford to let them take her alive. They'd put her on trial for espionage, find her guilty and lock her away in some hole for the rest of her days.

Stanish knew what she had to do, and she wasn't going to do it for Ishaq Madari. He'd spurned her love after she'd given her heart to him. She had no defense for her actions, no way to answer the charge of high treason. She had allied herself with terrorists and criminals, and now she would pay for that alliance with her life.

She entered the portal that led to her cabin but just before she reached it she turned and entered another door. It led into the engine compartment area. One thing she had left in her satchel was a couple of grenades. More than enough to take out the engine room and sink this thing to the bottom of the Mediterranean.

Stanish locked the door behind her and searched until she found something to wedge under the handle. She kept the lights out and used a red-lensed flashlight to prepare the two grenades. She wasn't exactly an expert with engines but she had quite a bit of knowledge in sabotage— one of the classes she'd followed with relish at Quantico. As with most yachts of this size, each of the two engines was diesel and boasted nearly three thousand horsepower. They drove a twin-screw propulsion system with a capacity of nearly a quarter-million liters and supported a range of 7,000 nautical miles.

Its length at the waterline was approximately 246 feet, so she knew she'd have to plant the grenades low to damage the engines and yet successfully penetrate the steel hull effectively enough to take on water. Diesel wasn't nearly as explosive as gasoline but it was highly flammable and would spread quickly to the more combustible parts of the engine. The intense heat from igniting that much diesel would easily reach a temperature capable of melting the aluminum superstructure to slag.

Stanish willed her shaking hands to stop as she primed the grenades and set one at the base near the compressor. She placed the second one near the fuel lines of the other and then yanked the pin. After priming it, she walked on shaky legs to the first one and pulled the pin, then sat adjacent to it and bowed her head.

"Whatever power may exist, whatever god, forgive me," she said in a choked whisper at tears began to flow from her eyes. "Forgive me..."

HAWKINS AND ENCIZO met two more armed crew members near the stern of the yacht. The men were hovered over what looked like an intricate control panel. When they saw the commandos approaching, they hesitated just a moment. At first it looked as though they might resist but when the men saw the Phoenix Force pair had the drop on them, they raised their hands.

Hawkins relieved them of their weapons and ordered them to sit facing a nearby stanchion while Encizo made a quick study of the controls. A flash of movement to his right caused Hawkins to look toward the starboard side. He saw through his NVGs the fleeting image of a lone figure dash belowdecks through a door just beneath the ladder well that led to the bridge.

Hawkins keyed up his headset. "Six to Leader."

"Go."

"We have two crew neutralized and my partner's inspecting the device now," Hawkins related. "But be advised I just spotted a single crewmember access a door immediately below the bridge on the starboard side. Proceed with caution."

"Understood, Six. Leader, out," came McCarter's snappish reply.

Hawkins frowned but couldn't say he blamed the boss. Madari's seeming ability to outwit them at every turn had bothered McCarter, a lot more than he would have ever admitted to his teammates, and his nerves had just about reached the fraying point. Were it anyone else but David McCarter, Hawkins might have worried about continued effective leadership under the circumstances, but the former SAS veteran was a rock-solid combatant and a pro all the way. He'd be all right.

The trio came into view and McCarter immediately tossed them a salute as they descended the steps from the starboard walkway to the main deck. They fanned out as their training had dictated time and again, muzzles sweeping the deck and ready for any threat that might emerge. Hawkins kept one eye on their activity and the other on the prisoners.

Finally, no longer able to contain his curiosity, he directed his voice at Encizo. "Well, is that it?"

"Yeah," Encizo said, flipping his goggles up so he could scrutinize the panel in greater detail. "Yeah...I think this is it."

"Bingo," Hawkins replied.

"Easy. It ain't over yet."

"Hey, I don't get much joy in this life. Don't take what I got."

This drew a chuckle from Encizo. "Okay, pal—okay."

As soon as they cleared the perimeter, McCarter pointed at the door Hawkins had indicated before. James tossed a salute and moved alongside it while Manning approached at the opposite side. McCarter got into position at about a thirty-degree angle to James and then gestured for Manning to open it as he shoved back his NVGs.

McCarter pushed through as soon as Manning got it open. The corridor was lit fairly well, just as McCarter had suspected it might be. He was glad he'd used foresight to disengage his goggles and avoid being temporarily blinded by the lights. McCarter brought his MP-5 into play as he saw movement at the other end, but he realized it was unarmed crew members and they were in nothing but modes of half-dress. Apparently they'd been bunked down when the assault began.

Before he could decide what to do, the sudden rumble of an explosion and the rattle of the decking beneath his feet caused him to duck involuntarily. The explosion was followed by a second, this one more pronounced, a heartbeat later.

"What the hell was that?" James inquired, shouting to be heard over the sounds of a restless Mediterranean.

Manning swore under his breath. "I think somebody just blew the engine. Those sounded like ordnance—most probably grenades. Did you feel the shift in our speed? We're slowing very quickly."

McCarter felt his heart leap into his throat. "If they blew the engines then we might also be—"

"Taking on water!" James finished.

McCarter spit a few curses before keying up his transmitter. "Leader to Eagle One."

Grimaldi's voice rang in the headsets of the entire Phoenix Force team a moment later. "Go, Leader."

"Emergency evac. I say again, bring her in for emergency evac. Somebody blew the engines and we may be sinking."

"Copy, Leader. We're on our way."

McCarter switched to tactical frequency. "Clear the channel. We're burned, mates! Abandon ship!"

CHAPTER TWENTY-FOUR

There were two things that went through McCarter's mind as he and his teammates made for the back of the yacht where Grimaldi would pick them up.

The first was how much time they had to get off the yacht before it started taking on water. The second was how to evacuate the remaining passengers. It might have contented some men to let the crewmembers drown but that wasn't McCarter's style—it sure as hell wasn't something of which his colleagues and friends would approve. And McCarter wasn't a murderer or a heartless killer. He killed out of loyalty and duty, and then only as a last resort.

These men, while they had resisted Phoenix Force, were mostly operating under orders and it wouldn't serve any purpose to leave them to the terror of the depths. No. He was the mission commander and it was his responsibility to make sure they got off safely. The problem he had was that they couldn't operate the two choppers that close together. Just not safe in this wind and given the choppy waters, the turbulence of which was increasing by the minute.

McCarter slapped Encizo's arm as he ran past and shouted to be heard. "Rafe! I need you to make sure the rest of the team gets aboard the chopper."

"What the hell you talking about?"

"The crew—" he pointed toward the survivors who were now cloistered together near the stern and looking a bit dumbstruck "—needs someone to evacuate them."

Encizo shook his head. "No dice, David! I'll stay behind and get them out. I have more experience."

"My mission, my call. Damn it, Rafe, that's an order! Now *go!*"

McCarter shoved Encizo astern and the Cuban didn't resist. He didn't like McCarter's decision but he knew the Phoenix Force leader was correct. It was his prerogative to make it right, and his first duty was to obey orders irrespective of what it might cost them. There was nothing unethical or illegal about McCarter's command, and so Encizo knew the best thing he could do was to obey it.

Even as he made his way toward the stern where the six survivors stood, McCarter figured the situation to be pretty grave. It would take at least eight minutes for his teammates to get aboard that chopper. Grimaldi would have to hold position above a yacht on an ever-more-turbulent Mediterranean. Each warrior would have to ascend a sixty-foot rescue ladder in full gear at an average of two minutes per man. On top of all that, the other chopper couldn't get close enough to take those off the stern for safety reasons. A sinking boat in waters this rough could shift and spin around in very unpredictable fashions, and to put the two Seahawks in proximity under such conditions wasn't just unsafe, it was plain stupid.

McCarter reached the others and shouted, "Any of you speak English?"

One of the men raised his hand.

"You got lifeboats?"

The man nodded and pointed to the port side.

McCarter gestured for him to lead the way and indicated the others should follow. True to his predictions, the boat suddenly shifted and tossed nearly all of them prone to the deck. Only one man remained standing, obviously having better sea legs than the rest. McCarter quickly gained his feet. He felt pain in the middle finger of his left hand and realized he'd broken it when it got pinned between his weapon and the deck. McCarter cursed and then unslung the MP-5 and tossed it over the side. No point in carrying any more than necessary—he still had his pistol in case one or more of the sailors thought to seize an advantage. McCarter shed his backpack, as well, and then directed the men to lower the lifeboat.

McCarter took notice of another boat toward the port side astern but he didn't think it a wise idea. Powerboats of that kind were okay on calmer waters but they could be death traps in this rolling sea and he had no idea if it even had enough fuel. It didn't look like a standard attachment, anyway. Plus, the lifeboats were equipped with life preservers that were visible after they had removed the tarps. Most importantly, this crew had obviously been drilled well; they were deploying the boat like clockwork, so he'd at least have a crew familiar with its capabilities and operation.

McCarter hesitated when the man who spoke English dropped the boat and then ordered him over the side, but McCarter realized in that moment this must have been one of the officers aboard the yacht. McCarter didn't think him the captain but he did realize that the guy felt it necessary to ensure the rest of them were on the boat before he felt comfortable abandoning ship. McCarter looked over the side and saw the others were already descending the ladder so he nodded at the man and then followed suit.

When his feet touched bottom he looked up and waited but he didn't see the man—not even a silhouette or movement. He heard the guy shout something in what sounded like Greek and then he realized the crewmembers were moving the boat away from the yacht. McCarter started yelling at them but they ignored him. Even when the Phoenix Force leader yanked his pistol from its holster he realized the futility of it. Yeah, the guy *had* been some sort of officer and he'd elected to go down with his ship.

McCarter couldn't understand it but he could respect it, and as they moved out from the yacht he saw the faint outline of the man who had chosen to stay behind. He knew the guy probably couldn't see it but McCarter tossed him a salute. It was in that moment he realized the guy had chosen to sacrifice his own life, maybe in an attempt to save the vessel and maybe because he'd seen McCarter wasn't going to leave them behind to just drown. Whatever the guy's reason, it left McCarter with an almost unexplainable sense of emptiness.

When they were well clear of the ship, McCarter saw the first vestiges of the damage. The explosive blasts had weakened the structure enough to cause damage. Fires within the superstructure of the yacht were now starting to cut through the hull. McCarter noted also that the stern of the ship had begun to dip ever so slightly and he knew before too long the ship would begin to capsize before it nosed hard down with its ass coming straight up.

Whoever had sabotaged the yacht had known what he was doing. McCarter couldn't help but wonder, but only a moment, if it hadn't been Madari. He quickly dismissed the thought. The guy didn't have that kind of honor. There had only been one of those EMP prototypes aboard that vessel and Madari had claimed to have more than that. Given the size of the lab at his island bunker and other intelligence to that point, McCarter couldn't believe Madari had been on the yacht.

No, the bastard was still alive and McCarter was certain he knew exactly where he was headed. They needed to get out of this theater as quickly as possible and get back to the States. And he needed to report to Stony Man their findings here and exactly what they had encountered. McCarter's earbud signaled for attention.

"Go ahead!" he shouted.

"You okay, Leader One?"

"Wet and cold, mate," he replied. "But I'll live."

"Stand by," Grimaldi said. "We have you on IFR and the second chopper's moving in to extract you. And you might want to hurry because we've been informed by the *Resolute* we may soon have some company."

McCarter pressed his lips together in puzzlement. Then he asked, "Company from whom, Eagle One?"

"Libyan Air Force?" Captain Samuel Garth shook his head. "What the hell are you talking about, Number One?"

"That's what they say, sir. Claim our choppers have entered Libyan air space and they're warning us off."

"Tell them we're in the middle of—" he shook his head "—never mind, give me the phone."

Jankovich handed it to him and Garth said immediately, "This is American destroyer USS *Resolute,* Captain Garth commanding. To whom am I speaking?"

"This is Colonel Ahmed al-Yunis, Libyan Air Force."

"Sir, I understand you've threatened to dispatch aircraft to deter our aircraft you claim to be within your airspace."

"I don't *claim* them to be in my airspace, Captain," al-Yunis replied. "They *are* in our airspace. The observed airspace of my country is twelve nautical miles, and your aircraft are at nine miles. That's three miles inside the acceptable zone and they have failed to answer our calls of warning. I can only assume—"

"I beg your pardon, Colonel, but you can't assume anything. If your systems have picked them up then you must also realize there's a yacht there in distress, a yacht belonging to a citizen of Greece. We were asked to assist in their rescue."

"We know all about the yacht, Captain."

"You do?"

"That's correct. They sent a distress call to us more than two hours ago advising that they were experiencing trouble with one of their engines and requesting permission to dock at Derna. We granted that permission and once they entered Libyan waters they became our responsibility. So it is *you* who are interfering in this incident."

"We've been advised the ship is taking on water, sir," Garth said. "We were very close and heard their distress call so I sent two choppers to evacuate the crew."

Garth was mindful to maintain tact and diplomatic communications at all times, as well as to observe military courtesies. Technically, the colonel outranked him and it wouldn't do to say anything that could be misconstrued as disrespectful. Despite the fact he had tremendous authority and power at his disposal, Garth knew the call was being recorded and he knew the Libyans would also be recording.

Garth continued. "With all due respect, Colonel—"

"Captain, we have repeatedly warned your craft to cease and desist whatever they are doing and to leave our boundaries immediately. They have chosen not to reply to us, and so I'm left with no choice but assume their intent is hostile."

Something clutched at Garth's stomach but he did his best to ignore it. He wanted to engage this pompous ass with a scathing retort but he didn't dare. The President had not authorized him to create an international incident, only to get their mission accomplished at whatever cost. He was about to render more excuses, stalling the man for time, when Jankovich hissed at him.

"What?" Garth asked a little more forcefully than he'd intended.

"It's the mission leader, sir," Jankovich said. "He says they are clear and returning at best possible speed."

Garth nodded, raised a fist high in a sign of victory and then returned his attention to al-Yunis. "Colonel, there's obviously been some sort of mix-up here. But let me assure you our intentions are non-hostile toward Libya or any other foreign powers. I have, in fact, recalled the choppers. You are free to take whatever action you choose."

"You will order those aircraft to remain where they are and be prepared to receive Libyan military investigators."

"I'm afraid that's not possible, Colonel al-Yunis."

"And why not?"

"Because they've already left your airspace, just as you requested, and are now in international waters. You have no jurisdiction at this point."

"Are you tempting me to use force?" al-Yunis demanded, the apoplexy in his tone nearly palpable.

"I'm doing nothing of the kind, sir," Garth replied. "But let me be *very* clear when I say that those aircraft and the men aboard them are members of the United

States Navy and they are now flying under the international waters protected by NATO treaty. Therefore, any attempt to shoot down or deter those craft while in said airspace will be considered a hostile act and I am authorized to respond with the fullest force at my disposal to neutralize any such act. Am I being clear?"

A long, almost toxic silence followed but al-Yunis finally muttered an acknowledgment in the affirmative before disconnecting the call.

AFTER TURNING THE crew over to the SPs for holding until they could be debriefed, and delivering a short verbal report to Garth and Jankovich, Phoenix Force assembled in a temporary and isolated area aboard the ship set aside for their privacy. They had bunks, hot chow and showers at their disposal—leaving each man on the team with a new appreciation for U.S. naval hospitality.

"You know, this reminds of—" Hawkins began.

"Save it for your blog, Hawk," James cut in cheerily.

Hawkins laughingly flipped him the bird. "What a buzz kill."

"All right, stifle the guffaws for just a bloody moment, won't you?"

They gave the Phoenix Force leader their undivided attention. "We a got a bit of time to rest up before we lift off."

"How long is a bit?" Manning asked.

"About two hours, give or take. Jack's advised he needs to do a full work-up on the helicopter we brought from Athens...refuel and so forth. As soon as I hear from him, we'll be struts off here and headed back to our plane."

"Then home, sweet home?" Hawkins asked.

"Yeah. But I don't know how sweet it's going to be. I just got off the horn with the Farm. They were disappointed that we couldn't save the ship but understanding. Barb wanted me to personally let each of you know how glad she is we all came through this scrape alive."

"Score one for the good guys," James said, licking his finger and swiping an imaginary one in the air.

"Don't celebrate yet, mate. We got a long haul back and once we arrive we'll need to provide backup to Able Team."

"What's the problem?" Encizo asked.

"Seems that Madari's still alive," McCarter said. "And from every scrap of intelligence they've gathered at that end, Madari's been in bed with Steinham the entire time."

"Steinham?" Manning shook his head. "You mean the defense guy who sent those Cyclops people after us?"

"Exactly," McCarter said. "Except it wasn't us he sent Cyclops after, it was Stanish. Remember?"

"Yeah, and let's not forget she's still in the wind," Hawkins interjected.

McCarter frowned. "Wrong. She's dead."

"That confirmed?" Encizo asked.

"About as confirmed as I think we're going to get. I managed to talk to one of those crewmen we rescued through a Greek interpreter they had aboard. Seems she was the one who lit off the fuses on the yacht. She blew up the engines and he's a hundred percent convinced she blew herself up with them."

"What the hell for?" James asked.

McCarter shook his head with a sad expression. "I don't bloody know, Cal. I guess she had some sort of thing going with Madari, or near as I could gather from sailor boy. She was brought aboard some time earlier yesterday afternoon. She and the captain got into a quarrel over something and she ended up shooting him, although apparently it sounds as if she did so in self-defense."

Encizo muttered something under his breath and then said, "Too bad. A real waste—you know?"

"I know." McCarter cleared his throat. "Anyway, I don't know what drove that woman but I think she was a bit of a bloody loon. And while we don't know her reasons, we do know she was aboard and Madari wasn't. So our thought this yacht was a decoy was spot-on."

"So if Madari's not headed to Libya and he has the weapons, what makes us think he'll go to America?" Manning asked. "Why not just take Dratshev and the prototypes somewhere else and keep working on them? Build more and perfect them. I mean, Madari doesn't actually think he change the tide of political and social unrest in Libya with just a few weapons. Right?"

"I don't know what the guy's thinking," McCarter said. "But if he's anything like Mishka, he's probably a bit of a loon himself. And they're convinced that Madari's going to the States so he can settle a score with Steinham. I guess he's figuring he can test the weapons and get his revenge on Steinham. Kill two birds with one stone."

"Makes sense," Hawkins said.

"So what's the play, then?" James asked.

"There's a meeting of defense contractors at 2000 local time in Washington on Friday."

"That's tomorrow!" Hawkins interjected.

"We're ahead of them by eight hours, chief."

"Ah, yeah—forgot about that. Sorry."

"We need to get there in time to back Able Team. They don't have the resources capable of covering every avenue, and they don't want to rely on trying to put together something with the FBI or Secret Service on such short notice."

"Just how many attendees are we talking at this conference?" Manning asked.

"Damn near five hundred."

James let out a low whistle. "They use those EMPs on a crowd of that size it'll be a mass slaughter."

"Exactly what has the Farm worried. And why they want us to beat feet back there as quick as our arses will carry us. So let's get our gear checked and weapons inventoried so we can give them to Grimaldi to load. Then you'll have a little time to get cleaned up and eat. We'll go in pairs. I'll go last with Jack."

As they broke up to attend to their individual tasks and made small talk with one another, McCarter assessed each of them with a once-over. His chest swelled with pride. They'd done more than their fair share, accomplished everything asked of them, and without complaint they were going to head straight into the face of another terror storm undaunted. They were one hell of a team, and the best friends for which any warrior could ever ask.

CHAPTER TWENTY-FIVE

Cyclops Base Camp, Virginia

Riley Braden dragged his tired body through the door of the HQ building at the Cyclops base camp. Every muscle ached. All he wanted was a hot shower and comfortable bunk, but he could see by the expression on Colonel Jack Cyrus's face that wasn't going to happen. Braden ordered his two teammates to go do what it was he couldn't and then slung his gear pack on a nearby table and dropped into a chair like deadweight.

"I can tell you don't have much good news for me, Jack."

They were alone so he dispensed with the military formalities.

Cyrus propped his butt on the corner of his desk and folded his arms. He seemed almost pained, something he rarely demonstrated unless he had really bad news to communicate.

"I'm afraid you're right."

"Well, don't keep me in suspense. What's going on?"

"First, I owe you an apology."

"Huh? What the hell are you talking about?"

Cyrus sighed and looked toward the ceiling, obviously trying to collect his thoughts. "Riley, we've known each other for a long time. We grew up together, we joined the military together and we even served side by side on a few missions."

"That's the bad news?"

"No."

"Well then, quit taking us on a walk down memory lane and get to telling me why you're apologizing to me."

"My point is that we've known each other a long time—you know me probably better than anyone. And you know how personally I take the safety of the men under my command. I allowed my judgment to get clouded by this contract with Steinham. As a result, I jeopardized you by allowing this mission—no...this *farce*—to go on. I should have been stronger and fought Steinham on it."

Braden was definitely lost now. It wasn't so much the words or tone in Cyrus's voice, but the haunted look that seemed chiseled into his features. "Who says the mission was a farce?"

"I do," Cyrus said. "Steinham's been playing us for suckers from the beginning. He's been in cahoots with Madari all this time. You remember when he told us that they tried to create EMP weapons but their research didn't lead them anywhere?"

"Yeah, sure."

Cyrus nodded, rose and circled the desk to sit in his own seat before continuing. "DCDI had a five-year R and D contract with the U.S. government to come up with some technology related to EMP weaponry. It was only supposed to be for large-weapon tech, but Steinham was convinced he could bring it to small-arms technology, too. When it got close to the end of the contract and he realized they weren't going to be able to come up with something substantial, Steinham cooked up the scheme to kidnap Oleg Dratshev."

"What? That's insane—defense contracts aren't supposed to be in the business of kidnapping and collaboration with fanatics."

"Agreed. But he didn't think Madari was a fanatic, except about wanting to institute democratic rule in Libya. Steinham thought he could accomplish dual purposes that would solidify the United States as a technological power in the world."

"We already are," Braden interjected.

Cyrus shook his head. "We're falling behind quickly, Riley. We're sucking the hind tit to countries like China and the Saudis. They've been putting their money and resources into something tangible while we've been stuffing the straw man by torchlight."

"Did you know about this, Jack?"

Cyrus shook his head. "I knew as much about it as you did, and that's the honest truth. I didn't know he'd put himself in bed with Madari."

"So then what happened? Why did Madari betray him?"

"Steinham tells me it's because the government transferred some of his tech to the Libyans, the same Libyans that were responsible for killing Madari's family and exiling him."

"You believe him?"

Cyrus splayed his hands and shrugged. "I have no reason *not* to. But now Steinham's convinced Madari is coming here to kill him. And he's asking for our protection."

Braden sat for a long moment, his throat burning as he tried to stuff his anger deep in his gut. He quietly replied, "Let the bastard burn, Jack."

"Under other circumstances I wouldn't hesitate. But the fact is we have a contract with him and we're bound to honor it. Honor and duty are the only two things we have left, and I won't sully the name of Cyclops or any of the brave men who have sacrificed what America stands for."

"Cyclops doesn't stand for Steinham."

"No, it doesn't. But we *do* stand for the safety of this nation and despite the fact we fight for money I cannot stand idly by and let Madari waste innocent Americans."

"What are you talking about?"

"We pulled the bacon of an American SOG unit out of the fire last night. They told us that there's evidence to support the possibility Madari has managed to develop some prototypes of these energy pulse weapons. Hell, I don't understand all the technical bullshit, but I got the gist based on what they described to me. And Steinham confirmed this is a very real threat. If Madari comes after Steinham, he won't care who else gets in the way."

"You're saying Madari's not concerned about collateral damage."

"Right. He wants one thing and that is to kill Steinham—but he also wants to know these weapons will work so he can use them to fight his personal war with the Libyan government."

"So he's not a freedom fighter, he's a terrorist."

"I'd say if he couldn't care less about innocent bystanders then…yeah. He's a terrorist and we have to view him as such."

"Well, sounds like Steinham fixed us all real good. Didn't he?"

"No, I was responsible for letting myself be suckered by him." Cyrus shook his head. "I didn't do right by you, Riley. I didn't do right by any of us. I'm the CO of Cyclops.

The safety and welfare of every man in my command is my responsibility, including yours."

"And it's just that attitude that explains why we joined up." Braden scratched absently at his five-day beard. "I can only speak for myself, Jack. But I'm up for whatever you think is best. I don't want to be on the team that's protecting Steinham, but I'm more than happy to meet Madari head-on."

Cyrus nodded slowly, the relief evident in his expression. "Thank you, Riley."

"Don't mention it." Braden climbed to his feet, came to attention and then saluted. "And now, Colonel, if you don't mind, I'd like to get cleaned up."

Cyrus stood and returned the salute, then checked his watch. "You have about six hours. Get some sleep and I'll have you roused when I'm ready. I'll be working through strategy and tactics for this mission. We're going to make sure everyone comes out of it alive."

Braden turned and started to leave but then thought better of it and stopped. "Colonel?"

"Yeah."

"That SOG unit you helped."

"What about them?"

"We ran into a similar outfit in Belarus. They were also on a mission to find Madari. They let us go and advised we should stay out of it because they couldn't guarantee we wouldn't get caught on opposite sides of the line next time."

Cyrus nodded. "I had a very similar conversation with these men."

"You think they're together?"

"I don't know," Cyrus replied. "It's possible. But if they are, based on what I've seen of their skills, Madari won't stand a snowball's chance in hell of going up against them—doesn't matter how many prototypes he's got."

"You may want to account for their involvement. If we know what's going on with Madari, then it's a pretty good bet they know, as well. They may already be preparing for him to come."

"I'll take it under advisement. But I won't let it deter us from our mission under any circumstances. One way or another, we're going to stop Madari. Let's just hope we don't clash with these special operators."

"And if we do?"

"We'll burn that bridge when we come to it, Major."

"Yes, sir."

Even as Braden departed for the officer barracks, he thought about the team they'd encountered in Belarus. He'd seen those men in action, too. He'd watched them take out the security at the alleged FSB safehouse and he'd talked with their leader at some length. Braden had developed a significant amount of respect for those men. And for the very first time, he wondered if Cyclops could survive another such encounter.

FOR THE FIRST time he could remember in a long time, Ishaq Madari felt nervous.

A torrential downpour and hazy skies had delayed the landing of his plane, and it took even longer to await investigators from the U.S. Immigration and Customs Enforcement to complete their inspection. Madari felt they were a bit more thorough than under normal circumstances but he remained as congenial as possible. His passport and other documents, forged naturally along with the credentials he'd provided for Dratshev, were pristine and hardly got more than a cursory glance. No, the ICE officials seemed more interested in the aircraft aboard in which he'd smuggled the prototypes.

"Your flight plan indicates you came here by way of Athens," the lead agent said.

"Yes. Is there a problem?"

"Not at all, Mr. Darmi. Your documents are all in order and the inspectors are just about finished looking over your cargo. You're in technical materials exports?"

"Yes, sir."

"And what is that, exactly?"

"Mostly raw materials, substrates and purified aluminum. A little bit of silver, but as you've noted there we have pre-paid the duties and export fees on those, and they are in very small quantities." Madari tried for an ingratiating smile. "These materials are utilized mostly in computers and such, for the manufacture of chips."

The customs officer seemed to ignore the little lesson, choosing to grunt as an acknowledgment of what he'd just been told.

"And what again is the purpose of your visit to the United States?"

"I'm here strictly on business. I am to attend a meeting in Washington and when that's completed I'll return here and fly home."

The officer nodded and then paused as one of the inspectors came up behind him and whispered in his ear. The guy listened, although not apparently too intently, and then muttered something in reply before returning his full attention to Madari.

"I've just been informed our inspection is complete." The ICE guy handed Madari his passport and other documents, which included the equipment manifest.

Fortunately the disassembled weapons were so futuristic-looking it appeared they had fooled even hardened U.S. customs inspectors. Beside the fact, they obviously had other pressing duties and other aircraft to inspect, and this wasn't the first time Madari had visited the United States—or so that's what all his documentation indicated.

"You have a nice evening, sir."

Within five minutes the inspectors were off the plane and on to their next assignment. Madari breathed a sigh of relief as he watched them drive away. He realized a sheen of sweat had formed on his upper lip, moistening his trimmed mustache, and he wiped at it with irritation. Madari indulged in a moment of self-rebuke—he shouldn't have allowed them to make him that nervous. Only his years of experience as a security officer had helped him to remain rock-steady.

Madari shook it off and turned his attention to Dratshev, who had sat calmly aboard the plane and witnessed the entire exchange. Dratshev smiled. "You seem edgy."

"I'm not," Madari lied. "I was just becoming irritated with them. They were taking too long and I thought perhaps our cover had been blown."

"That would most certainly have ruined your plans."

"Of course."

"So now I'm curious to know exactly what your intentions are, and if there's ever a chance you will release me. Or did you just plan to murder me in cold blood once I'd accomplished your purpose?"

Dratshev's cavalier attitude irritated Madari but he could understand it. Dratshev had been an unwilling ally from the start, and had done what he had only out of scientific curiosity. A part of Madari had thought to kill Dratshev, but another part thought he'd be a useful tool in the future. And they still didn't have a hundred percent guarantee that the devices he'd designed would actually work in the long-term sense.

"To be perfectly honest, I haven't decided. If I release you, Oleg…what would you do with your freedom?"

"It depends on where you release me. I'd prefer not to be let go here in America. And if you choose to kill me then I'd hope you would at least have the common courtesy to ship my remains back to my mother country. Despite the fact they have done nothing to promote my research and hard work, it is still my home."

"A reasonable request and one I will honor. You have my word."

"I would much rather have my freedom."

"All in good time," Madari said. "For now, you'll remain here under guard."

"You only brought a crew of four. You have many more weapons than that at your disposal and that won't leave any guards."

"Those men are strictly acting as handlers for the prototypes. In fact, I have a significant force that should be arriving shortly to make the transfer. They will be the ones to actually use the weapons for the operation I have in mind. Don't worry—we shall return victorious. But in case we don't, and if there's any doubt in your mind, rest assured our failure will mean your death. Of this you can be certain."

Washington, D.C.

"IRONMAN, WE JUST got a call from Bear," announced Schwarz.

Lyons and Blancanales were at the dining-room table

of an apartment Stony Man Farm maintained in the city, checking their equipment and working to restock Betty from their previous ventures.

Lyons didn't even look up, focused on his task as he set the mag he'd been loading on the table and replied, "What about?"

"He says they got a bead on Madari. He just landed via plane in Norfolk."

"Norfolk?" Blancanales echoed. He looked at Lyons. "Why Norfolk?"

Silence dropped like a lead weight as the three urban commandos exchanged knowing glances. They'd all reached the same conclusion in that moment, realizing with horror that they'd made a tactical miscalculation.

Lyons said, "There wouldn't be any reason for Madari to go there unless…"

"The target wasn't Steinham at all," Blancanales said. "The target is Cyclops."

"Grab your shit, boys," Lyons said. "We need to get there and now."

"You want us to get Betty loaded?" Schwarz asked.

"Yeah."

Blancanales said, "Ironman—your call, but it might be faster to commandeer a chopper."

"Doubtful," Lyons said with a dismissive wave. "By the time we got to Dulles, transferred our equipment and got airborne, we could just about be there."

His teammates nodded in unison as they began to gather their equipment and head for Black Betty, which they'd parked downstairs. Lyons considered asking Stony Man for local military support, maybe something from Craney Island, but quickly dismissed the idea. Not only would that violate the rules for use of military force on U.S. soil but there would be a whole lot of publicity around it.

The Cyclops camp was in a very remote region, and if they could confine the use of the EMP prototypes to that area it would pose much less of a hazard to innocent bystanders. Sadly, it bothered Lyons that he had no way of warning Cyrus. They were in a remote area with no means of communication—part of their attempt to remain isolated and off the radar. Electronics would have made them vulnerable to hacking, part of the reason Cyrus had bought the land under trust in the first place.

"I don't understand it," Blancanales said as they climbed aboard Black Betty. "How the hell could Madari have known about Cyclops and the location of their training site?"

"Probably had Steinham's place bugged," Lyons replied.

"Makes sense," Schwarz agreed. "They managed to plant a bug on Ironman without any of us knowing it for some time. It would only stand to reason Madari's resources stretch far enough to get inside Steinham's organization."

"Not to mention everybody he's dealt with," Lyons added.

"That means we have a much larger security concern," Blancanales said. "For all we know, Madari could have an entire army of hired guns at his disposal operating right here on U.S. soil. I'm sure he wouldn't be stupid enough to go up against Cyclops with just a few novice dudes toting prototype weapons."

"That's a troublesome thought," Lyons replied. "Blast it, we can't be everywhere at once! Gadgets, did you get an ETA on Phoenix Force?"

"They're still about six hours out," Schwarz replied.

"Let's contact the Farm and let them know what we got," Lyons said. "At least David and friends will know there's been a change in plans."

"*If* there's a change in plans," Blancanales said. "Madari may still plan to deal with Steinham after he's hit Cyclops."

"That doesn't make much sense," Schwarz said.

"It does from a tactical standpoint. Madari isn't going after Cyclops to hurt Steinham. He's going after them so they can hurt him."

Lyons's ice-blue eyes flashed with wicked resolve. "Not if we hurt him first."

CHAPTER TWENTY-SIX

Rural Virginia

The electromagnetic pulse wave that hit the sentry shack wasn't anything for which Colonel Jack Cyrus or any of his men could have prepared. There was no way to shield against such a pulse, except maybe in a bunker deep underground, and absolutely no way to repel a beam of such magnitude. Even coming from a small rifle like the one Madari's terrorist fighter used, the results were far greater than anyone could have imagined.

For a heartbeat it seemed as though nothing extraordinary happened—then the unthinkable occurred right in front of every man in Madari's force. The shack seemed to both implode and eject. Everything made of metal turned to slag and anything not nailed down seemed to almost explode. The effect of the weapon on the bodies of the two sentries inside was even more spectacular.

Perhaps the better description might have been gruesome.

The two men were separated from their limbs, as shoulders and legs were ripped from sockets. One of the men caught a sufficient enough part of the pulse that it actually tore his head from his body. Blood and bodily fluids splattered the inside of the shack and were immediately charbroiled, the blood reaching boiling temperatures in a matter of milliseconds. Then the shack came utterly apart and its remains were projected in every direction.

The man who had fired the weapon lowered it and swore under his breath, looking at the pair on either side of him. These two were armed with merely conventional assault rifles, and neither of them could help but look at their comrade who was wielding a weapon of unbelievably fearsome power. No bazooka or RPG could have done that kind of damage in that moment. In fact, nothing short of a miniature nuclear bomb could have performed in the same fashion.

"Quit staring at each other and get moving!" their team leader ordered.

The trio burst from cover and sprinted toward the makeshift road of mud and sand. There was a complement of twenty-five men in all, each a trained member of the Libyan rebel forces and all with some measure of combat experience. In addition, Madari had equipped them with most of the EMP prototypes; an understandable choice considering theirs was the more daunting task.

The thing that had worried the commander of the group the most was what sort of resistance they faced inside. The Cyclops team was, according to all of Madari's intelligence, no more than a dozen strong. Each of them was much more experienced than the majority of this force if numbered in combined pairs. The 2:1 ratio was only adequate given the tremendous firepower and advanced weapons at their disposal, as the onset of their attack had just so clearly demonstrated.

Once the three point men were inside the perimeter, the team leader gave the signal through their transmitters. With a roar of engines, two dump trucks—modified to serve as personnel carriers—breached the perimeter and raced up the road. Each of the trucks had ten men with the EMP small-arms split equally between them, three per vehicle.

They also had a trailer towing one of the two large-scale weapons Madari had smuggled into the country. It had taken their teams some time to accurately assemble the weaponry, but Madari had assured the group commander that time was on their side.

"The Americans are stupid," he'd said. "Careless. They are unprepared for anything like this."

That hadn't really allayed the force commander's concerns, but he knew better than to argue. He didn't think putting their faith in superior firepower alone was wise. Experienced men and a good battle plan were the keys to victory in any combat strategy, something that could not be substituted by superior numbers or equipment—this had been proved time and again. Still, the commander had to admit after seeing the capabilities of the EMP prototypes that they stood a *very* good chance of being victorious this night.

The trucks rolled up the muddy rutted lane, which opened onto the main camp. The man they had managed to get inside the camp and gather pictures and intelligence had indicated the locations of the key buildings they needed to hit. The first stage of the plan called for them to use the heavy weapons to take out the barracks. From there, they would move the assault to the other buildings. Madari had left one directive: no prisoners. It was to be a scorched-earth assault and the commander of the attack force relished the idea. Tonight, to the Libyan revolutionaries would go the spoils of war.

And the Americans would learn what it meant to taste the revenge of freedom fighters!

THE OCCUPANTS OF the two vehicles seemed so intent on whatever their mission, they failed to notice the vehicle parked in the shadows of the trees less than fifty yards from the entrance to the camp. Of course, it was good reason. The matte-black, Kevlar-lined body of Black Betty was not only designed to repel radar but also other types of tracking. It could blend into the night as few others of its kind, and the men of Able Team were thankful for that much.

"Looks like your hypothesis was correct, Ironman," Blancanales remarked from his position behind the wheel.

"I can't take all the credit," Lyons said. He looked at his friend with a cheesy grin and added, "Madari's hardly an evil mastermind."

"Yeah, well, he's an evil something."

"Did you see what that weapon did?" Schwarz asked.

Blancanales groaned. "Oh, for the third time, *yes,* Gadgets. For pity sake we were all sitting right here."

"That's enough chatter," Lyons growled. "Let's do this. Gadgets, keep your eyes and ears open. I don't want to get blown to hell by one of those EMP weapons."

"It's not going to be easy to avoid," Blancanales said as he started the engine and eased the van from the dense foliage. "Are you sure it wasn't a good idea to just warn them?"

"I'm sure," Lyons said. "We'll be much better off taking them by surprise."

"I feel for those two sentries," Blancanales said.

Lyons grit his teeth. "I know. I do, too. But there wasn't

anything we could do about it. We didn't know they were
going to go that route, and if we did I'm still not sure there
was anything we could do about it. Besides, they knew
the risks of being in a PMC. Hell, we take the same risk
every day."

With that, Blancanales gunned the engine and bore
down on the entrance to the camp. Madari's terrorists had
left two sentries behind, and Lyons had already decided
on the best way to handle them. Just as they reached proximity, he rolled down his window and yanked the pin on
an M-67 fragmentation grenade. Blancanales slowed the
van and Lyons leaned out the window.

"Hey there, fellas!" he shouted as he reached out his
hand and dropped the grenade at their feet. "Happen to
know the way to Hell?"

The pair was so stunned by the brashness of the move
they failed to notice the grenade until it was too late. They
got what Lyons would later describe as "two of the dumb-
est looks I've ever seen on a terrorist's face" just before
the grenade went off. The explosion blew them to bits,
rendering them to a fate not too dissimilar to the one suffered by their victims in the guard shack, but by that time
Black Betty had cleared the effective blast area. Only a
charring smudge had been left on her bumper in the wake
of the blast.

WHEN TWO OF the Cyclops men coming out of the barracks saw the massive dump trucks, they weren't sure
what to think. It was an odd time of night for deliveries,
and they hadn't heard about Colonel Cyrus ordering any
new equipment. It took only a moment for them to realize
this was too highly irregular to be anything but trouble.
Both men whirled and sprinted for the barracks to warn

their comrades, but in that span of precious time the terrorists were already pouring out of the trucks.

The commander, who had been riding shotgun in one of the dump trucks, leaped from his perch and began to direct his men. He had opted not to take possession of one of the EMP prototypes, concerned that if something went wrong they could well end up without leadership. These men had trained month after month under his guidance, and he did not think them prepared enough to operate on their own.

As they fanned out to take up supporting positions for those with the EMPs, the commander shouting orders, none of them bothered to check their flank. As far as they knew, they were covered by the pair of sentries they had left behind. So they took no notice of the sleek, matte-black van that arrived just as they were preparing to deploy the EMP rifles against the barracks building.

"SEE THEM?" Blancanales asked.

"I see them. All right, you guys, we take out the ones with the funny-looking rifles first. That should level the playing field and buy Cyrus's men enough time to pull their asses together."

"Roger that," Schwarz said.

Blancanales brought the van to a halt and swung it into a position so they could use it most effectively for cover. The three warriors then bailed with full assault rifles in play. Lyons and Blancanales were toting M-16 A3s with 40 mm grenade launchers mounted below them. Schwarz had opted to bring a heavier weapon into the mix, dropping from the back of the van with an Mk 43 machine gun. The latest variant of the classic M-60 design, and identical to the M-60 E4 light machine gun with the exception of a slightly shorter barrel, the weapon was rugged and dependable, and Schwarz couldn't think of another crew weapon he'd prefer to have in such a situation.

By the time the majority of the Libyan terrorists realized they were no longer on the offensive and should now take up a defensive posture, it was much too late. Lyons and Blancanales scraped knees and elbows hitting the ground but the maneuver saved them from what scant couple of volleys the terrorists did manage to get off. Then it all went to hell for them.

Lyons caught his closest target on the first short burst he triggered. The 5.56 mm rounds tore through the man's gut and drove him to the ground. Lyons followed with a second burst, two rounds catching the figure next to his previous target in the chest and the third one clipping the top of his skull and blowing it off in a spray of bone fragments and bloody fluid.

Blancanales delivered his own destructive volleys with the same deadly accuracy as his teammate. He wasn't unfamiliar with combat by any means, but that was only overshadowed by his immense understanding of the capabilities of the M-16 A3. He'd utilized every known variant of the weapon since entering the U.S. military and even beyond that as trusted member of Able Team. With the right ammunition and in the hands of a trained marksman, the weapon was one of the most accurate in the world.

A terrorist toting one of the EMP weapons quickly found this out as Blancanales triggered two successive bursts that landed on target. Some of the bullets shattered the delicate pieces of the prototype while others punctured abdominal organs, lungs and heart. Blood erupted from nearly every orifice left by the rounds, and a couple even continued on an outward path that left splotchy patterns on the man's back—visible only because the impact spun him with the force of the autofire.

Blancanales delivered another volley, holding low, but it fell short and chewed the dirt as his intended target backpedaled to find cover behind one of the trucks. The moment of advantage in surprise for Able Team had passed and the terrorists were now getting organized. Some grabbed the nearest cover of the trucks while others went prone and began to set up interlocking fields of fire.

Lyons and Blancanales low-crawled toward the cover of the rear of Betty as Schwarz took a knee near the rear bumper and eased back the trigger. The M-60 E4 shimmied in his hands as he pounded the terrorist force with an endless stream of 7.62 mm NATO rounds, the familiar chug-chug-chug of the weapon somewhat like music to his ears.

What the Able Team warriors failed to notice, however, was that one of the men holding an EMP prototype seemed undaunted in completing his mission: the destruction of the Cyclops mercenaries.

Colonel Jack Cyrus was leaned over the conference table in the planning room, studying a map and technical blueprints of the DCDI facilities when the sound of autofire in the distance reached him. He whipped his head around and stared at the windows that were shuttered with thin, steel-brushed lead. He dashed to one after a moment of verifying he had indeed heard the shooting. There'd been no training exercise scheduled to his recollection.

Cyrus flipped one of the metal shutters aside—and what he saw horrified him. Two trucks with canvas tops were parked within a couple dozen yards of the building. A staggered line of armed men had set up position and were firing in the direction of the buildings; as well, others seemed to be exchanging fire with unseen foes to their flank.

"What the he—?"

Cyrus never got to finish the thought as rounds began to pelt the exterior wall of the HQ building, which was a modified Quonset hut. Cyrus slapped the shutter closed and fastened it, and then rushed from the planning room and headed straight to the spare armory. The sounds of combat were growing more intense by the moment, but Cyrus pushed any distractions from his mind as he selected an AR-15 from the rack. He added to it a bandolier of six full magazines and half a dozen grenades.

Cyrus moved to another area and yanked his flak jacket off a rotary hanger system. He donned the Kevlar vest, then slung the bandolier over his body, slammed a fresh magazine into the assault rifle and put the weapon in battery. Cyrus pivoted on his heel and charged down the hallway to a side entrance. He'd come out on the far side of the building, which would give him the advantage. He could come up on the invader's flank.

Cyrus had worked hard to make his company a success. He wasn't about to let these thugs take that away from him. He couldn't imagine who his enemy was but he had a pretty good guess. Madari. Nothing else made sense.

Well, he'd planned to make his stand and if he had to do it then better to do it right here on his own turf.

Cyrus punched through the door and into the steaming night. Humidity was high and mugginess hit his face like a wave. He wheeled to the left and moved up the side of the HQ building, weapon held in a ready state. He reached the corner and peered around it. From this vantage point he could see who had engaged the enemy to their rear—he recognized the sleek van—no mistaking the men who were fighting alongside it.

Cyrus grinned. Those tough bastards, he thought.

Cyrus saw one of the terrorists raise something to his shoulder. It had a super-long barrel with a boxy stock. It looked strange and awkward, like something out of a science fiction movie, and yet it must have been light because the terrorist seemed to wield it with uncanny ease. For a moment nothing appeared to happen and then the air around the barrel shimmered with heat. Cyrus realized with terror that it was one of the EMP prototypes and immediately raised his rifle and triggered a sustained burst.

He was a moment too late.

The EMP blast hit the front of the Quonset hut at the main doors. The area around them sparked and then the metal melted and the heavy wooden doors were blown off the hinges. The wood ignited and most shards were turned into charred embers. Sparks flew from the metal as the microwave beams from the EMP connected with the heavy tin material of the HQ building.

Cyrus continued to hold back the trigger as he swept the terrorists indiscriminately. There was no room for dainty here, or to pick and choose targets. The man who had fired the weapon finally fell to the sustained volley Cyrus directed at him and the others around him. One of the dead terrorist's comrades managed to reach the weapon and get his hands on it. He rose and aimed it in Cyrus's direction.

Cyrus ceased firing, raised the rifle to his shoulder

and triggered two short bursts. The first set missed but on the second—jam! Cyrus cursed and moved immediately to field procedure for clearing the jam. At one point, he risked a glance and realized that the man was aiming at him but nothing was happening. Cyrus returned to clearing the jam, got his weapon back into action and raised the rifle to his shoulder once more. He took careful aim and just as he squeezed the trigger he realized his body was on fire. A moment later he could no longer see and then his brain boiled in its own fluids. His body imploded at the cellular level as his blood boiled. Flesh was irradiated from his bones in the blink of an eye.

But by that time Jack Cyrus was no longer aware any of it was happening.

THE WEAPON THAT killed Cyrus also killed the terrorist who fired it.

Lyons saw the death of the mercenary leader, a grisly sight to be sure, but he also saw the results of whatever went terribly wrong with the EMP prototype that had been fired at him. The weapon seemed to explode in the terrorist's hands and the liquid helium was immediately converted to gas with the temperature change. The inhalation of the gas ruptured the terrorist's lungs, depriving his body of oxygen, and he immediately slumped to ground.

"Did you see that?" Lyons shouted to Blancanales and Schwarz as he dropped another terrorist with a fresh salvo from his M-16.

"Hard to miss!" Blancanales replied.

"Look out!" Schwarz shouted.

His teammates looked in the direction he was pointing and noticed that one of the terrorists had turned the last working EMP weapon in their direction. They scrambled to their feet and for a brief moment Lyons thought he felt the air around his body heat up.

The Able Team warriors managed to get clear of the beam before it struck Black Betty. The gasoline engine erupted under exposure of the electromagnetic pulse and few seconds later the gas tank ignited. The blast was powerful enough to lift the van off the ground. Tires melted, the undercarriage split from front axle to back, and all the glass in the front seemed to dissolve to gritty, shiny shards.

Able Team reached the wood line and crashed through the brush to obscure their movements. Lyons verified they were all right before he led them along the line of trees to come up on the right flank. Fortunately, mercenaries were now emerging from the barracks with weapons in hand and putting up a hell of a fight against the intruders. The Libyan terrorists now seemed disoriented, their ranks falling quickly under the marksmanship of the Cyclops combatants.

Lyons turned to Blancanales. "Hey, Pol, that one remaining man with the EMP is hiding behind one of those trucks."

"Probably waiting for his weapon to recharge," Schwarz remarked.

"Let's help out the Cyclops boys and take out those trucks," Lyons said.

Blancanales nodded. "Agreed."

The pair knelt in unison and brought their grenade launchers to bear. The wanted to hit the trucks simultaneously, so once Lyons verified they had target acquisition he counted it down from three. The twin 40 mm HE grenades arced through the air so fast they weren't visible to the naked eye. They struck at nearly the same time and blew the trucks apart. Superheated fragments of metal and plastic were transformed into shrapnel that performed grisly work on the terrorists, some large enough to shear limbs from bodies while others penetrated vital organs with the effectiveness of bullets.

Able Team followed up with a barrage of sustained fire from their weapons, sending the surviving entourage into complete disarray. Combined with the charging Cyclops defenders, their weapons held low and sweeping the terrorists in a merciless crossfire, the stance of the attackers was short-lived indeed.

Eventually the onslaught ceased and left only the stench of burned gunpowder and scorched flesh and blood in its wake. For a long while Lyons and his teammates remained in place. The Cyclops mercenaries would be on high alert and trigger-happy, most likely ready to shoot at anything that moved.

Finally, Lyons cupped his mouth to be heard and said, "This is Irons! Is Major Braden with you?"

A man in camouflage battle dress and toting an MP-5 stepped from the assemblage. "I'm Braden."

"We're done here, and we're coming out with weapons at neutral position."

The Able Team leader knew that, while they had neutralized the threat to Cyrus, they still had to locate Dratshev, and they were running out of time.

CHAPTER TWENTY-SEVEN

Washington, D.C.

Ishaq Madari stared through the night-vision binoculars and studied the grounds of the DCDI facilities. He'd come here for only one purpose—destroy everything important to David Steinham. He smiled as he thought about how the pristine buildings with their tall, clean lines, room-size windows and penthouse gardens would look when his team had finished with them. The most titillating thing about that thought was that Steinham had financed the very devices that would ultimately bring about his destruction.

Madari congratulated himself on his ingenuity. Splitting his teams into two units, one to take out the main source of defense in Norfolk while the other came here, had been a stroke of sheer brilliance. He wondered for a moment if he was turning into some sort of egomaniac but he quickly dispelled the thought. Even now, as he lowered the binoculars and checked the dash clock on the panel truck, Madari realized the attack against Steinham's mercenaries was well under way.

In fact, it's probably already over, he mused.

Madari looked in the side mirror but he saw no vehicles. The street was completely deserted. Odd—he would have thought there'd be some traffic on a Friday night.

It was then that Madari remembered Steinham was at a conference and probably so were a lot of his staff.

It hadn't been enough to just kill Steinham in Madari's mind. He had to humiliate the man, turn his technology and his facilities—the only real source of Steinham's wealth and power—into smoldering ashes. This strategy had a far more powerful effect than just pointing a gun at a man's head and pulling the trigger. Any ape could do that. No, this was much better because it would strip Steinham of the things that were really important to him, ripping away the facade and exposing him for the weak and pathetic fool he was. In a way, Madari viewed this as a way to utterly emasculate the defense contractor. This was a just recompense for what Steinham had done to Libya.

A good many of Madari's men had sacrificed, some even paying the ultimate price, to defend the cause. Madari would make sure each and every sacrifice hadn't been in vain. He would crush Steinham beneath his foot like a cockroach. That would not only teach Steinham but anyone else that to interfere with the affairs of the Libyan revolution and the goals of its sons was futile and foolish.

Madari now had in his possession the ultimate power in advanced military technology and he planned to use it.

He looked at his watch and ordered the panel truck driver to wait. Madari then opened the door, dropped to the sidewalk and moved to the back. He rapped twice on the panel door and stepped back as it swung out. Ten men emerged from the truck, half of whom had prototypes in hand. The rest carried conventional weapons, mostly sub-guns, and those with EMP small arms had similar weaponry strapped to their backs in case they had to abandon their primary arsenal.

Madari didn't care about how much human life he took. He wasn't a murderer, anyway; he was a freedom fighter and liberator of his people. All he wanted to do was to make sure these weapons could pass the ultimate test. If Dratshev's genius proved out, he didn't see any problem in taking down the powers in Libya. He would burn the palaces and buildings of the elite to the ground, destroying the symbols of tyranny and oppression and replacing the dictatorship with a democratic system of government. Then and only then would he be able to rest and enjoy a long and happy life with Mishka.

Madari shook himself from his daydreaming as the last of the troops unloaded. He closed the doors of the panel van and then gestured for them to spread out. They did exactly as they had been drilling for months, one of the men under the watchful eye of the team leader, breaching the fifteen-foot chain-link fence with insulated wire cutters. As it turned out, the fence wasn't electrified but Madari saw no reason to take chances.

Once they had a large enough hole, the men began to push through and cross the perimeter, forming a skirmish line and walking across the manicured grounds on approach to the first building. They had nearly reached it and were about to concentrate their fire at very specific points on the ground floor when shots rang out to their left. From a copse of trees on a nearby hill, Madari could make out muzzle-flashes. He recalled from the blueprints that this specific area served as sort of park for the employees.

Someone had transformed it into a defensive position and with good reason. It provided high ground and adequate cover from conventional weapons fire. It was too bad for whoever had planned the defense that they weren't up against conventional weapons. Madari shouted at his men to concentrate their firepower on that hill and destroy the defenders. Their efforts were wasted. Madari still had the upper hand.

The battle with his enemies would end abruptly for them before it really started.

MADARI HAD APPARENTLY forgotten one of the cardinal rules of warfare: never underestimate your enemy.

The warriors of Phoenix Force were about to hammer that fact home, an especially pleasurable task for Gary Manning. The "guns" firing at the terrorists were actually a series of dummy barrels Manning painstakingly implemented as soon as they arrived at the DCDI facilities. The idea had been to get Madari to turn any EMP weaponry on a relatively benign target. Stony Man Farm had assisted in clearing the area by a radius of several blocks in every direction once the vehicle in which Madari departed the airport in Norfolk had been identified by ICE agents.

In all likelihood, Madari had thought he would be able to destroy the DCDI facilities unchallenged—he'd completely miscalculated both his capabilities and the resolve of his enemy. Phoenix Force had arrived more than an hour ahead of schedule. Minutes before, Able Team had advised them of their victory at the Cyclops base and the capabilities of the weapons, as well as the exploit that caused the devices to blow apart if fired without sufficient time to recharge.

Not that it mattered. McCarter's plan had originally been to not give them the opportunity to use them but Hawkins had come up with the brilliant idea to create a decoy. By setting the terrorists up with something to di-

rect the EMP fire at—a park with trees on a remote area
of the grounds totally devoid of human occupation—they
could mitigate damage and force Madari's hand sooner
than he'd planned.

Unfortunately for the terrorists who were now focused
on nonexistent threat from the private park, their blind
obedience to Madari would nail the lids on their respective coffins. The air shimmered around the barrels of the
five weapons, these much smaller than the ones Madari
had left with the Norfolk team. The trees ignited and
their trunks were instantly charred by weapons, one even
being ripped from the ground by the combined force of
two beams.

It was the moment Phoenix Force had awaited and as
soon as McCarter gave his signal, the five warriors broke
from their various points of concealment and charged
the Libyan terror group. They moved as one fluid strike
unit—all but James toting MP-5s they held high and at
the ready—as they approached the group. The terrorists
were so focused on the damage they had done, relishing
in what they assumed to be their first victory, they took
no notice of the approaching threat.

Madari was the first to see the oncoming commandos and he waved at his men, screaming for them to do
something. They whirled; a few confused, a few with
enough awareness to bring their weapons to bear, most
taken utterly by surprise. Whatever the reaction of each
man, they all hesitated and Phoenix Force seized the advantage. All the death and destruction they had faced the
past few days, the utter frustrations of being outwitted
at every turn, were channeled into the marksmanship of
these five men.

Hawkins was first to draw blood, sighting on a terrorist holding an EMP and triggering a 3-round burst. The 9 mm Parabellum rounds connected with the terrorist's chest, punching and lifting him off his feet. He triggered his EMP prototype reflexively and true to Lyons's claim, the thing burst apart in a cloud of helium gas. Hawkins was already tracking on a new target, getting this one with a double-tap to the head. The man's face appeared to split vertically, the pressure of the air built up from the path of the bullets cracking bone before the soft lead noses actually struck brain matter.

As the man crumpled to the slick grass, damp with a recent rain, Hawkins saw the first man he'd shot take a knee and bring a weapon to bear. He couldn't get there in time so Hawkins did the only thing he could and threw his body to the ground. Rounds from the terrorist's SMG burned the air so close above him he could hear the reports from their passing.

Manning, who had just taken another of the terrorists toting an EMP weapon, saw his friend's plight and broke from his next target to assist Hawkins. The Canadian was a crack shot with a rifle and at this distance he couldn't miss. He fired two 3-round bursts, the first striking the terrorist in the chest. Just as with Hawkins, the impact seemed to drive the man back but not bring him down permanently.

Manning swore and went prone before keying up his transmitter. "Body armor! They're wearing body armor!"

CALVIN JAMES GRIMACED on hearing Manning's announcement. Body armor was definitely not something on which they'd counted. He wondered a moment why Able Team hadn't told them about that, but then his reflexes took over and he went to ground. He looked over his right shoulder where he expected to see McCarter on his flank but the Phoenix Force leader was no longer visible.

James concentrated on the trouble ahead as he disengaged the safety of the M-203 grenade launcher attached to his Colt M-16 Commando. A carbine variant of the standard assault rifle, James preferred the weapon to more conventional hardware like the FN FNC, since he could carry heavy ordnance. In this case, his preference would save the lives of his friends. He snap-aimed through the leaf sight and triggered the M-203. He followed that by ejecting the smoking shell and loading a second. Ten yards estimated to the left and he stroked the trigger a second time.

The grenades blew on impact. The first HE fell a bit short but it was enough to cause the terrorists to pause for thought. That proved to James's advantage because the second blast landed amid a cluster of three terrorists who were lost for cover and apparently disoriented by the proximity of the first HE grenade that was still raining grass, mud and other detritus upon them when the second one went up. The force of the blast lifted each of the terrorists from his feet as flame and superheated shrapnel cut through flesh with effect.

James grinned as he slammed home another shell and prepared to deliver more punishment on the enemies of peace.

ENCIZO AND MCCARTER had both obviously been thinking the same thing and acted in concert on that hunch.

They broke from the straight approach and crossed roughly parallel to the terrorist position so that the remainder of the team members was out of the line of fire. When they were in suitable range, the pair checked each other with nods and then yanked smokers from their web gear harnesses. The smoke was white and thick as they tossed the canisters with all the force they could muster. It was proving difficult enough for the terrorists to take Phoenix Force in the dark, especially since they didn't have an equal advantage with night-vision equipment. The blanket of smoke that poured from those canisters only made the situation worse for them.

As the smoke began to thicken, Encizo and McCarter opened full-auto with their MP-5s. The goal at this point was to keep heads down long enough to give the other three time to beat a hasty retreat, which they didn't hesitate to do once they spotted the smoke. By this time the terrorists were utterly disoriented and McCarter knew the time to implement their backup plan was now.

"Leader to Eagle One," McCarter said.

Grimaldi's voice came back immediately and steady. "Go, Leader."

"You have the ball. Repeat, you have the ball."

"Roger. I copy. I have the ball."

That exchange rang as sweet relief in the ears of the five Phoenix Force warriors who now turned and beat a very hasty retreat from the battleground. The smoke had started to dissipate and the surviving terrorists were about to understand the error of their ways in a most permanent fashion. The next sounds were the blades of the Boeing AH-64D Longbow Apache helicopter as Grimaldi rocketed over the buildings and made a true course toward the massive smoke screen.

THE SIGNATURES OF the terrorists materialized in the APG-78 radar, a modern marvel of targeting technology not fooled by smoke or weather. With verification from McCarter that his team was clear, Grimaldi let loose.

"Hell hath no fury like 70 mm rockets," Grimaldi said.

Half of the dozen Hydra 70 rockets blasted from the M-261 launcher configured with WDU-4A/A APERS warheads. Each rocket weighed almost ten pounds and contained more than two thousand fléchettes weighing in at 20 grains each. The terrorists could provide no defense against such awesome power. When the rockets hit, they blew in a sight nothing less than spectacular to behold. Sparks, flame, mud and bodies were blown apart as more than twelve thousand pieces of shrapnel heated to greater than five hundred degrees burned and tore their way through tender flesh. Not even the body armor they wore could suppress the effects of that power, and especially not when Grimaldi followed with five hundred rounds from the 30 mm cannon.

Grimaldi heard a squelch in his ears as the voice of McCarter came on. "Nice work, Eagle One! The bloody drinks are on me when this is done."

"Gratzi," Grimaldi replied.

"And be advised, the driver seems to be getting away."

"Roger, but alas no. He just *thinks* he is."

"Copy that."

As the chopper buzzed from the scene to deal with the would-be getaway driver, the men of Phoenix Force approached the devastation with caution. Fires from clothing and the smell of burning human flesh caused a nauseating cloud to roil into the comparatively tranquil night sky. All that really remained were divots of charred ash and clay, the telltale remnants of the rocket impacts, and bodies strewed around in various modes of dismemberment.

Death had been Madari's sword and he'd reaped that which he'd yielded without regard, nothing more or less to it. As the flames dispersed and McCarter got close, he looked for confirmation that Madari had indeed perished in the attack. He didn't get it, but something in his gut told him it was truly over. He wished some sense of satisfaction would come, but it didn't. The past days had been a whirlwind of blow and counterblow, little more. While he wanted to find closure, he couldn't.

And that was the most frustrating feeling of all.

Norfolk, Virginia

AT DIRECTION FROM the Oval Office to the deputy director of Homeland Security, the ICE agents at the airport had been told not to attempt to seize Madari's plane or to apprehend anyone aboard. Instead they were to wait for the arrival of three men who, when they finally made their appearance more than three hours later, smelled like smoke. And death.

The lead ICE agent who had originally questioned Madari squinted at them. "You guys been fighting a war or something?"

"Something," Schwarz said with a grin.

"How about we skip the twenty-questions game and you bring us up to speed," Lyons said in a flat and icy tone. He was in no mood to cross swords with another agency at present. After briefing Major Braden and leaving the Cyclops compound, Able Team had hustled to the airport.

"We've had the plane under observation since the orders came down to wait for your arrival."

"Any idea how many are inside?" Blancanales asked.

The agent shook his head. "No, but we're guessing at least three."

"Pilots?" Lyons inquired.

"No. We actually took them into custody in the pilot lounge to prevent them from returning to the plane. We didn't want it to take off."

Lyons nodded. "Very shrewd. Nice work, but we'll take it from here."

"What're you going to do?"

It was Schwarz who said, "Maybe we'll book a flight to Acapulco."

The agent looked puzzled at first. "Huh? Oh...ha. I get it."

"And you'd probably wished you hadn't," Blancanales said.

"Okay," Lyons told his friends. "Let's nut up and do this."

ABLE TEAM FIGURED a rear approach would serve best to reach the plane undetected. As far as the occupants were concerned, they had no reason to suspect anything was wrong, so company wasn't expected.

Lyons carried a 12-gauge combat shotgun. Blancanales and Schwarz had opted for pistols, and Blancanales carried a tear gas canister in the cargo pocket of his fatigue pants. Lyons had point with Blancanales behind him and Schwarz covering rear flank. They moved soundlessly across the tarmac, single-file, with Schwarz facing the opposite direction and being guided by Blancanales's hand on his shoulder.

Lyons held up a fist when they reached the tail of the plane that brought them to a halt. He then turned to converse in a whisper with the other two. "What do you guys think?"

"Seems quiet enough," Blancanales replied.

"Can you see the door?" Schwarz asked.

"It's open and the step-ramp is down and locked," Lyons said.

"Sounds as if they weren't preparing to leave in a hurry."

Blancanales reached into his cargo pants and withdrew the tear-gas grenade. "Shall we?"

Lyons nodded and gestured for Blancanales to take up point. They continued in similar fashion with Lyons in the middle now. While the scattergun made the best weapon for an op of this nature, he didn't want to risk blowing a hole in Blancanales's back. As they neared the door, Lyons crouched and duck-walked under the plane, moved parallel up the starboard side and then crouched and returned to the side of their original approach.

Lyons now faced toward the rear of the plane, shotgun held low but at the ready.

Schwarz had his Beretta 93-R aimed at a high point in the doorway of the aircraft.

Blancanales made his way to the foot of the ramp. Keeping to the side, he risked a glance up but didn't see any movement. The plane was fairly large but chances were good that the tear gas canister would bring any occupants out quickly and with minimal risk to the Able Team warriors.

Blancanales nodded at Lyons and then yanked the pin on the tear gas canister. Lyons raised three fingers and counted backward. When he reached zero, Blancanales lobbed the canister overhand and it bounced off the top step and rolled through the hatchway. A loud pop ensued, drawing a shout from the interior. Other voices joined in a chorus of surprise as the plane rapidly began to fill with smoke, some of it gushing from the door but most staying inside.

Able Team readied their weapons and when the first occupants emerged, choking and wiping their eyes, they started screaming for the men to get their hands up. One man after the next debarked until it came to the fourth man. He reached into his waistband and yanked at a pistol. Lyons shouted a warning and then raised the scatter-gun and squeezed the trigger. The 12-gauge shell filled with No. 2 and 00 shot blew a fist-size hole in the guy's chest. His weapon flew backward and into the smoky plane. The body stood erect a moment and then teetered off the steps facedown, making several dull thumps before it settled into a heap at the base of the steps.

The other men began to shout protests, fearful they'd get blown away in the same fashion. Blancanales and Schwarz kept trying to out-shout them, waving their arms for the men to get on their bellies.

"Face down!" Blancanales kept saying.

They couldn't be sure the men even spoke English but the waving and gun pointing seemed sufficient to communicate their desire. After the men were neutralized, Schwarz and Blancanales relieved them of their side arms while Lyons kept one eye on them and the other on the hatchway.

Lyons was about to suggest they clear the plane when another man emerged. He was tall and lanky, but sickly looking in a strange sort of way—as the kind of look in men who suffered horrific childhood diseases. In his hand was the pistol the Libyan terrorist had lost when he'd stupidly resisted. This guy wasn't Libyan, though, as became apparent to the Able Team commandos.

Lyons raised his shotgun. "Stop, Dratshev! Don't be stupid."

Schwarz and Blancanales had no choice but to keep their pistols trained on the three men on the ground. They couldn't risk losing any of them. Lyons would just have to work through this one on his own.

"If you're going to kill me, I wish to hell you'd do it and get it over with," Dratshev said.

Oddly, the scientist sat on the top step, fished into his coat pocket and withdrew a single cigarette. He studied it a moment, coughing and squinting as the tears welled in his eyes. They could hear him wheezing now, fighting for air. Obviously he suffered from some sort of respiratory problem and the tear gas had exacerbated the condition.

Dratshev cursed under his breath at noticing the cigarette was cracked halfway down. He bit off that end, spit it away and then lit it. He took a deep breath but immediately began to cough and involuntarily he spit the cigarette out. It bounced down the steps in a shower of sparks and the eyes of all three followed its path just a moment.

When they looked at Dratshev he had the barrel of the pistol pointed to his own head.

"What the hell are you doing?" Lyons demanded.

Dratshev's expressed remained morose and in the dim light his eyes appeared only more sunken. "It is no use. I've dedicated my life to science and this is the end it has bought me. I let my curiosity get the better of me and it cost lives. Now Madari has left me to die in this stinking dung hole instead of in my homeland. Though even that's a farce since my own country betrayed me."

"Look," Blancanales said, keeping his voice calm and

steady. Lyons forced himself not to smile—always the Politician. "Look…Dr. Dratshev. It doesn't have to be like this. We know you were coerced. That should count for something. You can help *us*—you can undo what you've done. Nobody understands these weapons better than you. If you die, it dies with you."

"Maybe—" Dratshev's voice choked and he broke into another fit of coughing. Then he continued. "Maybe that won't be such a bad thing. There are worse hells in this life than you may ever know, sir. And I cannot, for one, be a part of them."

"Dr. Dratshev, please don't—"

The crack of the pistol took all present by surprise. The side of Dratshev's head seemed to crumple in a spray of blood, bone and brain matter. The pistol clattered down the steps and his body slumped at a cruel angle before sliding backward into the hatchway. His sightless eyes were still open as his face disappeared from view.

"Damn," Lyons muttered. He looked at Blancanales. "Sorry, Pol. There wasn't anything you could have done. Some things are just beyond our control."

Blancanales nodded but Lyons could see it was of no comfort—empty words for an empty victory.

"Well," Schwarz said, "at least for now Madari's reign of domination had come to an end and America can sleep a bit easier tonight. Hell, we can *all* sleep a bit easier tonight."

"Yeah," Carl Lyons replied. "And that has to count for something. Right, Pol?"

"I guess it does at that, Ironman," he replied.

* * * * *

The Executioner®
Don Pendleton's
MAXIMUM CHAOS

The mob will stop at nothing to free a ruthless killer

Desperate to escape conviction, the head of a powerful mob orders the kidnapping of a federal prosecutor's daughter. If the mobster isn't freed, if anyone contacts the authorities, the girl will be killed. Backed into a corner, her father must rely on the one man who can help: Mack Bolan.

Finding the girl won't be easy. Plus, with an innocent life at stake, going in guns blazing is a risk Bolan can't take. His only choice is to pit the crime syndicate against their rivals. The mob is about to get a visit from the Executioner. And this time he's handing out death penalties.

Available October wherever books and ebooks are sold.

GOLD EAGLE®